FACE BLIND

ALSO BY RAYMOND BENSON

FICTION

Evil Hours

James Bond 007 Novels
The Man With the Red Tattoo
Never Dream of Dying
DoubleShot
High Time to Kill
The Facts of Death
Zero Minus Ten
Die Another Day
(based on the screenplay by Neal Purvis & Robert Wade)
The World is Not Enough
(based on the screenplay by Neal Purvis & Robert Wade and Bruce Feirstein)
Tomorrow Never Dies (based on the screenplay by Bruce Feirstein)

NON-FICTION

The Pocket Essentials Guide to Jethro Tull
The James Bond Bedside Companion

www.raymondbenson.com

FACE BLIND

A Novel

by

Raymond Benson

Published in Great Britain by Twenty First Century Publishers Ltd in conjunction with UPSO in December 2003.

A catalogue record of this book is available from the British Library.

ISBN: 1-904433-10-3

Cover design: chalk drawing by Fred Piechoczek.

To order further copies of Face Blind or other books published by Twenty First Century Publishers Ltd please visit: www.twentyfirstcenturypublishers.com

For Randi

ACKNOWLEDGEMENTS

The author and publisher wish to acknowledge the help of Cecilia Burman, Jordan Charter, the Fulton County, Ohio Sheriff's Office, and the Fulton County Health Center.

For more information on face blindness, visit www.prosopagnosia.com.

PROSOPAGNOSIA (n.)
From Greek [*prosp* = face; *agnosia* = lack of knowledge].
Face-blindness; a neurological condition that renders a person incapable of recognizing faces. It is unrelated to the person's ability to see faces. Someone with perfect vision can suffer from prosopagnosia. It is also unrelated to the person's IQ. In the normal brain there is a center that is dedicated to face recognition. Prosopagnosia arises when that special center becomes damaged or is otherwise unable to perform its function.

Chapter 1

A small piece appeared in the New York Daily News two days after the incident had occurred. It was the first mention of the event but it wouldn't be the last. Before long, it would become one of New York City's great unsolved cases and a mystery that would keep the police scratching their heads for years to come.

SLAYINGS AT WRITER'S HOME

> Police are baffled by the scene of multiple slayings inside the townhouse owned by writer John Cozzone, located on the Upper East Side of Manhattan. Two men and one woman were found dead in the home. One man and the woman had been shot to death, but the other man had been stabbed. The identities of the victims are being held until further investigation is completed.
>
> Cozzone was not one of the slain individuals. Police are searching for the writer, who had a fleeting taste of fame and success in the mid-70s as the author of two best-selling novels, *The Apples of the Cosmos* and *The Loose Lips of Lucretia Leone*. Police are still trying to discern what relationship the victims had to Cozzone, but preliminary scrutiny indicates that the townhouse was the scene of a drug deal gone bad.

A day after the story appeared, John Cozzone's location was made known to the New York police, and this revelation only made the mystery even more puzzling.

The investigating officer was certain that someone, somewhere, knew what had taken place in that townhouse on a warm June evening at a time when most people in Manhattan were having their dinners, or watching television, or attending the theatre.

The officer was correct, more or less. Indeed, one individual did know what had occurred in John Cozzone's home that evening, for the person in question was present when it happened. The problem was that this witness could no more accurately detail the whos or the whys of the incident than the domestic housecat that was also in the house at the time.

To do so, one would have to possess an omniscient perspective of all the personages involved, travel back in time two weeks before the incident, and start at the beginning.

Chapter 2

"Hey, baby, howzit goin'?"

The words echoed in her brain. The greasy voice with its implied menace resonated through the dream as it had always done, filling her countenance with dread and panic. The familiar pattern repeated itself as she looked back to see where the voice had come from. As usual, there was nothing but the endless avenue stretching off into darkness, completely devoid of pedestrians and traffic. It was as if First Avenue had become part of a gigantic ghost city where no human soul traversed. The silence, as they say, was deafening. The shadows stretched toward her with slow, creeping tentacles, beckoning her to stand still so that they could ensnare her and pull her into the black unknown.

Hannah turned to run – but as is the case in dreams of this ilk, her legs felt heavy and it took a tremendous effort just to raise her foot. More anxiety enveloped her as she struggled to move forward, fighting against an unseen force that rendered the muscles in her legs powerless.

"Hey, baby, where ya goin'?"

The baritone male voice was intensely malevolent, infused with the underbelly of lust and perverse desire that women often experienced while walking the streets of Manhattan. Sexist remarks went with the territory if one happened to be female and the sad fact remained that youth and attractiveness made the target stand out even more.

"Don't rush off, baby, you wanna party?"

Hannah strained to move one leg in front of the other and run up the deserted avenue toward her apartment building. It was still several blocks away. Why was it so dark? Even the street lamps were dim and spooky. Why was no one around? There wasn't a single car, truck, or bus moving uptown, and that was not only unusual – it was simply impossible at eleven o'clock on a weeknight. Manhattan was the city that never slept! Traffic noise was *always* present, even in the middle of the night.

My God, Hannah thought, *she was all alone.*

Of course, in the back of her mind, she knew that it was just the weird dream logic. She hadn't really been alone when the real incident occurred. There *had* been traffic – lots of it – and there were people on the sidewalks. Still, because of the late hour, the avenue was less populated than it would have been if it were broad daylight. Hannah almost never walked the streets late at night but she had been forced to do so when the Number 1 bus broke down and she had no patience to wait for the next one. She had been tired and was fighting a cold. What she had wanted more than anything was to get home, have some hot tea, crawl into bed, and fall asleep with Panther curled up on top of the blanket.

Instead she got the creep.

"Hey, baby! I'm comin' after ya!"

That's when she knew he was behind her in the dream. Hannah looked back again, just as she had done in real life, but she didn't see anyone. She *felt* him, though. The creep was back there, just a few feet away, sneaking up with claws outstretched. Hannah faced forward once again and ran, but the rules of the dream world prohibited her from making much progress. Even when it had happened on that fateful night in May, Hannah had felt as if she couldn't move quickly enough.

Nevertheless, she pressed forward. Only two blocks to go. She passed Wong's Laundry and the Love drug store and skirted across the street against the red light. It didn't matter, as there was no crosstown traffic. Even on the Upper East Side near her building the city was eerily empty.

As she passed the little pizza joint where she often picked up slices, Hannah heard the running steps on the pavement behind her. That was the cue to scream for help, but nothing came out. Her throat was twisted and dry. The dream logic made it worse, for her scream came out as a mere whisper. Of course, no one heard her. There was no one *to* hear her.

"Come 'ere, baby! I'm right behind ya!"

Terror gripped her heart as she pushed her small frame forward with all her might. She made it across the last street and was steps away from the five-floor brownstone where she lived with her cat. She knew that the creep was still back there, though, just seconds away. Timing was crucial.

She pushed the glass door open and burst into the small inner foyer, where the metal mailboxes lined the wall and a locked security door prevented visitors from entering the building without first using the intercom to communicate with tenants. Normally she would have stopped to open her mailbox and collect what bills had come that day –

she never got letters – but that thought didn't cross her mind. Her goal was to simply get the key into the security door and get inside before the creep was upon her.

She had always berated herself for carrying too many keys. She had four keys just to get into her apartment – one for the security door and three for her own door. There was a mailbox key and several others that opened various things at the bank where she worked.

Her hands shook as she pulled out the bundle of keys and fumbled for the right one. She plunged it into the lock on the door, but the dream wouldn't let her do it. The key turned to rubber and bent grotesquely. Wrong key. She tried the other one that looked identical to the security door key and found that it went into the lock easily, but then she was unable to turn it. Something was wrong.

Please, oh God, please!

She felt the outer door swing open behind her and the rush of cold air as the creep made his presence known.

"Hey, baby. This where you live? You gonna invite me inside?"

Hannah tried to scream again, then started to turn and defend herself. She wanted to beat the creep senseless, but she was a petite woman weighing all of one hundred and five pounds. Before she could spin around, however, the blow sent her crashing into the security door. She would never forget the pain and shock of that moment's violence, the sensation that a hole had been gorged into the back of her head.

As she fell to the tiled floor in the small cubicle, she gazed at the intruder to get a good look at him before she passed out. But the dream had its own script and the ending never changed.

The creep had no face.

***

Hannah awoke with a start, jerking her body in a defensive reaction to the nightmare. When she realized that she was safe, in bed in her apartment, she sighed loudly and fell back into her pillow. Her heart was pounding and the sheets were damp.

It had happened again.

"Damn," she muttered. The awful dreams occurred so frequently that one would think she'd be used to them by now.

A mournful "meow" forced her to open her eyes again. Panther was standing at the foot of the bed, eyeing her with concern. A black shorthaired domestic, the cat had been her constant companion for seven years.

"Sorry, Panther," she said. "Did I scare you?"

The cat meowed again and began to rub his head and body against the bulge beneath the sheets that was her leg.

Hannah looked at the alarm clock by the bed and saw that it was nearly time to get up anyway. She reached over, switched the alarm over to radio, and slowly sat up on the bed.

The sunlight streamed through the blinds at the other end of her railroad efficiency. It wasn't large by any means, really just one big room that had three sections – a living area, a kitchen, and a bedroom space – and an attached bathroom. The rent was miraculously inexpensive for Manhattan, it was close enough to her job that she could walk, and it provided plenty of room for a thirty-four-year-old single woman and her cat. She didn't need a fancy apartment. She never entertained, she never had guests, and she didn't date. Hannah liked it that way.

She stood, walked into the kitchen, grabbed the kettle, filled it with water from the faucet, and placed the kettle on the stove. She turned on the burner, then went to the bathroom. When she was done, Hannah went back to the kitchen, opened the pantry, and retrieved Panther's food from the shelf. The cat maneuvered between and around her legs, meowing in his predictable, needy fashion.

"Hold your horses, Panther," she mumbled. She poured the food into his bowl and then gave him fresh water. By now the water in the kettle was boiling. Hannah took her favorite coffee cup from the drainboard, placed the filter holder on top of the cup, pulled a fresh filter from the package in the cupboard, then got the packet of Starbuck's ground coffee from the fridge. She dumped a couple of measured spoonfuls into the filter, then poured the hot water on top. As it seeped through into the cup, she removed the knee-length maroon T-shirt that she had slept in for three years, and got into the shower.

After the ritual cleansing, Hannah dressed for work in blue jeans and a New York Marathon T-shirt. Every day was "Casual Day" at her office. She was lucky.

She sat at the little dining table with her cup of coffee and sipped it slowly while listening to the news on the radio, peeling and eating a banana from the fruit basket, and watching Panther eat. She hadn't quite shaken off the dregs of the nightmare and she knew it would linger for hours. Hannah was used to it. For five years she had dreamt the same thing, over and over…

When she was done, Hannah returned to the bathroom and brushed her teeth. Then she looked into the mirror and studied what she saw.

It was always the same. The blonde hair looked all right – straight and thin, shoulder-length, not needing much styling. The rest was blank as usual. She knew that it was her face she was looking at, but every day she felt as if she were peering at a stranger. Hannah refused to put on make-up and hadn't done so since the incident. Besides, she would only make a mess of it if she tried.

She had been told throughout her life that she was naturally pretty. Perhaps she had been… before. She certainly didn't think of herself in those terms now. It didn't matter to her. She simply didn't care anymore if she were pretty or not.

Proceeding to the final part of the morning ritual, Hannah opened the mirror to reveal the medicine cabinet. She took the small container of one hundred-milligram Zoloft tablets, shook out one and a half, and swallowed them with water from the tap.

Hannah took a look at the litter box under the sink and made sure that it was full and needed no cleaning, then went out to the living area to gather her purse and keys. In her free hand she picked up a duffel bag full of dirty laundry. She shut off the light, gave Panther a stroke or two, then opened the door.

She lived on the third floor of the brownstone walkup. Most of her neighbors kept to themselves, just as she did, but as she went down to the second floor, Liz opened her door and stuck her head out.

"Oh, hi Hannah," the woman said. "I thought I heard your feet on the stairs."

Hannah wasn't sure what that was supposed to mean. She had tiny feet and always trod lightly. Any amount of noise in the stairwell echoed throughout the building and she was usually careful not to create any.

"Hi, Liz."

"You wanna come in for some coffee?" Liz asked. She opened the door wider to reveal that she was wearing a stained, pink terrycloth robe that barely contained her large bust. Liz Rosenthal was a big woman with a weight problem and brown hair cut like the Beatles circa 1964. Brightly displayed on the top of her bulbous right breast was a tattoo of a heart with a nail through it. Around her neck she wore a gold *chai.*

"No, thanks, I just had some." Hannah stopped in front of Liz's door long enough to be polite. "I have to get to work."

Liz was in her early forties, or so Hannah guessed. The woman was a lesbian and made no attempts to hide it. Hannah had seen Liz with other women over the years, but lately she had been alone. Liz was probably the closest thing to a friend that Hannah had, but the relationship was not entirely comfortable. Hannah felt that Liz wanted to make something more of it, since Hannah was always by herself, too. Nevertheless, she had given Liz a set of her apartment keys, just in case something happened to her. That way Liz could get in to feed Panther if she had to.

"I thought you set your own hours," Liz said in her thick New Jersey accent.

"I do. But I also have deadlines."

"Mmmm. So how *is* your famous cousin?"

"Okay, I guess. He's not really that famous."

Liz shrugged. "If you say so."

"You're up early," Hannah said. "Did you work last night?"

"Yeah, I got in around four. Couldn't sleep much. The usual."

Hannah nodded and then shuffled her feet. "Well, I gotta go. See you later."

"Have a good day, honey," Liz said. She smiled and shut the door.

Hannah descended the steps to the ground floor and left the building. As she passed through the inner foyer, the nightmare came back to her and she felt a sudden chill. She told herself that she should have moved after the incident, but finding a place as good as this one for the price was practically impossible. It was out of the question. Still, it was rare that she didn't feel uneasy entering or exiting her own apartment building.

It was a beautiful Thursday in June. First Avenue was bustling with activity. Rush hour traffic was in full force, the sidewalk was littered with people dashing off to work, and shop owners were opening their places of business. Hannah walked south two blocks to Wong's Laundry, where old Mr. Wong greeted her warmly.

"Good morning, Miss McCleary," he said, pronouncing it "McCreary," as he always did.

"Good morning, Mister Wong," she said. "I'll pick these up this afternoon, okay?"

"Okay." He wrote out a ticket and gave her the stub. "See you later."

"Thank you."

She walked back outside and continued her path south. Before the incident, she would have walked over to Second Avenue and caught the bus to go downtown to the bank where she used to work. Now all she had to do was walk nine blocks and over one avenue to John's townhouse. She had been fortunate in finding a job where she could walk to work, stay out of the public eye, and deal with as few people as possible.

This was important to Hannah, for her cousin John, Mr. Wong, and Liz were probably the three or four people – maximum – that she would recognize that day.

Chapter 3

"The patient suffers from acute depression as a result of a divorce three months ago."

The doctor's voice resonated in Bill Cutler's ear as he typed, flying through the transcription on autopilot. Cutler didn't mind doing Dr. Berger's tapes. He was one of the few physicians who spoke slowly and succinctly in consideration of the typists, and everyone in the office loved him for it. Dr. Berger also seemed to be intelligent and thoughtful. Cutler enjoyed Berger's tapes because they were often entertaining and sometimes educational. Cutler had learned a great deal about psychoanalysis from working on Berger's patient reports. The entire office staff wanted to work on Dr. Berger's tapes. In contrast, no one wanted Dr. Lazar's tapes. She was a psychiatrist who spoke in broken sentences and in a strange foreign accent. Transcriptionists spent more time correcting her grammar and looking up words she didn't know how to pronounce in English than they did typing the patient reports.

"Prescription for Zoloft, one fifty milligram tablet q.d."

Cutler thought it was amazing that there were so many people taking anti-depressants these days. One would think that everyone in America was suicidal. He didn't get it. He had never understood why people had to see doctors and take medicines to overcome depression. When he was depressed he got stoned or drunk, picked up a girl, and fucked her brains out. He always felt like a new man the next morning, as long as he had kicked out the girl before going to sleep. He didn't much like to wake up next to anyone.

"Next patient is Eileen Charles, forty-five years old, in on a med maintenance visit."

Cutler glanced at his watch. It was almost time for him to leave for his audition. Not that it would make any difference in his life. After fourteen years in the big city, Cutler had never been seen on the stage. He had been cast a few times in off-off-Broadway showcases and the like, but he had never made it through an entire rehearsal process to opening night. The directors always fired him, and it wasn't because he couldn't act. Cutler knew that he was a good actor, possibly one of the best in New York. They usually got rid of him because he was "difficult."

It had been a long time since he had been given another chance. These days he was in that nebulous age range. Being thirty-five might be great if you were Tom Cruise or Brad Pitt, but it was the kiss of death if you were an unknown actor with no credits. He was always "too old," or "too young," or "not tall enough," or "not short enough," or "too good-looking," or "too much like a soap opera guy," or whatever. Still, he was determined to be an actor, make it to Broadway someday, win a Tony or two, then move to Hollywood and be in the movies.

At least they couldn't say he wasn't ambitious. Most of the time, though, people said that Bill Cutler wasn't a very nice guy and he knew it to be true.

Cutler had grown up with a much older brother and an alcoholic single mother who didn't care. Patrick was ten years older than Bill, so by the time Bill was old enough to be on his own, Patrick had long gone to seek his fortune and his mother was in the twilight zone. Thus young William was allowed to get away with anything. This freedom instilled valuable traits of self-reliance in the boy, but it also eventually nurtured an adult that felt he was entitled to whatever he wanted. He had never been afraid to speak his mind, confront authority, buck the system, and roll the dice. When he was a teenager, his classmates and teachers thought him extremely arrogant.

Added to his extroverted and presumptuous personality was the fact that he was remarkably good-looking. He had no trouble attracting the opposite sex; the problems arose when women quickly learned that he was a cad. What few relationships he had enjoyed as a younger man were short-lived and painful. As he progressed into his thirties, he used women only for a quick fix of pleasure, then discarded them as if they were yesterday's newspapers.

In short, Bill Cutler was a calculated misogynist. His own therapist had told him so, and Cutler accepted it as fact. It went hand in hand with some of the more darker and suppressed aspects of Cutler's psychological makeup that he didn't like to dwell on too often.

He finished the current transcription, slipped off the earphones, and went to the coffee machine. Debbie and Kathy were typing away, diligently putting in their forty hours a week. As manager of MedScript Inc., Cutler had it pretty good as far as day-jobs went. He had always been a fast typist and he had picked up medical transcription quickly at a temp job when he first came to New York. It was a way to make ends meet, although he was beginning to think that he was going to be a medical transcriptionist forever.

Acting was what he really wanted to do, of course. Unfortunately, that career path had been interrupted by what he referred to privately as the "dark time." He could have continued to audition then but he chose not to do so. He had been too angry and depressed.

During that period, his rich brother Patrick had created MedScript. After Bill's probation was over, Patrick did his little brother the "favor" of allowing him to manage the company. Patrick was always concocting get-rich-quick schemes and, surprisingly, most of them worked. Patrick, who in reality was Bill's half-brother, was a millionaire. He had invested wisely as soon as he was out of high school and had started a chain of temporary help outfits that made a ton of money in no time. Despite the age difference between them and the lack of sharing both parents, Bill and Patrick looked remarkably alike. Patrick was also single, having been through one failed marriage, and spent most of his time wheeling and dealing and chasing his own herd of women.

On the other side of the coin, it seemed that every get-rich-quick scheme that Bill came up with failed miserably. Patrick continually denigrated him for being a "loser," and only gave him the job of managing MedScript because Bill was a fast typist and because he was family. Beyond that, Patrick was none too subtle in showing his contempt for Bill.

Bill hated his brother. He thought Patrick was a smarmy prick who didn't give a damn about anything but his money. Patrick often treated Bill with disdain, as if his younger sibling was a huge failure. He constantly derided Bill for his acting aspirations, saying that it was a dead-end and that Bill had no talent.

When the legal and medical problems began, Patrick wanted to disown his brother. Bill always wondered what had made Patrick have a change of heart after the probation. Perhaps it was the fact that their mother had died.

Fuck him, Bill thought. At least Patrick trusted his little brother enough to give him some responsibility in one of the fat cat's companies. What Patrick didn't know was that Bill often ran off to auditions in the middle of the day. Big deal. Cutler knew that he would make up his time and that he was the best transcriptionist in the office, much less the boss. He never made mistakes in his typing, he knew how to spell every impossible medical term in the book, and could even get through Dr.

Lazar's tapes without complaining too much. Unfortunately, he could barely keep staff for very long. Debbie and Kathy were new, and Cutler gave them two more weeks before they got fed up with his bullshit and quit. The longest he had kept an employee was six months.

Fuck 'em. That was Cutler's attitude. If they didn't want the job, fine. He had learned to work for a living while pursuing the things he really wanted to do. He hated typing doctors' reports as much as the next person, but it beat being a waiter by a long shot.

The phone rang. Cutler picked up the receiver before Debbie could get it.

"MedScript, may I help you?" he asked in a game-show voice.

"What the hell kind of voice is that?" Patrick asked, annoyed.

"What are you talking about? It's a friendly, enthusiastic voice," Bill said defensively.

"Bill, just talk in your normal voice, okay? You don't have to do this weird shit on the phone, all right?"

"Fine." Bill wanted to say something else but didn't.

"I'm calling to find out if you've filed the tax return for the quarter."

"Not yet. It's on the agenda this week."

"Shit, Bill, it's due on the fifteenth. I don't want it to be late, we'll get a penalty."

"Big deal, Patrick, most companies file late, or they get an extension, or they pay the goddamned penalty. It isn't that much."

"Fine, Bill, we'll take it out of your salary, how'll that be?"

"Look, Patrick, I said I'd do it. Don't worry about it!"

"All right. How's the new help?"

"They're fine. We haven't lost anyone this month."

"Okay. Keep up the good work. I have to call some of the other shops." He hung up without saying goodbye.

The prick, Cutler thought. The guy always ended his conversations with "Keep up the good work," even if the entire dialogue had been a dressing down.

He went back to his desk and went on to the next patient.

> *"Jill Thompson is a forty-two year old woman who is suffering from depression due to the death of her husband in a car accident. Apparently the husband died without life insurance and Mrs. Thompson is possibly going to lose her apartment."*

Awww, too bad. Cutler had little sympathy for these people.

"Have prescribed Prozac and recommended that she see a therapist. Will refer her to Dr. Miller."

Cutler grunted to himself and removed the little black book from his shoulder bag that he had propped on the shelf behind him. It contained the addresses and phone numbers for the few people he knew in the city, but it also held what he called his Quest List. Cutler opened the book and turned to the last of the entries. With a ballpoint pen he added the name, "Jill Thompson." He then opened the accordion file that contained the patients' records. Whenever doctors submitted a day's dictated tapes to be transcribed, they were placed in an accordion file that also included the corresponding patients' manila folders. That way, when the tapes and transcripts were returned to the doctors' offices downstairs, the staff could easily file the transcripts with the patient records, and then file away the records.

Of course, the patients' files contained all of the necessary information – address, phone number, health insurance, social security number… and countless other personal and private tidbits.

Cutler jotted down Jill Thompson's address and phone number, then put away the file. He finished the tape, printed out the string of transcripts, and placed them all back into the accordion file. He then walked to the front of the room and placed the file into the "Finished" basket, where it would be picked up and messengered back to the doctors' offices. MedScript Inc.'s clients included a number of practices in the same mid-town area building. Turnaround time was guaranteed to be twenty-four hours. Usually the workload was unbelievably impossible. Other times, like today, it was relatively light. This was because the doctors themselves got behind in their dictation and ended up submitting two weeks' worth of tapes in one go.

Cutler waved at Kathy and Debbie as he slung his bag over his shoulder. Debbie pulled out her earphones.

"I'm off to an audition," he said. "I'll be back in a couple of hours."

Debbie was used to the supervisor leaving them alone. She merely nodded and went back to typing.

***

The audition sucked, as usual. Cutler felt justified in giving the director the finger as soon as the twerp said, "We'll keep your resume on file, thank you very much." Cutler thought that the little shit looked like a snot-nosed kid right out of college. Typical of the off-off-Broadway scene.

One of these days, Cutler thought. One of these days he'd show 'em all. He'd show the world what a tremendously gifted actor he was. He could assume any character, any voice, and any mannerism. There were times when he'd shown up at work in disguise and fooled the others for a few minutes before he'd reveal his true self. They often thought he was a flake, a little crazy, but they usually laughed. Once he showed up in drag. That *really* threw them. He had them going for fifteen minutes.

Cutler left the East Village and took the subway back to mid-town. As he walked toward the office, he looked at his watch. He had been gone forty-five minutes. He could afford to stay away from work a while longer. Why not have a bit of fun?

He pulled out the Quest List and examined it. The three pages that made up the list were comprised of names – female names – along with their addresses and phone numbers. Nearly all of them he had picked up from the medical transcriptions. Of the twenty-two names, he had successfully slept with seventeen of them. Not bad. Three of the others turned out to be ugly as sin, and as for the other two, he could never finagle a meeting. He hadn't yet given the shove to the last one he had slept with, a pathetic divorcee with two kids. Nancy. There was just enough time to give her the heave-ho. There was also this new one, Jill Thompson. Too old, but at least he could have some fun with her.

It wasn't safe to use his cell phone. Cutler found one of the dying breeds of pay phones on the street and inserted the coins. He dialed Jill Thompson's number. After three rings, a woman answered.

"Hello?" She sounded tired. Put out. He knew exactly what she might have looked like.

"Mrs. Thompson?" he said, exhibiting his best Price-is-Right voice.

"Yes?"

"Good morning, this is Ron Jeremy from the – " He quickly consulted the notes he had made from the patient's file. " – Hartford Insurance Group."

"Yes?"

"I'm calling to inform you that we have made a *terrible* mistake. It concerns your late husband's life insurance."

"My husband… you people told me that my husband didn't have life insurance," the woman said.

"That's just the point, Mrs. Thompson. He *did* have insurance. We've just discovered that there was a clerical error in our claims department. Mrs. Thompson, your husband left you with a $500,000 insurance policy!"

There was silence at the other end.

"Mrs. Thompson?"

"I'm here… I just… Really? Oh, my God. Harold, you dear! Oh, my God. Thank you, Lord!"

"I thought you'd like to know as soon as possible."

"Well, why didn't you find this out sooner? I've been to your offices, I consulted the man who handled our policies, I wrote letters…"

"I understand your frustration, ma'am. That's why I wanted to let you know that you can come to our mid-town office this afternoon and pick up a check if you'd like."

"A check?"

"That's right, you'll get the entire amount today. Normally we would distribute it over time, but seeing as we're the ones who made a dreadful mistake, Hartford would like to make it up to you."

The woman was crying. Cutler savored the sound. "Oh, thank you, sir," she sobbed. "Thank you. Tell me your name again?"

"Ron Jeremy."

"I'm writing this down," the woman said. "Now, where do I go?"

Cutler looked across the street and saw it. Peepland Adult Video and Novelties.

"You need to go to Sixth Avenue and 42nd Street. We're two doors east of Sixth Avenue on 42nd." He gave her the address of the porno shop. "Just go right in and tell the man in front that you want to see Ron Jeremy."

"Oh, thank you! Thank you very much!" The woman was ecstatic.

"You're quite welcome. Have a good day!" Cutler hung up and laughed aloud. Boy, would she be in for a surprise when she walked into the porno shop and asked for Ron Jeremy, who was one of the sleaziest actors working in that industry!

Cutler took a pen and marked out the name "Jill Thompson" from the Quest List. Now it was time to call Nancy. He had put it off for far too long, mainly because she was good in bed. The poor woman was saddled with two kids and very little income, barely took care of herself, and smoked like a chimney. Nevertheless, she had a body to die for and did things to him that most men only dream about. It was too bad that she got hooked on him and expected him to bail her out of her awful situation.

He dialed the number and waited.

"Hello?"

"Nancy, it's Eric," he said, using the name she knew him by and the southern accent he had perfected by watching old westerns on television.

"Eric! You bastard, where have you been?"

Great, she was pissed off. Not surprising.

"I've been out of town, baby. How are you?"

"How am I? Why couldn't you call? I've been wondering what the hell happened to you!"

"Sorry, babe. I wasn't in a position to call."

"Don't give me that shit, anyone can pick up a phone at anytime."

"Nancy, it's only been a week."

"What do you mean? You sleep with me one night and then disappear for a week? Where are you now? Are you coming over?"

"Not if you're gonna be mad at me," he said.

"Oh, Eric, I'm furious with you, but I promise to be good. Come see me, please? I need to see you. I miss you so much."

"Where are the kids?"

"At their father's."

"Right. Listen, Nancy, I have something I gotta tell ya."

"What."

"I'm gettin' married. My high school sweetheart. We saw each other at our high school reunion this past week. That's where I was. We've decided that we were meant for each other."

There was silence on the other end. Finally, she muttered, "What did you say?"

"I'm gonna get married. I wanted you to be the first to know."

"You... you son of a bitch. You wanted me to be the *first to know*?"

"Yeah. You wanna come to the wedding?"

"You bastard piece of shit!" she screamed at him. "I hope you rot in hell!" She slammed the phone down.

Cutler had to chuckle. He shook his head, took the pen, and scratched out Nancy's name from the Quest List. He knew that what he had done was cruel. He was well aware that it was a shitty thing to do. It's just that his therapist had insisted that he find a hobby to distract him from the temptation of things he *used* to do, and this was what he had come up with.

Cutler replaced the black book in his shoulder bag, left the phone booth, and walked back toward the office as he whistled "Hi Ho, Hi Ho" along the way.

Chapter 4

Dominic DeLauria spent his last night at Rikers alone in his cell for the first time in five years. He felt bad about his cellmate, which was a rare thing for him to do. Usually he didn't care one whit about others, but Lane had befriended him and was a decent enough guy.

Nevertheless, what had happened on Wednesday didn't prevent DeLauria from focusing on his release. No longer would he have to answer the question, "What are you gonna do when you get out?" Everyone at Rikers knew that he was about to be released on parole, and for the past week that question was all he heard.

"I'm gonna fuck your mother," he'd answer. It got a laugh, most of the time. If someone didn't like it, the guy knew enough not to mess with DeLauria and let it go.

Wednesday had begun like any other day. DeLauria had finished his lunch of oatmeal and bread, left the mess, and wandered outside to the yard to have a smoke.

Only one more day, he remembered thinking. Eight long years. He had some catching up to do.

He lit the Marlborough, inhaled, and held the smoke as if it were a joint. It felt good. He wondered if he would get used to walking into a store in Manhattan and buying cigarettes again. Obtaining them in prison was an expensive nuisance. Things were certainly going to be different on the outside.

Some of the others in the general population were shooting hoops. DeLauria never played ball in prison. He didn't care to socialize with what would have to be teammates. He had always preferred the gym and its extensive workout equipment. He had kept in shape during his incarceration; in fact he was probably in better condition now than when he went inside. The strict regimen had sculpted his already hard body into a massive machine of muscle. DeLauria looked to be ten years younger than his well-preserved forty-two. It felt good.

He stared at the other inmates, watched the guys playing basketball, kept an eye on the skinheads by the wall… then noticed his cellmate standing on the other side of the court. *What a bitter, broken man*, DeLauria thought. Like almost everyone, Tim Lane insisted that he was innocent and was falsely convicted, but DeLauria didn't believe him. He had a knack for discerning whether a person was lying or not. DeLauria wasn't too familiar with the details of the crime aside from what Lane had told him. Something about an assault on a woman in Manhattan that got him ten years. It was Lane's second offense for sexual assault, so in DeLauria's opinion Lane got off lucky. The guy had served five years so far.

DeLauria strolled over to Lane and offered him a cigarette.

"No, thanks," Lane said.

"Same old story, huh?" DeLauria asked.

"Yeah, I got them Rikers Island Blues again," Lane said.

More than once an inmate mistakenly thought DeLauria and Lane were related. They were both of medium-height, had dark hair, and, like DeLauria, Lane probably had some Italian blood in him. When they first became cellmates, DeLauria wanted nothing to do with Lane. He didn't want a friend. But Lane had some street smarts and was no punk. He had admitted to DeLauria about being involved with some petty robberies, a hold-up or two, and a previous assault on a woman. Over time, the two men warmed to each other. DeLauria eventually thought Lane was all right. As far as cellmates go, he could have done much worse.

"So, Dom, you counting the hours?" Lane asked.

DeLauria rarely smiled, but he did now. His cold, brown eyes glittered beneath the wave of black hair.

"Seventeen hours and thirty two minutes," DeLauria replied. "Tomorrow morning I'm the fuck outta here."

"I'm not gonna ask you what you're gonna do when you get to the city."

"Thanks."

"But I imagine you're gonna kick some butt."

"You're damn right."

Lane sighed. "I guess I have about three more years before I can get out on parole. Maybe two."

The pair began to walk around the perimeter of the yard, ignoring the stares from the various cliques of blacks, Hispanics, Asians, and skinheads. It took guts to avoid belonging to any particular group in prison. Neither DeLauria nor Lane catered to it. In many ways, both men had earned the respect of their fellow inmates by not conforming.

"You talked to your lawyer?" DeLauria asked.

"Yeah. I'm fucked, so I might as well get used to it."

"Never get used to it."

Lane shrugged again. "Fuck it."

They walked in silence for a few moments as DeLauria finished the cigarette and then tossed the butt to the ground. He stepped on it, relishing the feel of crushing something under his shoe.

"I tell you," Lane said. "If I could get out tomorrow, I'd go after that silly bitch and *really* assault her. She doesn't know what assault *is*."

"If you didn't do it, why did she identify you?"

"Hell, I don't know. You know how it is. She probably never really saw the guy's face, and the police told her that I was likely the guy. So she went along with it and said, 'Yeah, that's him.'"

"Sounds like your lawyer didn't do you much good."

"Nah, he wasn't worth shit. I swear when she pointed at me, she wasn't even looking at me. I mean, she was *looking* at me, but it didn't seem like she was *seeing* me, you know what I mean?"

"Maybe."

"It's like she was looking past me, and she pointed at me just to put an end to it."

DeLauria noticed one of the black Muslims staring at them and could almost smell the hatred oozing out of the guy.

"Tim, your friend Hassim is giving you the evil eye," he said.

Lane looked over and met the man's gaze. "That asshole," he said. "He thinks I ratted on him at lunch the other day."

"He'll never forgive you for beatin' him when you got into that scrape. How long ago was that?"

"Four fuckin' months, man," Lane replied. "Guy holds a grudge."

They continued to walk, ignoring the man named Hassim.

"DeLauria!"

It was one of the guards calling from the entrance to the yard. DeLauria looked up and stared at the man.

"Come here!"

"What's up?" Lane asked.

"Dunno. I'll see you later," De Lauria said and walked across the yard to the guard. The man was holding a clipboard.

"I just need your signature on this. It's regarding your release tomorrow morning. Tried to find you in your cell earlier but Sergeant

Duffy said you were out here."

DeLauria shrugged and took the pen. He signed his name and gave the pen back to the officer.

"Very good," the man said.

DeLauria started to ask, "What time will I – " but he was interrupted by a loud cry from the other side of the yard. He and the guard both turned toward the noise and saw that several of the black Muslim gang members had grouped together to mask what appeared to be a scuffle. There was a flash of movement and then it was over as soon as it had begun. In an instant, the men dispersed in different directions, leaving a white guy lying on the ground. His orange jumpsuit was covered in blood.

It was Timothy Lane.

***

Hassim was caught a few minutes after the attack. The guards searched him and found a box cutter that he had somehow smuggled out of the workroom. He was taken away amidst the protests of his pals.

DeLauria thought they were all scum. He thanked whatever God there was that he was getting out of this hellhole.

He was released from prison on Thursday morning at eight o'clock. He had eighty-two dollars and was dressed in the civilian clothes he had been wearing when he was arrested eight years ago on racketeering and money laundering charges. The DA had been unable to pin the murder rap on him. And lucky for DeLauria, the DA didn't link the other murders to him either. DeLauria was always careful to do it differently each time.

It had been his second time in prison. The first stint was when he was twenty. He served two years for beating a guy senseless behind Rocky's Italian Restaurant in Brooklyn. DeLauria got time off for good behavior. It didn't hurt that Pontecorva had the judge in his pocket.

Now he was out. Money wouldn't be a problem. Pontecorva took care of his men, especially ones who took a fall for the family. All DeLauria had to do was go into Manhattan and pop into Lou's down in Little Italy. The boys there would set him up with a place to live and the means to start his life again. They would also supply him with weapons, the tools of his trade. The work would come after that.

DeLauria flagged a taxi and got in.

"Broome and Mott," he said.

Chapter 5

On Friday, Hannah awoke, performed her morning routine, and walked to work as usual. She approached the four-story townhouse situated in the East 60s between Second and Third Avenues and noticed that the door was open. A black BMW was parked in front, its trunk open. As she walked toward the door, John Cozzone stepped out, carrying a suitcase.

"Hannah, hello!" he said.

"Hi John," she said. "Going somewhere?"

"Yeah, I am. Go on in and get situated, and I'll be in shortly to give you the details."

Hannah nodded and went inside. She loved the townhouse. She would just as soon spend her time working there than be at home, day or night. John was a bit of a slob, though. Weren't all men? He wasn't terribly organized, either, and that's where she came in.

Upon entering, there was a small parlor to the left that was rarely used. It was a catch-all sitting room, but John mostly utilized it to sit and put on or remove his winter coat and boots during the winter if he had to go out in the snow. There was a large picture window that looked out to the street. To the right of the entry hall was a coat closet and the beginning of the stairs leading up to the second floor. Straight ahead, past a storage closet beneath the stairs, opposite the ground floor bathroom, the entry hall led to the spacious living room. An open-walled kitchen adjoined the living room, connected by counters where one could sit on barstools and be a part of conversations in either space. A dining area occupied a section of the living room, but it was rarely used. John and his guests usually sat at the kitchen "bar."

Hannah went up to the second floor. Originally there were two bedrooms and a bathroom on the second floor but John had converted one bedroom into his office and the other into a library. Hannah never went into the library – it was terribly disorganized and was full of books, videos, old vinyl record albums, and a lot of junk. The master bedroom and bath were on the third floor, and two more bedrooms, used as guestrooms, occupied the fourth floor.

Upon entering the office, the first thing Hannah noticed, as she usually did, was the smell of marijuana. John had been partaking again, probably as recently as an hour ago. The room was a mess but her personal work area was clean and neat. He had put in a desk, computer, printer, and phone just for her on the opposite side of the room from his own cluttered workspace.

She set down purse and examined the several post-it notes that he had left for her. The thick manuscript was open where she had left it a day earlier, ready to continue typing.

Several author photographs of John stared at her from their frames on the walls. These were mounted next to reproductions of book jackets – a few in English but mostly from other countries. Tucked behind her desk were a few large cardboard posters that advertised John's appearances at local bookstores. He had kept them as souvenirs but had done nothing with them.

The two worldwide bestsellers John had written in the seventies had kept him wealthy and somewhat famous, but he had yet to deliver a new book of any substance. Hannah sometimes wondered if the royalties from those two books actually still supported his extravagant lifestyle. John Cozzone lived like a rock star – he resided in a luxurious and expensive townhouse with infrequent maid service, he seemed to have a different model-type girlfriend every month, he drove a BMW and had a private garage in which to keep it, and he obviously did a lot of drugs. Hannah wasn't into that kind of scene at all, which contributed to her awe of the man.

John Cozzone was in his early fifties, handsome, dark, a little weather-beaten, and had a slim, toned body. Although Hannah couldn't see his face well, even when she stared at his photographs, she knew that he was good-looking. She liked the way he smelled, a musky, tobacco scent that permeated him, his clothes, and the whole house. Hannah had to admit that she had a schoolgirl crush on him, even though he was a distant cousin.

Hannah turned away from the photos, walked out of the office and headed toward the kitchen downstairs. She desperately needed a cup of coffee to get started. John had one of those fancy Cuisinart machines and he kept the best gourmet coffee in the fridge. Hannah thought she probably drank too much coffee, because the caffeine sometimes brought on anxiety attacks. The only way to combat that was to have a glass of hard liquor, usually something like whiskey or bourbon.

Hannah was surprised to see a woman already at the coffee maker in the kitchen. The woman had her back to her, but Hannah could see that she was young and beautiful. She had shoulder-length blonde hair and was wearing tight blue jeans. Her blouse was tied at the mid-rift, exposing her waistline. The tip of a tattoo on her left rear cheek peeked out the top of her jeans. Hannah didn't think she had met her before, but it was difficult to say at this point.

The woman heard her and turned.

"Oh, hello, Hannah," she said. "How are you?"

"Fine." Hannah stood there, trying to figure out if the woman was familiar.

"Come on in, I'm just finished. You want some coffee?"

"Please."

The woman turned, held her cup in her left hand, and offered her right hand to Hannah. "We met last week. I'm Sophia."

Hannah remembered meeting her now. The girls John brought home were all the same. Again, it was difficult to see the face with any kind of clarity that made sense, but Hannah could see that she was yet another model-type.

"Hi," she said, shaking the hand.

"So what is it you really do for John?" Sophia asked.

Hannah felt intimidated by her. The woman exuded a strong, almost menacing, vibe. There was something tough about her, as if she had lived on the edge for a long time.

Hannah looked at the floor and explained, "I type his manuscripts, do personal assistant stuff, that kind of thing."

"A glorified secretary?"

"I guess."

"But he says you're related, too?"

Hannah nodded. "He's my cousin. A distant cousin. My mother's sister's first husband's son from a previous marriage. So we're not really related by blood. Just complicated familial politics."

Sophia laughed. "I get it. How long have you known him?"

"Just a few years. He got in touch with me after my – after I left my last job, at a bank. He had heard from his mother that I was living nearby or something. She's dead now so he has no other family and neither do I. He offered me a job. It's been very convenient for both of us." She moved away from Sophia so that she wouldn't have to look at the girl's face.

"Lucky you. Get to make your own hours and stuff, huh."

Hannah nodded as she made her coffee. "Oh, he gives me deadlines and little tasks to do. But mostly it's typing his new work."

John entered just in time to hear that. "And it's *brilliant,* right, Hannah?"

Hannah laughed. "I just type it, John. I'm not a critic."

Sophia turned to John and put her arm around his neck. "So, baby, are you really going to publish something besides *The Apples of the Cosmos*?"

"I did publish something besides that!" he said, giving her a kiss on the cheek.

"Oh yeah, that other one. *The Loose Lips of Somebody.*"

"*The Loose Lips of Lucretia Leone,*" Hannah answered.

"That's it," Sophia said, winking at Hannah. "I think they were published around the time I was *born.*"

"Watch it," John said, "or I won't take you with me."

Hannah could see that John was hurt by Sophia's comment but he pretended that it didn't matter. He gave the girl a squeeze and moved back into the hall, saying, "I've got a couple more things to get and we'll be ready to go. Hannah, let's go to the office."

She followed him as Sophia said, "See you later, Hannah."

"Bye," Hannah said, over her shoulder.

As they went up the stairs, Hannah figured that if Sophia and John were going away together somewhere, then there must be something between them that was more than his usual one-night stands. John entered the office and closed the door behind Hannah.

"How do you like her, Hannah?" he asked.

Hannah shrugged. How was she supposed to have an opinion? "She's nice, I guess, but she kinda comes off as a bad girl."

"Oh, she's bad, all right," Cozzone said with innuendo. "*Very* bad!"

Hannah turned away. He obviously liked her a lot. "I don't like the way she teases you."

"Yeah, she does that," he agreed, smiling sheepishly. "She's right, you know. I haven't published anything in over twenty-five years. It's humiliating." He went to his desk and opened one of the drawers. He rummaged through it until he found what he was looking for – a shiny, long silver letter opener. He began to open the pile of mail that sat on his desk.

Hannah said, "I'm sure most writers would be very happy to have just published the two books you did write. They've sold millions."

John slit open each envelope, glanced at the contents and either tossed the mail into the trash or stuck it into a "to do" basket on the desk. "That's what I like about you, Hannah, you're an optimist."

"Oh, but I'm not, John, not really."

"No?"

She sat down at her desk. "You don't know me that well if you think I'm an optimist."

"Well, you are when you're around me," he said. "But come to think of it, you do seem a little shy. Reserved, you know what I mean?" She nodded and looked down.

"Sorry, I didn't mean to embarrass you," he said.

"That's all right."

He finished with the mail and took a moment to admire the letter opener.

"That's a nice letter opener," she said.

"Book of the Month Club gave it to me. I suppose I should use it more often. It's sharp as hell." He shrugged, opened the desk drawer, and tossed it in. "Well. Anyway, I guess you've figured out that Sophia and I are going away for a few days. We're going to Chicago, driving the Beemer. A road trip. We'll be gone at least a week, maybe more. Should be a lot of fun." He moved to his desk and picked up an empty shoulder bag that had been slung over the chair.

"How long have you been seeing her?" Hannah asked quietly.

"Hmmm?"

"Never mind."

"How long have I been seeing Sophia?"

Hannah nodded.

"Less than a month. Haven't you met her before? She's quite a girl. Comes from a well-connected Italian family." He went over to the safe that sat on the floor near his desk. He squatted and worked on the combination. "Anyway, I need you to housesit for me, can you do that? Do you mind sleeping here?"

Hannah blinked. "No."

"You can use the master bedroom if you'd like. Or one of the guestrooms, I don't care."

That would be great, she thought. The master bedroom was equipped with all kinds of high-tech entertainment equipment, a huge bed, and a private bathroom with a Jacuzzi. She did wonder why it was necessary for her to sleep there if she was going to be working every day while he was gone. He answered before she could ask.

"I'd feel better if it appeared that someone was here at night," he said. "You understand." He opened the safe and pulled out a couple of packages wrapped in brown paper. He placed them carefully inside the open shoulder bag.

"Sure," she said.

"I mean, you don't have to stay here all the time. If you need to go home and, you know, get your mail, and stuff, do so."

"Can I bring Panther here?" she asked.

"Panther?" John closed the safe and locked it. He stood, zipping up the shoulder bag and slinging it onto his back.

"My cat."

"Oh yeah. Sure. I don't mind. He won't freak out being somewhere new?"

"I don't know, he's never been anywhere else."

"Well, then it will be an adventure for him."

"Thanks."

"Now, let's see," he said, stepping over to her desk. "I'll probably be gone about a week. You can reach me on my cell phone if you have to, but try not to call unless it's an emergency, all right?"

"Sure."

"Finish up the manuscript, that's the first order of business. Take any messages that come in on the answering machine. No need to call anyone back, we'll just let them stew until I come home. Collect the mail from inside the front door and stack it on my desk. There are some plants in the living room and bedrooms… you might water them once while I'm gone. Oh, and Manuel over at Boxes and Copies called me earlier. The copies of the manuscript you finished the other day are ready to be picked up. If you can do that for me, I'd appreciate it. Any questions?"

"I don't think so."

"Feel free to use the TV, the stereo, whatever you want." He wagged a finger at her and said, sternly, "But no boyfriends!"

Hannah snorted and said, "Yeah, right."

"Actually, if you want to entertain a boyfriend over here, be my guest."

"I don't have any boyfriends."

John reached out and touched her chin. "No? Well, you should."

Hannah felt her stomach suddenly lurch into the upper regions of her chest. He smiled at her and walked out of the office. Hannah wasn't completely sure, but she thought that might have been the first time he'd ever touched her aside from shaking hands.

She sat at the desk and turned on the computer. Might as well get to work. She'd go home later, pack a bag, and carry Panther over in his travel case.

Hannah worked for fifteen minutes when she heard John call, "Hannah? We're leaving!"

She got up and went to the landing. John and Sophia were in the foyer on the first floor.

"Have a good time," she said.

"Thanks, you too," he said. They both waved at her and then went out the door.

Hannah sighed. She was alone in John Cozzone's townhouse. She could play queen of the castle.

She moved back into the office and sat. John's faces on the wall stared down at her, but they were all different and yet all the same. He might have been anyone on the street and she wouldn't know the difference. He could very well be Timothy Edward Lane and she wouldn't know him. After all, the two men were of similar build.

Timothy Lane. Hannah shuddered as the name popped into her head. It invariably did, especially the days after one of her nightmares. Timothy Lane. The man who had assaulted and tried to rape her in the foyer of her building five years ago.

Or did he?

Hannah sometimes broke out in a sweat if she thought about it too much. She tried to tell herself to forget about it, that the detective had been right. The detective had said that Lane was "most likely" her attacker. She was unable to identify him from a lineup, but she had stood in court and pointed at him. She believed in the detective, so she accused the one they had arrested.

"That's the man," she had said, indicating Lane, who sat there with his mouth open, aghast, like he would kill her if he had the chance.

Well, he was locked away now. She was safe.

So why did she always feel so guilty when she thought about Lane?

After a moment, she dug into her purse and pulled out the business card that had been given to her five years ago.

SAM BLAINE
Detective First Grade
37th Precinct

She dialed the number on the card and waited. The gruff voice that she remembered so well came from an answering machine.

"You have reached Detective Sam Blaine at the 37th Precinct. I can't take your call at the moment, so please leave a message at the beep and I'll return your call as soon as I can. If this is an emergency, dial…"

Hannah waited for the tone and then said, hesitantly, "Uhm, Detective Blaine? This is Hannah McCleary. I haven't talked to you in a while and I thought I'd just see if there has been, you know, any other arrests for crimes that were similar to mine? I was… well, I've been curious. Never mind, you don't have to call me back. I'll try you again sometime. Bye."

Hannah had disliked her experience with the police. While they had been sympathetic to her ordeal, they were very gruff and hard. After the attack and her release from the hospital, she had to spend a lot of time at the police station and the place terrified her. She never felt comfortable there and the men in uniforms frightened her as much as any would-be rapist. Considering everything she read about police corruption and other dubious traits, Hannah simply didn't trust them. She knew that it was an irrational reaction but she was not a rational person. Hannah was well aware that she had a lot of problems.

She decided to start to work but the temptation to explore the townhouse was too great. She needed to get up and walk around, settle her nerves. For some reason, it had set her heart racing when John had touched her on the chin. The adrenaline rush brought back the unpleasant sensations she had experienced the night she was attacked. That fear, mixed with the guilt she felt when she thought of Timothy Lane, made her extremely uneasy.

Hannah walked up the stairs, past the third floor, and into John's messy bedroom. Clothes were scattered all over the floor and furniture – discarded boxer shorts, socks, trousers, gym shorts. There was female clothing, too. A bra and panties lay on the floor and a red cocktail dress was flung over a chair. Sophia's, most likely.

She suddenly had an inexplicable desire to look through her cousin's closet and chest-of-drawers. These were where people hid their most private things. Underwear, of course, but also keepsakes like love letters, drugs, and other dark secrets. Hannah felt a thrill as she opened the drawers one by one and carefully rummaged through the apparel. At first it appeared that there was nothing of interest other than Jockey briefs and socks, until the bottom drawer yielded a black box that caught Hannah's attention. She pulled it out and examined it. It was made of leather and had a gold clasp, not unlike a jewel box. Ever curious, she flipped the latch and opened the treasure chest.

A handgun and two boxes of ammunition lay inside.

What would her cousin be doing with a gun? she wondered. Why would he need one?

She had an intense desire to pick it up and hold it, but she shivered and decided not to touch it. She knew nothing about guns, didn't like them, wouldn't know a revolver from an automatic. She quickly closed the box and carefully placed it back in the drawer the way she had found it.

She stood and gazed around the room again. The king-size bed was unmade. Hannah approached it slowly. The room smelled of sex and John Cozzone's musky odor. She reached out and touched the sheets. There was a wet spot that was now cool to the touch. A pair of John's briefs was tucked under the blanket. Hannah pulled them out and hesitantly smelled them.

Inexplicably, tears came to Hannah's eyes. She sat on the bed and lay back. There was a mirror over the bed. She could see her figure stretched out above her, but the face was still an enigma, a blank slate, a doll with no features.

Hannah pulled the sheets on top of her body and snuggled into them. She inhaled the smell of John's pillow and then the tears began to flow freely.

Chapter 6

Bill Cutler had reluctantly agreed to meet Patrick for lunch. It was a ritual they went though once a month, even though it almost always turned out to be unpleasant for both of them. Patrick came into the city from New Rochelle, where he owned a large house. They would meet at Patrick's favorite mid-town restaurant, a small Italian place on W. 47th Street that was within walking distance of MedScript. Patrick never once asked Bill if he would prefer going somewhere of his choice.

Bill was late, as usual. As he sauntered in, he noticed that Patrick sat at the table with his precious Bloody Mary, drumming his fingers and looking at his watch.

"Sorry, I had to finish a transcript," Bill said, taking the seat across the table from his brother.

Patrick sighed and shook his head. "I don't know why I bother," he muttered.

"Would you rather dine alone?" Bill asked a little too loudly. Some of the other guests looked up from their meals. "I'll be happy to go down the street and grab a slice of pizza and leave you in peace."

"Oh, lower your voice, for Chrissakes. Can't we have a decent meal together for once?"

"Hey, you started it."

"Forget it. What are you having?"

"Mind if I look at the menu?"

"Fine."

The waiter stepped up to the table and took Bill's drink order. Unlike his brother, he liked variety. This time he ordered a gin and tonic.

"I thought you hated gin," Patrick remarked.

"What do you know what I like or not?"

"All right, stop. Listen, I want to talk to you about something."

"What?"

"You know I'm shopping around for a townhouse in Manhattan. I think I might have found a nice one on the Upper West Side. You want to come look at it with me?"

"What for?"

Patrick shrugged. "I thought I could get a second opinion."

"You want *my* opinion? Since when have you ever asked my opinion?"

"Sheesh, Bill, I'm trying to be friendly. And besides, if I buy a townhouse it will be in the family."

"What family?"

"You and me. We're all we've got, right?"

The waiter brought Bill's drink. Bill grabbed it from him and took a big swig. "You're right, Patrick. I love you, man."

The waiter sensed the tension. "Should I come back in a few minutes?"

"No, I'm ready," Patrick said. He ordered his usual lasagna. Bill sighed and ordered spaghetti and meatballs.

The two men stayed quiet for a few minutes as they simmered down. Finally, Bill asked, "What did you think of my proposal to expand MedScript's services?"

Patrick raised his eyebrows. "I read it. I don't know, Bill, MedScript is a specialized company. We do medical transcription. To start farming out temporary nursing help is a whole different ballgame. You have to hire good people and the screening process could be problematic. Good nurses are hard to come by. Medical personnel become targets for all kinds of lawsuits. Like all of your other schemes, this one's full of potential disasters."

Bill nodded, "Yeah. You never like any of my ideas."

"Bill, that's because most of them aren't realistic. You don't think them through. You come up with the bare concept for something and don't realize that there's much more to it. You don't plan ahead and study all the angles. Business is like chess. You have to anticipate all the moves and counter-moves."

Bill had no argument for that. It's the same thing that he'd heard over and over from his brother. The "life as a chessboard" speech. Bill wanted to shove a Rook up his brother's ass.

"Look," Bill said. "I know I've made some mistakes in my life. I haven't been the golden boy that you've managed to be your whole life. But I'm making a good go of MedScript, aren't I? I'm a damn good manager!"

"I didn't say you weren't."

"Well just listen to me every now and then. The expansion idea was just that... an idea. So it sucked. Why not encourage me to think about something else instead of shooting me down every time?"

"Okay, I'm sorry," Patrick said. "You're right."

Bill took a piece of bread and buttered it in silence. After a minute, Patrick asked, "How's the therapy going?"

"What therapy?"

"Come on, Bill."

"I stopped going."

"What?"

"I stopped going. It wasn't doing me any good."

"What are you talking about?" Patrick was clearly agitated. "You're supposed to be in therapy. It's part of the terms of – "

"I know what it is, Patrick," Bill said, trying his best to control his temper. "My P.O. doesn't give a shit. I told him that the therapy was doing me more harm than good, which it was. It made me think *more* about that... stuff... than when I'm not in therapy. Really, Patrick, I'm doing all right. Trust me."

"Hmmm, that sounds a lot like famous last words."

That was it. Bill threw his napkin down on the table, stood, and walked out of the restaurant.

***

Bill wasn't happy that Dr. Lazar's tapes were left for him. Debbie and Kathy had carefully avoided taking the doctor's accordion file and now it was the only one left in the bin. Bill considered making an excuse to leave the office – anything to avoid having to work on it. Unfortunately, he had just heard from the pediatrics offices located on the first floor. A big batch of tapes was coming that afternoon. They were going to be swamped, so he needed to take that tape and finish it before the dam broke. He cursed under his breath and grabbed the file.

He set up the folders and removed the two tapes the file contained. Cutler estimated that there was two or two-and-a-half hours of work there. Fine, he thought. He'd zip through them and then take a long coffee break. As long as his snotty-nosed brother didn't call and ask for something trivial, he might just make it.

Dr. Lazar's annoying dictation droned into his ear for over an hour before he stopped to take a pee break. The woman simply didn't know how to speak into a tape recorder. She hesitated, spoke too slowly, repeated herself, and didn't talk in complete sentences. And that *accent.* Most Eastern Europeans he could understand pretty well, but this woman took the cake. Half the time she sounded like a parody of Nazi interrogators. "*Ve hav vays of making you talk!*"

Cutler glared at the two young typists as he walked toward the men's room, which was located out in the hall. He could have sworn that they snickered at each other. It was probably a conspiracy. "Let's fix it so that Bill gets Dr. Lazar's tapes." Currently the policy was that any accordion file was up for grabs as long as it was in the bin. Thus, the typists automatically took the easy doctors first. Cutler was strongly considering instigating a new rule stating that files had to be logged by time of day when they came in – that way they would have to be worked on in the order in which they arrived. No more leaving the lousy tapes for someone else.

Cutler did his business in the washroom and took his time getting back to his desk. He had a headache, so he opened a drawer, removed a bottle of ibuprofen, slung it down with a gulp of lukewarm coffee, and continued to work.

So far none of the patients interested him. No hot young nymphomaniacs who needed psychiatric help. No lonely single mothers. Just boring, depressed people who like to whine.

Toward the end of the second tape, Bill perked up as he typed the next patient report. He carefully made sense of the doctor's poor dictation and presented it neatly and intelligently.

"The patient's name is Hannah McCleary. Thirty-four years old. Extremely interesting case. She came to me a year ago from Dr. Bromfield."

Bill knew that Dr. Bromfield was a noted neurologist. His medical transcriptions came through the office, too.

"Miss McCleary suffers from a very rare neurological condition called 'prosopagnosia.'"

That was a new one. Bill frowned, stopped the tape, and took off the headset. He pulled out his medical dictionary and looked up the word so that he could spell it correctly. It wasn't there. He got up and went over to the common reference area, where the company kept an assortment of books. He found the one called *Disorders of the Brain* and looked up the word.

There it was – prosopagnosia. He read the entry with interest and found that it was the name of a very rare condition also known as "face blindness." Apparently a small portion of the brain was used exclusively for the identification of faces. The spot was located in the back of the head, slightly above the occipital region. A person normally stores the memories of the people he or she meets – faces – and accesses these files every time he or she looks at another human being. Usually, people have no problems recognizing their friends and relatives, as well as others that they don't know personally but whom they have encountered on an informal basis. Someone might not know the name of the security guard that stands at the bank of elevators on the first floor, but his face will be very familiar. A person with face blindness is unable to recognize people – even people they know extremely well, like relatives. The book cited a case in which a grown man was unable to distinguish his own son from two of his son's school friends. Only when the son spoke did the man know him. Another woman cited the example of running into a male colleague from work at a department store. Because he was encountered in an environment that he was not normally associated with, the woman did not recognize him. This was despite the fact that she worked next to him every day for years.

Extraordinary, Bill thought. How did one function with that handicap? It seemed unreal.

He continued to read. People diagnosed with prosopagnosia from birth usually developed methods for identifying others to compensate for the visual deficiency. These techniques included smell, voice recognition, hair color, size and weight of the person, and other subtle clues that told the viewer who the person might be. The condition was much more problematic in patients that developed it as an adult. Prosopagnosia could be caused by a head injury that effected the brain's face recognition center. In these rare cases, the patient usually had a very difficult time adjusting to the disability. More often than not, subjects with acquired face blindness tended to avoid social situations, crowds, and other circumstances that might require them to recognize and know people.

Bill closed the book and returned it to the shelf. He went back to his desk and continued working on the report.

"Dr. Bromfield's notes are in the patient's file. The patient was the victim of an attempted rape five years ago. She received a head injury but was otherwise physically unharmed. She recovered from a concussion but it left her with the prosopagnosia. Dealing with the condition has been difficult for the patient and Dr. Bromfield suggested that Miss McCleary enter psychotherapy. Apparently she did not get along with Dr. Miller, who I referred her to, so I am

referring her to Dr. Madison. Miss McCleary suffers from depression and anxiety, and as a result has withdrawn from any kind of social interaction that she can avoid. The patient struck me as extremely shy and introverted. She is already on 150 milligrams of Zoloft q.d. During my evaluation of her I have also concluded that she suffers from the emotional scarring from her ordeal, and she seems to have paranoid delusions. She stated more than once that she believes that the assailant who attacked her is still out there, despite the fact that the man was caught and convicted. One thing she stated that concerns me is that if she were to meet the man who did this to her, face-to-face, she would do her best to try and kill him.

"The next patient is…"

Bill stopped the tape. He sat a moment and contemplated what he had just heard. Was it for real? How could someone not recognize faces? Did this mean that the patient, this Hannah McCleary, wouldn't know someone she just met if she bumped into him an hour later?

He pulled out his black book and turned to the Quest List. He wrote down the name "Hannah McCleary," and made note of her address and phone number that was plainly displayed on her file. He also jotted down some of the things Dr. Lazar had said, then closed the book.

Bill leaned back in his chair, put his hands behind his head, and thought about his next great performance.

Chapter 7

"You sure these guys are cool?" Cozzone asked as he parked the BMW on Avenue A.

"Yeah, they work for the Pontecorva family," Sophia said. "They supply the stuff to the Castellanos. It's a deal that the two families have with each other. All in the spirit of cooperation, know what I mean?"

"I guess."

They had driven down Second Avenue and then cut over to the Lower East Side. After he turned off the engine, Sophia removed a Colt .45 from her handbag and began to check it like a pro.

"What the hell, Sophia!" Cozzone whispered.

"It's just to be safe. Come on, I know how to use it."

He gave her a grin, but his heart wasn't in it. "What kind of a bad girl have I gotten mixed up with?"

"The worst," she said, and then she leaned over, kissed him on the cheek, and stuffed the gun into her purse.

"They'll probably frisk you," she said. "I'm pretty sure I'll be okay. Oh, and don't tell them your real name. All they know is that the usual carriers aren't coming." She started to get out of the car.

"Hey, wait," Cozzone said, grabbing her arm. "Look, I feel funny about this. It's not the way I like to do business."

"What's wrong? You want to make a big score, don't you? That's what you've been saying."

"I know, I know. But I'd rather deal with people I know and trust."

"The people you know and trust are small time. You'll never get past distributing nickel and dime bags. If you want to move the quantities, you have to deal with the big boys. And big boys play with guns, so you have to take a risk. Think of it like Atlantic City. You're going in to make a bet."

"I've done all right," Cozzone said. "I've been able to pay the rent for years on what I sell."

"Hey, you're the one who was complaining about it. What's the matter, are you backing out?" Her tone indicated that she was almost put out.

"No, no."

"Well, what's the matter?"

He shrugged. "Just a little nervous about it, that's all."

"Well get over it," she said. "You've already got Ramon in Chicago waiting for the stuff. He's already lined up buyers, although I gotta admit I don't trust anyone with a name like *Ramon*. Anyway, if you back out now, it's gonna fuck up your reputation. No one will deal with you again."

Cozzone looked at the brown paper packages inside the shoulder bag. "Sophia, there's thirty grand in here."

"Yeah? So?"

"For me, that's a lot of money. What if they screw us?"

"I'll make sure they're won't screw us, John! Now, are going or not? Do I have to make a very embarrassing phone call?"

He sighed and then shook his head. "Let's go."

They got out of the car and walked west on 2nd Street. When they got to the old brownstone, she looked at him and said, "This is it."

They went inside the front door and she pushed the intercom button.

"Yeah?" It was a gruff male voice.

"Charlie?"

"Who's asking?"

She suddenly realized that she hadn't thought of an alias so she used the first name that came to her. "It's Hannah. Spits sent us."

There was a slight pause, during which Cozzone looked at her quizzically. "Hannah?" he mouthed.

She shook her head at him, indicating for him to shut up.

"Second floor," came the voice and then the door buzzed.

The building smelled old, mixed with the distinct odor of cat urine. They went up the creaky wooden steps, the noise reverberating throughout the narrow building. There was no way anyone could sneak up on these guys.

When they got to the landing, they found a very large man standing with his arms folded across his chest.

"Charlie?" she asked.

"No. Anthony. Charlie's inside." He jerked his head toward a door with the number "12" on it. He opened it and motioned them inside.

It was a sparsely furnished one-bedroom apartment. It looked as if no one really lived there. Cozzone suspected that it was merely a place where illegal transactions were made.

Anthony closed the door and locked it. "What did you say your name was?" he asked Sophia.

"Hannah."

The brute looked at Cozzone.

"Oh, I'm Vincent."

"Hello, Vincent. I gotta check your bag."

"Oh, sure." Cozzone handed him the shoulder bag. Anthony unzipped it and rummaged around. He didn't mess with the wrapped packages. The man placed the bag on the floor and then said, "I gotta frisk you."

"All right," Cozzone said. He held out his arms as the big man patted him down.

Satisfied, Anthony motioned to a round dining table that had four wicker chairs around it.

"Have a seat. Charlie will be right out," Anthony said.

"What about me, baby?" Sophia asked in a come-hither voice that Cozzone hadn't heard before. She raised her arms and presented her smashing model figure.

Anthony smiled slightly and said, "That's okay, honey. Have a seat." He went to the bedroom door, opened it, and disappeared.

Cozzone looked at her like she was crazy. "What are you trying to do?" he whispered.

"Hush," she said. "Just thought it'd be better to offer myself up for a frisking. I figured he wouldn't."

Cozzone took a seat at the table. "Sounded to me like you wanted him to fuck you."

"Shut up and just let me do the talking," she said, sitting next to him.

After a few moments, Anthony came back out, followed by a tall thin man with a mustache and graying hair. An ancient scar ran from the edge of his mouth to the back edge of his jaw, below the ear. He looked to be about fifty, whereas Anthony was probably in his thirties.

"Don't get up," the man said when Cozzone started to rise and extend his hand. "I'm Charlie Patrone."

"Vincent Pileggi," Cozzone said. "And this is…"

"I'm Hannah Vaccarino," Sophia said. "How you been, Charlie? Long time no see, baby."

"Do I know you?" he asked her, immune to her charms.

"You probably don't remember. We met at Christopher Rizzo's wedding a couple of years ago. In the Hamptons, baby."

"I don't remember you," Charlie said.

"Oh, but I remember you," she said sweetly. He sat at the table while Anthony stood beside him, ready to pounce on the couple if they made a false move.

"I understand Spits sent you?" he asked.

"That's right," Sophia said.

"We didn't know he was gonna send a lady," Patrone said.

"Hey, baby, as long as you get your money, what do you care, right?" she said, smiling, the come-on directed at both men. But Patrone remained stone-faced.

"Look, *baby,*" he said, carefully considering his words. "We're talking about a lot of money and a lot of product. We can party later, if you'd like, but first we conduct business like professionals."

Sophia wiped the smile off her face. "Sure, Charlie, whatever you say."

"You got the money, *baby*?" he asked.

"Yeah," she said. She looked at Cozzone, who opened the shoulder bag and took out the packets wrapped in brown paper. He slid them across the table to Patrone, who casually opened one with a switchblade that appeared in his hand out of nowhere. The stacks of green bills appeared to be fresh and new.

"Thirty thousand, as agreed," Sophia said.

Patrone studied the money in front of him, and then nodded at Anthony. The big man left the room.

"So where do you plan to distribute the product?" Patrone asked.

Cozzone said, "Chic – "

"Out of state," Sophia interrupted. "You don't have to worry. We're not messing with any of your territories."

Patrone simply nodded. Anthony returned with a gym bag. He placed it on the table and put a small mirror next to it. He then opened the bag, reached inside, and pulled out a zip-lock freezer bag full of white powder. He carefully opened it, scooped out a little with a tiny coke spoon, and lined it up on the mirror. He slid the mirror across the table to Sophia and handed her a short straw. Sophia took the straw and sampled the cocaine.

She sniffed hard, shook her head, and went, "Whoa, baby!" She licked her finger and scooped up the remains from the mirror and tasted it. "Wow, I can feel it already," she said. She looked at Cozzone. "It's good, baby."

"Then we have a deal?" Patrone asked. "Baby?"

"Yeah," she said. "Hey, can I use your bathroom a second? I really gotta pee."

Anthony and Patrone looked at each other, then Patrone shrugged. Anthony pointed to the bedroom. "It's right back there."

Sophia took her purse and left the room. Patrone reached over and stacked the money while Anthony sealed up the cocaine and placed it back in the gym bag.

"There are two bags," he said. "Eight pounds, total."

Cozzone's heart was pounding. They were now in possession with enough cocaine that, when cut and divided, would net them a half-million dollars, maybe more. It was the largest score he'd ever attempted.

"How long you known Spits?" Patrone asked.

"I don't know him," Cozzone said. "She does."

"So how come she calls the shots? Where are your balls, my friend?"

Cozzone just smiled. "She busted them a long time ago. She's a firecracker, ain't she?"

Patrone frowned. "If you say so." He stood. "Now if you'll excuse me, I have –"

The sudden loud recoil made Cozzone jump in his seat. Simultaneously, Patrone's chest burst outward. Blood and tissue splattered across the table and covered one of the empty chairs. Anthony whirled around, drawing a Heckler & Koch 9mm from a holster on his back, but he was stopped by another deafening crack. Anthony jerked backwards, dropped his handgun, and fell backwards.

Sophia stood in the bedroom doorway, the Colt in her hands, her eyes trained on the big man on the floor. Anthony struggled to reach for his gun but she pulled the trigger again. A portion of the bodyguard's upper back flew off and the man was still.

Cozzone couldn't move. He stared at Sophia as if she were mad.

"What the fuck, Sophia?" he swallowed.

"Come on, John, grab the money. Let's get the hell out of here," she said.

"What have you done?" he asked again, louder.

"What do you mean, what have I done? I just saved us thirty grand, that's what I've done. Now let's get out of here, fast!" She replaced the Colt in her purse, then grabbed the stacks of bills. She shoved them in the gym bag and slid it over to Cozzone. "Will you *move*?"

"Sophia, do you know who you just killed?" he asked, still unable to stand.

"Yeah, I know. That's why we gotta run. We have to get out of New York, and fast." She looked at him, waiting for him to stand. "Now, John!"

Trembling, he stood and took the gym and shoulder bags. They left the apartment quickly, sailed down the stairs, and casually walked out of the building. Without another word, they made it to the BMW and got in.

Back upstairs, Anthony opened and closed his eyes once.

***

"You could have warned me that you were going to do that," Cozzone said as he started the ignition.

"You would have freaked out," she said. "Let's go."

He pulled out and circled the block so that he could head uptown.

Sophia began to laugh.

"What's so funny?" he asked.

"Baby, we're rich! We're fucking rich!"

"We're fucking *dead* when Pontecorva finds out about this."

"He won't know who we are," Sophia said. "By the time they get their shit together to start looking for us, we'll be halfway to Chicago."

Cozzone turned the car west and headed towards the tunnel.

He had a very bad feeling about all of this.

Chapter 8

By mid-afternoon, Hannah had completed typing five chapters of Cozzone's manuscript. She was not particularly impressed with what she had read, but then again, she wasn't much of a critic. It certainly wasn't mass-market material. The novel was of a historical nature and dealt with intrigue during the Napoleonic wars. It wasn't her cup of tea.

She looked at her watch and decided it would be a good time to go home and take care of things before returning to Cozzone's apartment that evening. She needed to pick up her laundry, go to the bank, do some grocery shopping, and pack a bag.

Hannah locked up carefully with the key John had entrusted her with, then set out walking north. Boxes and Copies was right there on Second Avenue, so she stopped in. Manuel, the young Hispanic who ran the place, looked up from his computer and smiled.

"Hello, Miss Hannah," he said.

"Hello, Manuel." Hannah wondered if he ever left the place. The operation was a personal mailbox service, post office, and copy center. Cozzone did a lot of business there and frequently sent Hannah over to ship packages or mail things.

"You come to get your copies?" Manuel asked.

"I forget how much there is."

He didn't have to look. "Four reams."

"Oh," she said. "I'm on my way home and don't want to carry them. How about I stop by on the way back? I'll be coming back this evening."

"Whatever you like, Miss Hannah. How is Mister John?"

"He's good. Thanks, Manuel."

Hannah left the shop and then stopped by the ATM outside her bank to withdraw $100, more than enough to last her a few days. After that she went into D'Agostino's to buy some milk and cat food. She knew exactly where the items were located and had them in a basket within two minutes. The checkout line, she knew, would take much longer.

Nearly ten minutes later it was her turn to pay. The checker cheerfully said, "Hello, how are you today?" in a tone that implied that he knew her. "Has that cat of yours already eaten what you bought the other day?"

Hannah was aware that she must be a familiar customer in the store. She didn't recognize the young man at all, and of course she wouldn't. She had been friendly with several of the checkers, both men and women, but it was impossible to tell which one this was.

"I'm fine, thank you," she said, putting on her best front. Then she noticed the nametag that read: HELLO, MY NAME IS JAMES! MAY I HELP YOU?

"Nice to see you again, James," she said. "Yes, my Panther eats more like a horse than a cat."

"Well, if it's a *panther* then I can understand…" he replied, winking at her. She saw the wink but Hannah still had trouble making sense out of his face. She had to look just past the side of his head in order to discern his features accurately.

She took her groceries and carried them in front of her with both arms. The walk to her apartment was just another two short blocks. She stopped at the Laundry and saw that Mr. Wong wasn't there. One or both of his two sons were usually working in the shop, and she couldn't tell them apart. Hannah presented her claim slip and one boy gave her the duffel bag. She was just able to carry it by the pull-string and hold the bag of groceries, but had her home been any further away it would have been an impossible task.

She entered the building after some awkward manipulation of the bags and her keys, stopping only to open her mailbox. Inside was a brochure on Santa Fe, New Mexico that she had ordered over the Internet a while back because she liked to fantasize about taking a trip there someday. She knew that she never would, though.

Her footsteps echoed on the wooden stairs as she ascended toward her floor. Liz's door opened and the woman peeked out.

"Hi, Hannah," she said. "You need some help?" She was dressed in tight jeans and a white tank top that displayed her large, drooping breasts. No bra, of course.

Hannah was about to drop the grocery bag. "If you could…"

Liz stepped out of her apartment and caught the bag. "Got it."

Hannah set down the duffel bag and unlocked her door. "I'm glad I saw you," she said as she took the grocery bag from her neighbor. "I'm going to be spending the night at John's for a few days."

Liz raised her eyebrows. "Oh?"

"I'm house-sitting," Hannah said. "He's gone away with his girlfriend."

"Oh, well, that's nice. Maybe I can come see where the famous writer lives?"

Hannah shrugged. "Sure, I don't see why not. Maybe we can fix a dinner over there and watch something on TV. He's got this huge entertainment set-up."

"Sounds good. I'm off next Friday night. A week from tonight?"

Hannah shrugged again. "I guess that's all right, but I'm not sure when John's going to come back. He said it'd be at least a week, so that's probably okay."

"Good. I gotta get to work now. Tonight's Ladies Night."

Hannah looked at her sideways. "Isn't every night Ladies Night at your bar?"

"Yeah, but this is a night that we give free drinks to men who come dressed in drag. Ladies Night, get it?"

"I guess. So men come to your bar, too?"

"Sure. Even straight ones, hoping to pick up a couple of lesbians. Hah! In their dreams."

Panther slinked out into the hall and rubbed against Hannah's legs.

"Well, look who's hungry. I gotta put this stuff away and feed the cat," Hannah said.

"You need me to feed the cat while you're away?"

"No, I'm taking him with me. And I'll be in and out to check my mail and stuff."

"Listen, why don't you come down to the bar some night?" Liz asked. "I'll make sure you get a drink or two on the house."

Hannah looked at the floor. "I, uhm, I don't really like to go out in public much."

"I've noticed. Come on, you don't have to be a dyke to go there. Lots of straight people go."

"I don't know..."

"Well, think about it. I'm not twisting your arm or anything."

"Okay. Thanks."

"See ya around," Liz said as she headed back to her apartment.

"Bye."

Hannah shut her door and sighed. The last thing she wanted was to go someplace where she had to meet people. Social situations were bad news. She might be introduced to someone, and then five minutes later she wouldn't recognize the same person if she went away and came back. Just imagining the prospect of going to a public gathering produced anxiety. If the uneasiness became too much then Hannah would experience a panic attack, and that was truly awful.

She placed the grocery bag on the kitchen counter and dropped the duffel bag on the floor. As she opened the fridge to put the milk in, she noticed that the light on her answering machine was blinking. This was unusual, for Hannah almost never received messages. She punched the button and heard the coarse voice from the not-too-distant past.

"Hello, Miss McCleary, this is Detective Blaine returning your call. I'm not sure exactly what you meant by your message. If you were wondering if we ever arrested someone who might have also been a suspect in your case, the answer is no. We got the right man the first time. You don't ever have to worry about him again. If you have any further questions, don't hesitate to call."

For some reason, the detective's words didn't bring her much comfort. There was something about his certainty that seemed phony. It was almost as if he was convincing himself that he was right. She took what he said with a grain of salt. Was Timothy Edward Lane the right man? The detective seemed so sure. Why didn't she?

The answer was obvious. She hadn't known that she was face blind until after the trial. She knew that *something* was wrong, that her memory for recognizing people was somehow effected by the ordeal, but she had attributed that to the concussion. Her doctors had told her that she might experience things like that. It was several months after Lane had been convicted and sentenced to prison that she finally saw a neurologist and went through a battery of tests to determine why she thought she was going mad. No one would believe her when she said that she was unable to recognize anyone anymore. She couldn't remember the man who sold her coffee at Starbucks and she had trouble following movies on television because she couldn't tell the characters apart. Paranoia and fear overtook her until she had become distrustful of nearly everyone. At first she had the delusion that the whole world was against her and that every faceless stranger she met was a member of some kind of secret cult who wanted to punish her for sending an innocent man to jail.

Did she really believe Lane was innocent? Hannah couldn't say. Something in her gut, deep within her consciousness, screamed that she had made a terrible mistake. She had gone along with the cops and identified Lane as her attacker. Despite the lack of physical evidence, the jury took into account the fact that Lane was in the area and was caught twenty minutes later attempting to rob a convenience store. Another witness had seen Lane loitering on First Avenue around the same time that Hannah had made the walk home from work that fateful night. Lane had also been convicted for a previous assault but hadn't served much time. Circumstantial evidence, to be sure, but her positive identification sealed the man's destiny.

Her shrink had told her to try and put it behind her. The cops weren't usually wrong. If they felt that the man was guilty, then it must be so. Hannah told herself this over and over, but the dreams still haunted her and the guilt remained heavy in her heart.

Sometimes it made her want to scream with rage.

Hannah ignored the meowing cat at her legs and eyed the cupboard where she kept the bottle. Her shrink had told her that it wasn't good, that it would have negative interactions with her medication. Nevertheless, it calmed her. Often – too often – it was the only thing that worked.

Hannah opened the cupboard and removed the bottle of Jack Daniel's. She took a glass from the cabinet, opened the bottle, and poured the brown liquid into the glass. She opened the freezer, removed two cubes of ice from the automatic dispenser, and plopped them in. She downed the drink, coughed once, then tossed the ice into the sink.

"All right, Panther, here you go," she said.

She proceeded to feed the cat, then emptied the duffel bag so that she could put away her clean laundry. She then packed a small bag and prepared Panther's travel case. He immediately hid behind the couch when he saw it. An appearance of the travel case usually meant a trip to the vet.

"We're going on a vacation, Panther," she told him. "Don't worry, it's not the vet."

As an afterthought, she packed the bottle of Jack Daniel's and then went over to the lounge area to turn on the television. The news was on, but she rarely paid much attention to it. Mostly she just listened while she did other things because the faces were meaningless. There was some story on about a couple of gangsters being shot and killed in an apartment on the Lower East Side. Police thought it might be a drug-related incident and they were looking for a man and a woman for questioning.

Hannah opened a flat box that sat on the coffee table and pulled out several 8x10 glossy photographs of celebrities that she had purchased at a movie memorabilia shop. On the backs she had written the names of the actors and actresses. She shuffled the stack and put them on the table. Then, one by one, she studied the face on the top photo and attempted to identify the celebrity. It was her way of playing with Flash Cards.

"You're Tom Cruise," she said. She turned the photo over and saw that it was really Charlie Sheen. "Damn."

The next one. "Harrison Ford." Nope. George Clooney.

The next one was a woman. Sometimes they were easier because there were more attributes to consider – hair length, for example.

"Meg Ryan." Hannah turned the photo over. She got that one right.

The next one was another woman. "Diane Keaton." Nope. Susan Sarandon.

The phone rang.

Odd. Hannah never received calls. Two in one day was some kind of record.

She picked up the receiver. "Hello?"

"May I please speak to Hannah McCleary?" It was a man, a voice she had never heard before. He had a slick Boston accent.

"This is she."

"Hello, Miss McCleary. I'm Doctor Tom Cagle. I work with Doctor Lazar."

"Yes?"

"She recently referred you to a therapist, a Doctor Madison, is that right?"

"Yes. I have an appointment in a couple of days to see him."

"Ah, right. I'm calling because Doctor Madison will be unavailable. In fact, he's leaving the city. He's moving out to Long Island. Doctor Lazar asked me to take over your referral. Is that okay?"

"Sure, I guess so."

"Excellent. Anyway, I keep evening hours for therapy patients. Is that convenient for you?"

"Sure, I guess so."

"Good. I have some slots open next Thursday evening. That was the same day you were scheduled to see Doctor Madison. Can you come around seven-thirty?"

"Where are you?"

"Mid-town. East Fifty-fifth Street and Fifth. Is that good for you?"

"That's fine."

He gave her the address and his office phone number. "You don't have to cancel your appointment with Doctor Madison. We've taken care of that for you. And I'll let Doctor Lazar know that you'll be seeing me."

"Thanks."

"When are you supposed to see Doctor Lazar again?"

"Uhm, not for a few weeks. Three or four weeks, I think. I'd have to check my calendar."

"That's all right, I just wanted a ballpark estimation. Seeing me in the evening isn't going to interfere with your job, is it?"

"No, I can set my own hours."

"Really?" he asked. "That must be nice. What kind of work do you do?"

"I'm a personal assistant to an author."

"That must be interesting. Someone famous?"

"Sort of. John Cozzone. Have you heard of him?"

"Is that the guy who wrote *Apples of the Cosmos*?"

"That's him."

"Wow, that was a great book. It's been a long time since I read it. Has he done anything recently?"

"He's always writing, but he hasn't published anything in a while."

"Well. You can tell me more when we meet. I look forward to seeing you then next Thursday at seven-thirty."

"All right. Thanks. What was your name again?"

"Cagle. Tom Cagle." He definitely sounded as if he was a Kennedy with that accent.

"Got it," she said. "Thank you. Bye."

After he hung up, Hannah reflected that the doctor seemed very kind and friendly. She wondered what he looked like, but his face would mean no more to her than that of Tom Cruise. Or Charlie Sheen, for that matter.

Chapter 9

Dominic DeLauria got out of the taxi and pressed the button on the intercom that hung to the left of the imposing gate.

"Yeah?"

"It's Dominic."

The gate slowly swung open to reveal the long, curved driveway that led to the house. DeLauria walked in and strolled up the incline, past the exquisitely manicured hedges and Romanesque statuary that lined the drive, and on up to the guardhouse. Two of Pontecorva's bodyguards manned the guardhouse at all times. One of them waved DeLauria through and said, "Freddie's waitin' for you. Good to see you, Dom."

"Thanks." He went a further forty yards and rounded the bend to behold the huge Tudor mansion in Glen Cove where the Pontecorvas had lived for half a century. DeLauria had never known the Don, Pasquale Pontecorva, the man who had built the family from scratch from the dregs of a deadly mob war that occurred in the forties. When the old mafia families metamorphosed into the modern-day crime families, Pontecorva had been at the forefront. He was one of the first to see that drugs would be the big thing and invested heavily into creating a secure pipeline to import cocaine, heroin, and other nasty substances from various sources around the world.

Today his son Freddie ran the business. DeLauria had a great deal of respect for Freddie. Some said that Freddie was a better Don than his father was. Freddie had some kind of business degree from Harvard, he was cool, calm, and highly intelligent. In the twenty-two years DeLauria had been working for the Pontecorva family, he had never seen Freddie lose his temper or make a rash decision. Freddie also took care of his men, especially those who served time for something they had done for the family. While DeLauria was at Rikers, Freddie had kept DeLauria on the payroll. He had promised DeLauria that there would always be a place for him when he got out. For that, DeLauria would go to the ends of the earth for Freddie Pontecorva.

One of Freddie's goons, a guy they all called Tommy Salami, met DeLauria in front of the house.

"Hey, Dominic, you're looking good," Tommy said, giving DeLauria a bear hug.

"Thanks, Tommy. So are you."

"When did you get out?"

"What's today… Monday? It was last Thursday morning."

"They treat you all right in there? You didn't get fucked in the ass or anything, did you?"

"No, but you can kiss it for asking me that."

Tommy laughed and slapped DeLauria lightly on the cheek. "Good to have you back. Freddie's inside. Come on in."

They walked into the immaculate mansion that still looked as it did in the fifties when Pasquale Pontecorva bought and furnished the place. The décor was distinctly classical Roman, and it reminded DeLauria of Caesar's Palace in Vegas. The greeting hall was bright and sunny, surrounded by bulletproof glass windows. A running fountain occupied the middle of the room, the center of which was a statue of a naked Roman goddess holding a lyre.

Tommy led DeLauria through a hallway and into the spacious study that served as Freddie Pontecorva's office. The room was a contrast to the front of the house. It was furnished more like a lawyer's den. The walls were lined with books, mostly law books, and a large oak desk occupied one side of the room. An array of comfortable leather furniture pieces occupied the other half of the room – where Pontecorva could sit and meet with his men.

"Have a seat. Freddie will be right in," Tommy said. "What can I get you to drink?"

"Scotch and soda."

"Coming right up."

Tommy left the room and DeLauria sat in one of the large chairs. He had to wait only ten seconds before Pontecorva entered the room.

"Dom," he said, smiling wide. DeLauria stood and the two men embraced heartily. "It's good to see you."

"Thanks, Freddie. You, too."

Freddie Pontecorva was in his fifties. He was a heavy-set man without any fat on him. DeLauria thought the man must work out a lot, for the boss's bulk was made up of large, solid muscle. His wavy black hair had grayed a little, and the mustache now had salt and pepper in it, but for all intents and purposes the man looked the same.

"What, you have a painting of yourself up in the attic that ages? You look great," DeLauria said.

"Nah, I get old like everybody. I got some medical problems. I feel all right, though. Today, anyway. How about you? Looks like prison treated you pretty good."

"Fuck prison. I'm out now."

"Yes, you are. Ah, here's our drinks."

Tommy entered with a tray. DeLauria took his Scotch and soda, and there was something with orange juice for the Don.

"I'm keeping away from the alcohol," Pontecorva said. "It's straight O.J."

"Oh yeah?"

"Doctor's orders. High blood pressure, if you can believe it."

"But you look really healthy."

Pontecorva shook his head. "I feel fine, as long as I don't drink." He indicated his body as they sat down. "All this… *stuff*… is taking its toll. I need to lose weight."

"Ah, Freddie, you're a fucking mountain. It's rock solid. Maybe you should see a different doctor."

Pontecorva waved his hand and said, "Forget about that, let's talk about you. *Salud.*" He raised his glass and DeLauria did the same. The Scotch tasted good.

"So," Pontecorva continued. "Did the boys fix you up when you got into town?"

"Yeah, they did. I got a nice little place in lower Manhattan. Near Ground Zero."

Pontecorva nodded. "Real estate is good down there now. No one wants to live there. We got some good deals on a few buildings."

"I appreciate it. The piece is good, too."

"A Walther P99, if I remember right, is your weapon of choice?"

"Uh huh. Just what I like."

"That's James Bond's gun, you know."

"I thought he used a PPK?"

"That's in the old days. He upgraded with the times."

"I didn't know that."

"Yeah. So, you're set with some money?"

"I'm very comfortable, Freddie, thanks. You've been real good to me."

Pontecorva waved his hand again. "We take care of ours, Dom, you know that."

"I appreciate it. Now. What can I do for you? I'm anxious to get to work. It was pretty goddamn boring at Rikers."

"I'm glad you asked that, Dom. Something has come up and I need your… expertise."

"Sure, anything you say."

Pontecorva took a sip of his orange juice. "You remember Charlie Patrone?"

"Sure."

"He was killed on Friday."

"My Lord. How?"

"Apparently he was supposed to unload some coke to his usual carriers. But two strangers showed up to make the deal. A man and a woman. From what I understand, the woman was calling the shots."

"Why would Charlie allow two strangers to get near him?"

Pontecorva shrugged. "It was cleared through the usual go-between. I'm not real sure, but Charlie was expecting the strangers. Anyway, Charlie was killed and his man Anthony was wounded. Bad. He died Sunday morning, but he was able to tell us some things on Saturday."

"Like what?"

"The broad's name was Hannah. The guy's name was Vincent. She was a real sexpot, calling everyone 'baby,' and she made the hit like a pro. They took off with the coke, nearly eight pounds. Anthony thought they might be going to unload it in Chicago. The guy let that slip."

"That's your territory, isn't it?"

"No, the Castellanos run the mid-west. Still, it was our stuff."

"So you want me to find them?" DeLauria asked.

"You bet your ass I do. Not only do I want you to find them, I want you to scare the shit out of them for a couple of days. I want them pissing in their pants for a while before you take 'em out. And I want you to recover the coke – or the money they got from selling it."

"Do we know anything else about them?"

"No. But I suggest you start with the usual go-betweens."

"I was just gonna ask about them. Who are they?"

"We were cooperating with the Castellano family on some of our distribution. They have contacts in the mid-west and south that we don't have. They had agreed to stay out of our territories and give us fifteen per cent of the take, on top of what they pay for the stuff to begin with. I suggest you go see the people we deal with over there."

"So you got a name?"

"Yeah." Pontecorva reached into his pocket and pulled out a small slip of paper. He handed it over to DeLauria, who glanced at it, memorized the information on it, and then wadded the paper into a small ball. He then popped it into his mouth and took a swig of Scotch to wash it down.

Chapter 10

Hannah was enjoying the respite from her dreary one-room apartment on the Upper East Side. Lounging in John Cozzone's townhouse over the weekend had been pure luxury, and this was something she was definitely unused to. Even Panther seemed happy. He had many rooms to explore, several floors to mark as his territory, and dozens of objects to climb and perch upon. Hannah had been afraid that he would freak out and simply hide somewhere, but he purred constantly and rubbed himself on everything.

She was able to get quite a bit of work done, too. She had typed nearly half the manuscript in just a couple of days. Cozzone had left some drafts of other works-in-progress to do in case she finished the big project early. She figured she'd be able to get to them before he returned.

Hannah wondered how he was doing. Sophia seemed, well, interesting. Certainly attractive – at least that's what Hannah could discern. Good body, anyway. Her face was just like the ones on the covers of the women's magazines, and those were all alike. Hannah couldn't tell one from the other.

On Tuesday, Hannah decided to go home and check her mail. She also needed to pick up a bottle of ibuprofen from her own medicine cabinet. She had been experiencing headaches more often, and the one last night had been a doozy. It had kept her awake for hours. She attributed it to the swigs of whiskey that she partook before bedtime. She knew this was bad for her, but she did it anyway. In her own deranged way, she was well aware that she enjoyed wallowing in melancholy – especially if it was in a luxurious townhouse.

She got dressed in blue jeans and a sweatshirt, then left the apartment to walk the eighteen blocks up to her street. It was a beautiful summer day, and most people would relish walks around Manhattan at this time of year. Unfortunately, the walk she made between her apartment and Cozzone's was usually the furthest that Hannah dared to venture. She didn't like crowds. Subways were intolerable. The heavy-pedestrian traffic of mid-town frightened her. She dreaded going to her therapist appointment on Thursday, but she supposed she would have to face her fear and do it.

As she walked along First Avenue, she was reminded once again of the fateful night that she had been attacked. She clearly remembered passing by the various shops and restaurants that were closed at the time. If only one had been open that night, things might have been different. She could have ducked into one and saved herself from the predator.

"Hey baby, where ya goin'?"

She'd never forget those words.

"Hannah?"

The woman in front of her seemed familiar. Hannah knew the body and the hair color. Who was it?

"Are you lost? You looked like you were in another world!"

Hannah breathed a sigh of relief. It was Liz.

"Oh, Liz, hi," she said. "I'm sorry, I was daydreaming."

"I'll say. Whatcha doing?"

"I'm on my way home to check the mail and stuff. I haven't been there since before the weekend."

"I know. Hey, I'm glad I saw you. There was this guy outside our building just now. When I came outside he asked me if you lived there."

"Really? What guy?"

"I don't know who he was, he didn't say."

"What did he want me for?"

"I don't know."

"What did he look like?"

She shrugged. "Like anybody, I guess. Actually, he was pretty good looking, for a guy. Kinda like a soap opera actor. Dark hair, blue eyes, glasses, good shape. He had on a trenchcoat, like detectives wear."

"What did you tell him?"

"Only that you weren't home."

"You said I lived there?"

"Uhh, yeah, I guess I did. But I said you weren't home."

"Great."

"Sorry. Hey, are we going to have that dinner at your cousin's on Friday?"

"Sure, you still don't have to work?"

"No, I'm off. You got my phone number with you?"

"Yeah."

"Call me and let's set it up."

"Okay, see ya."

"Bye, Hannah."

Liz continued to walk south and Hannah headed on home. As she got closer, she saw a man that matched Liz's description. He was standing in front of the building. A chill ran up her spine and her heart suddenly increased its tempo, for Hannah was certain that the man was Timothy Lane. He was the same height and weight – the same *shape* – and exuded the same vibe.

But it *couldn't* be him! Lane was in jail!

The man appeared to be taking notes in a small pad, looking up at the building and at the windows. He wore a gray trenchcoat and indeed resembled a plainclothes cop. Hannah could see that the man had dark hair and wore glasses, but she was unable to make much sense of the rest of his face.

He looked up as she approached the door.

"Are you Miss McCleary?" he asked.

She turned, keeping her head down. "Yes?"

"I'm sorry to come around without calling first. I'm Detective Sean Flannery." He showed her a black wallet with a silver badge inside. She barely looked at it and nodded.

"Yes?"

"I'm handling your case now. Well, not officially, since your case is closed, but we sometimes compare suspects in cases to see if, well, to see if we have the right man in custody and so forth." The man had a slight southern accent.

"Where's Detective Blaine?"

"Detective Blaine?"

"He was the one who handled my case before."

"Right, Detective Blaine. He's not working the case anymore. He only works open cases," Flannery said.

"What can I do for you?"

"Well, I was wondering if you might have a cup of coffee with me. I'd like you tell me about what happened to you in your own words. I know I can read the court transcript and all that, but I like to hear it from the victim personally."

"What for?" she asked. "The man was caught and convicted."

"I realize that. But we have some other cases that are very similar to yours, you see. I have some mug shots of men who have been arrested over the last year, and I thought it might be useful for you to take a look at them. Just to get your reaction."

Hannah shook her head as she felt an abrupt burst of anxiety. "No, I can't do that." She didn't want to say that the faces would mean nothing to her.

"It would only take a few minutes…"

"No, I'm sorry, I can't." She turned away to enter her building.

"Wait, Miss McCleary, please." He came close to her and she could smell a strong, but not unpleasant, cologne.

"Detective…" she began.

"Flannery."

"Detective Flannery, I can't look at any more mug shots. I'm through with all that, don't you see? I've put it behind me. Or at least I've tried for five years to put it behind me. I'm still haunted by what happened and I just don't like to drag it up again. Please leave me alone."

"I understand how you feel, Hannah," he said, not unkindly. It struck her as odd that he used her first name. "I'd still like to buy you that cup of coffee, though. We don't… we don't have to talk about your case."

She looked at him. "I don't understand."

The man shuffled his feet and looked off down the street. He laughed and shrugged. "Well, to tell you the truth, I, uhm, I really didn't come here to talk about your case at all. I just… I wanted to meet you."

"Meet me?"

"You see, Detective Blaine, he had a photo of you that was used in the trial, you know, and I saw it and, well, I wanted to meet you."

Hannah didn't consider why Detective Blaine would still have a photo of her that could be seen by anyone at the precinct. The question in her mind was why would this man want to meet *her* by looking at a photograph?

"Is this a joke?" was all she could think of to ask.

"No, it's not. It's a sneaky way of meeting a woman, I must admit. I apologize," he said. "But Hannah, if you would permit me to say so, I was struck silly by your photograph. You… well, you're a very attractive woman. There. I said it."

"Look, Detective Flannery…"

"Call me Sean."

"I don't think so. I'm going inside to take something for my headache, and then I have to go back to work. Thank you for what you said, but goodbye." She turned to go inside.

"Wait, Hannah!" She stopped. He handed her a business card. "Look, here's my card. Take it. Please."

She hesitantly reached out and took the card.

"May I call you?" he asked. He seemed so sincere. "We can meet for a cup of coffee or something. Whatever, whenever. It'd make me very happy."

She had to admit that his insistence was endearing. The problem was that it was extremely difficult for her to believe that *any* man would want to meet her. She was not the type of woman with whom men fell in love simply by seeing her picture. Yet, this man seemed so kind.

"All right," she said, finally.

"Thank you. I'll see you sometime, then?"

She nodded and tried to smile. Flannery nodded back and said, "Goodbye." He then turned and walked down the avenue. He looked back once and waved, then continued walking.

Very strange, Hannah thought as she went inside. That had *never* happened to her in all her life. Did he really like her? A *detective*? Could this really be happening?

Suddenly she felt excited, a little nervous and apprehensive, but it wasn't an unpleasant feeling. For once, the anxiety felt *good.* Had providence just handed her a *man* that actually liked her? Had a miracle occurred?

Hannah's head was spinning. She let herself into her apartment and then realized she had forgotten why she was there. Oh yes, she had to check her mail. And take the ibuprofen. Funny, her headache had disappeared!

***

Bill Cutler removed the trenchcoat, folded it neatly, and placed it in the trunk of his '92 Toyota Corolla. He had been lucky to find a parking place so close to the woman's apartment. It was a decrepit old car, but it still worked and the mileage was still under 100,000. He would have liked to buy a new car, but when one lived in Manhattan, a car was an expensive luxury that wasn't really needed. He rarely used it. It cost a fortune to park it in Manhattan, so he rented space in Brooklyn for a third of the cost. Thus, the car usually stayed in its slot year-round.

Cutler removed the fake eyeglasses and stuck them inside his shirt pocket. He opened the car door and put on a tie, looking at his reflection in the passenger window as he did so.

The business card was a nice touch, he thought. He was pleased with himself for thinking of having some printed up. The badge was a prop from an old play that he had kept.

He then put on a navy blue sport jacket and grabbed a briefcase. He shut the door and locked the car.

Now he was a banker. Cutler assumed a stuffy, stiff posture and walked back to the avenue to wait for his prey. The ruse as "Detective Flannery" worked like a charm, just as the phone call from "Dr. Cagle" had. Cutler loved becoming new characters. It was a way to practice acting and also mark off conquests from his Quest List. What a wonderful hobby!

There was something about her that was familiar, but Cutler shrugged off the feeling. He had been surprised by how pretty Hannah McCleary was. He had expected a homely spinster, but the woman could be a beauty if she wore some makeup. It was true that she appeared a little mousy, certainly introverted and shy, but that was part of her charm. What she needed was a good fuck – that was obvious. Before long, he would have her eating out of his hand. He couldn't wait to see her passion face, the face she made in the throes of sexual pleasure.

First thing's first – another big test. Cutler wanted to make completely sure that the condition described in her medical report was correct.

He waited in front of a newsstand, pretending to browse the various papers and magazines on display until he saw her walking toward him on the avenue. She must be headed back to her job, so he planned to follow her from a distance to see where she worked.

With briefcase in hand, Cutler walked toward her, ready to meet her head on. She was twenty feet away and he could see that she still had that dreamy, faraway look in her eyes.

When they were upon each other, ready to pass, he said, "Hannah!"

She looked up at him, surprised.

"How are you? I haven't seen you in such a long time!" he said, feigning familiarity.

Hannah smiled and blinked. "Oh, hello, I'm fine." She didn't do a very good job of faking recognition. Cutler could see it clearly.

"You don't remember me, do you?" he asked.

Hannah looked down and shuffled her feet. "I'm sorry, I'm afraid I don't."

"I'm George from the bank. We all miss you, you know."

"Oh, hi. No, I changed jobs." She still wasn't sure who he was. "What… what are you doing up this way?"

"I'm on my way to see a client. Hey, it's nice to see you. I'll tell everyone hello for you!" With that, he continued on past her, not looking back at the bewildered woman. He waited a few moments, then turned around.

Hannah had continued walking south. She hadn't recognized him at all. Cutler had no idea if there was a George at her old job. If so, then he had gotten lucky. If there hadn't been, then it just added to her confusion.

Cutler crossed the avenue so that he could follow her from the opposite side. She'd never see him, and even if she did she wouldn't know who he was.

He was convinced. The girl's ability to recognize faces was nonexistent. Furthermore, the feeling that she was somehow familiar to him returned in full force. Cutler was fairly certain that he had met Hannah McCleary before, prior to the "dark time."

Chapter 11

"Spits" Spinozza wiped the sweat from his forehead as he jogged around Washington Square. He cleared his throat and spat to his left, a habit he had nurtured since he was eight years old. It's what blessed him with such an endearing nickname.

The jogging was just for show, of course. He really wasn't putting much effort into it. But if there were any cops watching he could easily use the exercise as an excuse for being there. What he was really doing was selling nickel and dime bags of cocaine to his regular customers. The routine was simple. When he saw one of them, he would stop running but continue to jog in place. He would slap hands with the guy and in doing so deposit a small plastic bag of white powder into the customer's palm. They would chat for another minute while Spits continued to prance, and then a final handshake would deliver the money from the customer to Spits. Spits would then take off jogging around the square again. He did this every day at noon for a full hour, and his customers knew to come and see him then. It worked like a charm.

Spits had completed a transaction with a strung-out New York University professor who was one of his regulars and had started running again. As he rounded a corner, he noticed a tall man standing in his path at the other end of the square. Spits had never seen him before, but the man was staring at him as if he were waiting for him. Perhaps he was a new customer, put on to him by one of the regulars? The guy looked too scary to be a cop. In fact, he looked like a Castellano goon.

Spits slowed the jogging as he approached the man.

"What's up, man?" he asked, out of breath.

"Your name Spits?"

Spits performed the action that warranted his nickname. "Yeah," he said, as he wiped his mouth. "Who the fuck are you?"

"Stop jogging."

There was something about the way the man made the command

that sent a chill up Spits' back. Normally he would have ignored a guy like that, but in this case the menace was clearly tangible. Spits stopped and tried to catch his breath.

"Do I know you?" he asked again.

"Who I am is not important," Dominic DeLauria said. "What's important is that I find out who you sent to meet Charlie Patrone the other day."

Spits felt his stomach jump into his chest. So that's what this was about.

"Why?" Spits asked. "Something happen?"

"You don't know?"

"No. What?"

"Patrone and his man were killed. Their stash was stolen. The Pontecorvas are not happy."

"Shit, man, I didn't know that! Honest!" Spits cried.

DeLauria put his arm around Spits' shoulders and walked him over to a bench.

"Relax. Sit down," he said. "We're just gonna talk."

Spits was still hopelessly attempting to catch his breath. "I swear I didn't think that was going to happen. Man, I'm sorry! Shit!"

"Who were they, Spits, and how is it that you sent them in your place?"

"Listen man, I think I was conned. This chick found me here and she said she was from the Castellano family. She didn't tell me her name."

"What did she look like?"

"I dunno, man, pretty. Well, pretty damn pretty. A fox. She looked too good to be a con artist, you know what I mean?"

"Go on."

"She was with a guy. He looked real familiar to me, but I couldn't place him. Not until later. Anyway, she said that Marco Castellano wanted her to pick up the week's shipment from Charlie instead of having me do it. I asked what am I supposed to do about my regular customers, and she said that Marco was gonna make it up to me in a week. This was last Wednesday, so that's today. I was expecting him to come around. In fact, I thought that's what I thought you were doing. I thought maybe Marco sent you."

"No, Marco Castellano didn't send me. Freddie Pontecorva sent me."

For once, Spits swallowed instead of spitting. He knew that meant trouble.

"This woman didn't give you her name?" DeLauria asked again.

Spits shook his head. "No. But the guy, I swear I knew him. I think he was that writer who was big about twenty years ago or so. John Cozzone. You know who he is?"

"No."

"He wrote a couple of best sellers in the seventies. I'd *swear* it was him. I guess he's a doper now, because the chick acted like they were gonna be distributing the stuff together. I don't know, she just knew so much about the operation that I figured she was legit. I shoulda checked with Marco first."

DeLauria nodded. "Is there anything else you can tell me about these two?"

Spits shook his head. "That's all I know. I swear."

"She didn't go by the name of 'Hannah,' did she?"

"Not that I know of. I never heard her name."

DeLauria sighed. "All right. Here's what we're gonna do. Come 'ere." He gestured for Spits to lean in so that DeLauria could whisper in his ear. As Spits did so, DeLauria thrust a Bowie knife into his victim's belly. Spits gasped and grunted once, and then he clutched DeLauria's shoulders as if he were confessing his sins to a dear friend. DeLauria forcefully pulled the knife up and into Spits' upper cavity. Then he withdrew the knife and wiped the blood on the victim's shirt. DeLauria immediately stood and walked away. Spits fell over, the blood spurting out of him as if he were a spigot. A girl nearby screamed. Two black kids playing basketball looked over and pointed. Someone yelled to call the cops.

DeLauria walked out of the square and got into a black sedan that was waiting at the curb. It sped away before anyone could get a positive I.D. on the license plate.

Inside the car, DeLauria told the driver, a kid named Favio, to take him home to his apartment in lower Manhattan. He was still holding the Bowie knife. He stuck it in the sheath that was strapped to his calf, under his trousers.

At least he had a lead, John Cozzone. DeLauria would find out more about this guy, learn where he lived, and discover what he was up to. Wherever Cozzone was, this "Hannah," would also be, if that was her real name.

***

"I can see the Sears Tower," Sophia said.

They were on the highway known as the Skyway, a toll road that curved around Lake Michigan from Indiana to Chicago.

"You know, we're really fucking late," Cozzone said as he passed a slow eighteen-wheeler. "Let's hope Ramon hasn't given up on us."

"I thought you said you called him last night."

"I did. All I got was voice mail. Hopefully he got the message."

"Maybe we shouldn't have spent so much time in Cleveland."

"Hey, you're the one who wanted to spend all day at the fucking Rock 'n' Roll Hall of Fame," Cozzone said. "You're the one who wanted to take a side trip to Philadelphia to see an old boyfriend who wasn't home. Jesus, we left New York last Friday and here it is Wednesday!"

"Look, I thought he'd pay us a lot more for the stuff than your guy in Chicago, okay? And as for Cleveland, I haven't had a goddamn vacation in years. So shoot me."

Cozzone shook his head. "That's the problem. I'm afraid somebody *will* after what you did in New York."

"Are you still whining about that? They'll never find us. Spits didn't know who we were. He's an asshole."

"I just don't like playing games with someone like Freddie Pontecorva. Or Marco Castellano. I may be Italian, but I'm not crazy."

"Just shut up and drive," Sophia said. "Marco Castellano's not gonna do anything to me. He's my cousin."

"Yeah, I know, and Carlo Castellano's your great uncle."

Cozzone was fuming. He had had just about enough of Sophia Castellano. She had been wonderful for the few weeks he had been seeing her, she was fantastic in bed, she looked like she just stepped out of the pages of a Victoria's Secret catalog, and she enjoyed drugs as much as he did. But she was beginning to be a First Class Bitch. Ever since he had agreed to go in with her on what they called the "Big Score," she had assumed control and insisted on calling the shots. Cozzone had been more than happy to let her have her way, but enough was enough. The killings in New York changed everything. Cozzone was too freaked out to enjoy himself. They hadn't had sex once in the five days since they left Manhattan. He wasn't sure he'd ever be able to go to bed with her again.

What did he know about her, really? Only that she was the great niece of the head of one of New York's alleged crime families. Carlo Castellano was the stuff of legends, a lot like his counterpart in the Pontecorva family. Cozzone knew quite a bit about how the Italian mafia worked these days because he had attempted to write a book about it. One thing was for sure – they didn't act like the mobsters of the golden age. Cozzone thought that TV show, *The Sopranos*, got it right. What was left of the crime families in New York generally cooperated with each other and worked together.

Sophia Cabrini had known how the two families operated with regard to cocaine distribution. It had been her idea to con the Pontecorvas out of a shipment. Cozzone now realized that he had been an idiot for going along with it. During the ride through Indiana, Sophia had revealed that she was on the outs with the Castellano family for certain "acts" she had committed when she was younger. Now Cozzone didn't trust her claim that the family would protect her if the Pontecorvas caught the two of them. She had proven in New York that she was dangerous, that she was a killer, and that she was unpredictable.

Frankly, she scared the shit out of him.

Chapter 12

Bill Cutler had spent all of Wednesday night turning MedScript's storage room into a doctor's office.

The room was located on an upper floor of the same building, which was inconvenient with regard to MedScript's needs, but it was the best that the building management could offer. Doctors' offices occupied the first three floors and other businesses took up the rest. The storeroom contained office supplies and spare furniture, including an unused desk. As manager of MedScript, he had the only key to the room. His brother didn't give a damn about it. Thus, he felt fairly confident that he could do anything he wanted with the room and no one would be the wiser.

The first thing he did was to get a sign made that read: "Tom Cagle, L.C.S.W." The initials stood for "Licensed Clinical Social Worker," a title he had picked up from medical tapes. The sign had a reusable adhesive on the back so that he could put it on the outside of the door when he wanted it there, and then remove it when he didn't.

The next thing he did was to find a place to store the excess supplies. These were made up of photocopy paper, desk supplies, cassette tapes, and the like. He decided that he could keep most of it in the trunk of his car, and the rest of it he could store at his apartment.

After the room was cleaned out, he re-arranged the spare furniture so that it appeared to be a respectable therapist's office. The desk remained, of course. There was a filing cabinet, a bookshelf, and a couple of easy chairs. Cutler bought a small table that could fit between the chairs and on which he could place a tissue box and an ashtray. No reason why patients shouldn't be allowed to smoke when they were revealing their souls! He stocked the bookshelf with several used books on psychology, substance abuse, and medical journals that he picked up at the Strand Bookstore.

Finally, the room was finished. His "patient," Hannah McCleary, would be arriving at 7:30 that evening. Best that he go back to MedScript and put in some hours before then.

***

Hannah arrived on time and knocked on Dr. Cagle's door.

Cutler had used theatrical spirit gum to paste on a fake mustache and had combed his hair differently in order to disguise his appearance somewhat. If what he had read about her condition was correct, then his patient would not recognize him as Detective Sean Flannery.

"Come in," he said as he opened the door. "You must be Hannah?"

"Yes," she said. She didn't perform a double take when she saw him, so Cutler figured that he was home free.

"You're right on time. Have a seat."

"What kind of office is this?" she asked.

"I beg your pardon?"

"I mean, there's no waiting room. What if you had someone else in here when I arrived?"

"Oh, don't worry about that," Cutler said. He had worked hard to achieve the accent he had first used on the phone, something a little like a Boston dialect. "I never schedule patients back to back. I do things a little differently, but I think you'll find that's why my patients like me." He chuckled at his own good humor and sat down behind the desk.

Hannah stood in the middle of the room, unsure of how to react to the unorthodox environment.

"Please," he said. "Sit down. Can I get you something to drink? Coffee? Soda?"

"No, thank you." Finally, she sat in one of the lounge chairs. "I've never been to a therapist like this before. Usually there's a couch and all."

"I don't believe in having my patients lie down when they talk. The point of all this is to discover things about yourself that might be causing problems. Sometimes this takes some work, and one can't work lying down. I'll never understand the whole lying down thing. I find that patients are able to talk better when they sit up."

"I see." She wouldn't look at him. Her eyes tended to dart all over the room, never focusing on any single object.

"If you'd feel more comfortable turning the chair to face another direction, that's quite all right," Cutler said. "Some patients open up more if they're facing the wall. You don't have to look right at me."

She shrugged. "I'm okay."

"Fine." He pulled out a folder and began to examine some papers he had placed inside of it for show. "Hannah McCleary. Doctor Lazar has told me about you, of course, but I'd like to hear a little from you. Why don't we start by you telling me a bit about yourself?"

Hannah looked lost. "What… what do you want to know?"

"Anything that comes into your mind. If you had to describe yourself to a biographer, how would you do it? Not how you look, but how you are as a person. What kind of person are you? How did you grow up to be the person you are now? Who is Hannah McCleary? What does she like, what does she dislike? What are her dreams and her goals? What is she afraid of? What are your hobbies? Really, tell me anything you'd like."

She still looked lost. "I don't know where to begin."

"All right, start with your childhood. Where are you from? What was your family like?"

She shrugged again and looked at the floor. Cutler noted that she was terribly shy. "I don't know, they were okay," she mumbled. "I grew up in Albany. I'm an only child. My mother was a librarian and my father sold insurance. My father died of a heart attack when I was six. My mother died of cancer when I was fourteen. I lived with an aunt for a while until I finished high school, and then I moved out into an apartment. I went to business school for two years, and then I came to New York. I've been here ever since."

"What did you study in college?"

"Business."

He gestured with his eyebrows, urging her to be more specific.

"Well, accounting, mostly. I'm good with numbers," she answered.

"I see. And did you find work in the big city?"

"Yeah. Someone I knew at school had a job in a bank here, so I had an 'in.' I worked downtown at Chase for several years until… well, until I couldn't…"

"Until what happened to you happened?" he asked gently.

She looked down again. "Yes."

"That was five years ago, right?"

"Yes."

"Before we get into that, tell me some more about yourself. What do you like to do? What do you *want* to do that you've never done?"

She was quiet for a few seconds and then she shrugged. "I don't know. I guess I used to like to go shopping. But I never had much money so I ended up not buying anything. I don't... I don't go shopping much anymore. I don't like crowds."

"What else? What do you like to do *now*?"

Cutler found her uneasiness painfully endearing. She was cute in a librarian sort of way. It was interesting that her mother had been one, for she was the stereotypical type of young librarian a schoolboy would have a crush on.

"I don't like to do much of anything now," she said. She had begun a nervous tic of pulling on her fingers.

"Do you go to movies? Read books?"

"I don't go to movies much. I can't follow them because I often can't keep the characters straight. I read magazines, mostly. Sometimes I'll read a book. I listen to the radio. I like music, I guess."

"Do you have many friends?"

She shook her head. "I don't have any friends. Well, I guess I have one or two. My neighbor, a floor below me, she's okay. Her name is Liz Rosenthal. She's... well, she's a lesbian and I think she likes me, if you know what I mean, but she's never made a big deal out of it. She comes over and we have coffee together, or I go to her apartment."

"I understand you're employed now?"

"Yes, I work for my cousin. He's a writer. I type his manuscripts. I'm sort of his personal assistant."

"Oh yes, you mentioned him on the phone."

"John Cozzone. He wrote *The Apples of the Cosmos* and *The Loose Lips of Lucretia Leone*."

"Oh, yes, I've heard of him. *The Apples of the Cosmos* was a big bestseller. I read it a long time ago. Was it twenty years ago?"

"More. It was in the seventies."

"It must be interesting working for him."

She shrugged. "It's okay. It's easy work and he lives within walking distance of my apartment."

"Oh? Where is that?"

"On East 63rd Street. It keeps me out of office buildings and off the streets. I... I don't like to deal with a lot of people."

"Let's talk about that a minute. Now, according to Doctor Lazar, you have this condition called prosopagnosia. Are people aware that you have this? By that, I mean your cousin, or your friend Liz?"

"No. They don't know. My cousin knows that I was assaulted, but no one really knows about the face blindness. When I first found out that I had it, I tried to tell some people. People from my old job at the bank.

People just don't believe me, you know? I mean, they look at me like I'm a little crazy. 'Face blindness? I've never heard of that! Are you sure?' It got to be where it was a pain trying to explain why I couldn't work in a bank anymore, or why I couldn't go to a party to see people I *might* know, or why I don't go to bars, or why I don't go out to meet people. I *can't* meet people. If I meet someone, I won't recognize him or her the next day. Unless there's something completely specific about them that I can remember, such as that they're really fat or they're bald or they have tattoos or a pierced nose or something like that."

Cutler was silent a moment. He hadn't fully realized the extent of her problem. This face blindness could be truly alienating.

"I think I understand how you must feel," was all he could say.

"No, you don't," she said. There was a hint of anger in her voice. "No one knows, except maybe someone else who has face blindness. I've found a handful of people like me on the Internet. Less than ten."

"You sound angry."

She looked away and shrugged. "I guess sometimes I am."

Cutler inhaled deeply and tried a different approach. "Hannah, what do you hope to get out of therapy?"

"I don't hope anything. Doctor Lazar wants me to come."

"I think Doctor Lazar wants me to help draw you out."

"I don't want to be drawn out."

"Hannah, even though you have a social… disability… it's unhealthy to stay cooped up in your apartment all the time. You *do* need to get out more. You *do* need to make friends. Don't you want to, say, fall in love?"

Hannah looked down. She continued to pull on her fingers and now she was biting her lower lip.

When she didn't speak for nearly a minute, Cutler asked, "Has there ever been a man in your life?"

She quickly shook her head. "No."

"I don't believe it. No boyfriends, ever?"

She shrugged. "There were some, I guess, when I was in college and all. Nothing serious."

"How would you feel if you suddenly met the man of your dreams and he didn't care one whit about you having face blindness?"

"I've had nightmares about that. I've dreamed that I'm at my own wedding and I can't recognize my husband among all the other men wearing tuxedoes at the reception." This time she laughed a little.

"Seriously, though, how would you feel?" he asked again.

She thought about it and finally said, "Well, sure, I'd like it. As a matter of fact, I..." Then she trailed off and looked at the bookshelf.

"What?"

"Nothing."

"What is it?"

"Well, I sort of met someone yesterday."

"Really?"

"He's a police detective. He wanted me to look at some mug shots. I don't know why, really, since the guy who... the guy who assaulted me was convicted already. Well, he said that's what he wanted, but then he said he really just wanted to meet me."

"Oh? Tell me more."

"He said he saw my picture at the precinct. The detective who handled my case before had it. He told me that he liked me and wanted me to have coffee with him."

"So why don't you?"

She shrugged in her inimitable way. "I don't know."

"What do you mean, you don't know?"

"I don't know! I can't imagine why he'd like someone like me."

"Why not? You're an attractive woman, Hannah. There's nothing wrong with you."

"There isn't?" she asked with sarcasm.

"No, there isn't. I'm quite sure if you were in a steady relationship, you wouldn't have any trouble recognizing your significant other."

She was quiet.

"Look, Hannah," he said. "You shouldn't be afraid to try. If it doesn't work out, then it doesn't work out, but how will you know if you don't try? It could turn out to be the best thing that ever happened to you. You never know about these things."

Her voice dropped to a whisper. "I don't know..."

"Hannah, what are you afraid of? Getting hurt? Everyone is afraid of getting hurt, even people who recognize faces."

He noticed that her eyes were welling up. She was on the verge of tears. "I have... nightmares. And headaches. And I'm scared a lot. For no reason."

This was a change in direction. She took a tissue, dabbed her eyes, and blew her nose. "Sorry," she said.

"That's quite all right. Can you tell me more about these feelings? How do they come about?"

She shrugged. "I don't know. They just... happen. You know, panic attacks. Anxiety. And then I'm depressed. I don't like it when it happens. I feel awful."

"What is it that you're thinking about when it happens?"

"I think about *him.*" She spat it out. "I think about the man who assaulted me, who tried to rape me, who hit me on the head and left me with this... thing."

"But he's been put away," Cutler said. "He can't hurt you anymore."

She put her head in her hands. "But... I just don't know..."

"What? Don't know what?"

"I don't know if he was really the man who did it."

Cutler sat forward in his chair. "Why not? Wasn't he convicted in a court of law?"

"Yes. But it was all circumstantial evidence, and I identified him in court as the man who did it. So the jury believed me."

"And?"

"And I really didn't recognize him! I just went along with what the police said. I thought that if the police said he did it, then I supposed he really did. I thought that if he were sent to prison then maybe I'd feel better. But I never felt better. I felt worse. I feel so..." She trailed off again and shook her head.

"You feel guilty," he said.

She eventually nodded.

Cutler was moved by her torment. Before, he had been enjoying playing the role of psychologist, turning it into an adventure, a playful exercise of acting. Now, however, he could see the pain and horror that the woman had been going through, and it *excited him.*

"But Hannah, you can never know for certain, isn't that right?" he asked.

"That's right."

"So put it behind you. The man is in prison. You can't let this eat you up. You're the victim here, not him."

"I can't help it. I relive the assault in my dreams. All the time."

"Do you see the man in your dreams?"

"No. He never has a face. He's more of a... feeling... than a person."

Cutler nodded, adapting a knowing expression. He looked at her for a few moments without saying anything. Hannah looked at the floor, pulled her fingers, bit her lip, and remained quiet.

Cutler glanced at his phony file and said, "I understand from Doctor Lazar that you said something to her, something about killing this man if you met him today?"

Hannah shook her head. "That was just something I said. You know."

"Did you mean it?"

She shrugged. "Yes and no."

"Please explain that answer."

"Of course I wouldn't really kill him. I don't think I could do that. But then, sometimes, when I'm alone and I feel that anxiety and I get a headache and begin to feel sorry for myself… then I really blame him. I hate him. I *do* want to kill him. Sometimes I fantasize that I find out where he lives or works, and I go there and I shoot him with a gun."

"Do you own a gun, Hannah?"

"No." Then she smiled mischievously. "But I know where to get one."

"You do?"

"Yeah, my cousin has one. I saw it."

"Oh dear," Cutler said. He took a moment to collect his thoughts. "You know, Hannah," he said, "it's quite all right to fantasize those things."

"It is?"

"Sure. Don't you feel better when you imagine this man getting blown away?"

"I guess."

"It would feel great, wouldn't it? In a fantasy, that is. To take a gun and shoot a hole in this man who hurt you?"

"Yes, it would."

"Sometimes it's good therapy to imagine something like that, or even pretend to do it. Play-act it. Let's do it now." He stood and gestured for her to do the same.

"What?"

"Stand up."

"Why?"

"Come on, you'll enjoy this."

"I, uh…" She hesitated, then stood.

Cutler went to his desk and opened a drawer. He took out a plastic toy gun and handed it to her. "Here, take this."

"What… what is this?"

"It's just a toy. Don't worry. Sometimes I have to use props and things like that in therapy sessions. Take it, it won't do anything."

She reached out and took hold of the gun. "Now what?"

"All right, let's say you've found out where this assailant lives."

"But he's in jail."

"I know, but let's pretend he isn't. Let's say they really did get the wrong man and you found out where the real assailant lives. You go there and you get inside his house. You wait for him in one of the rooms. You know he's coming home soon."

Hannah didn't know what to think. It was the most unorthodox therapy session she had heard of. "Look, I…"

"Trust me. Pretend you're playing a role. What would you do? Where would you go? Would you hide? Would you stand in the middle of the room? How would you go about killing this man?"

"I don't know."

"Think of it this way. What if shooting this man would suddenly cure you of your face blindness?"

She looked at him and then slowly nodded. "All right. I'd probably go over here and sit at his desk…" Hannah walked slowly around the room and sat in the doctor's chair.

"Good," Cutler said, encouraging her to go on. "And you wait… the gun is loaded, right?"

"Yes." She held the gun and pointed it at the door.

"Finally, you hear something downstairs. It's him, returning home. You hear his footsteps as he hangs up a jacket and starts up the stairs."

Cutler noticed that she was beginning to breathe heavy. She held the gun with both hands.

"You hear him reach the top and the footsteps grow louder. They're almost outside the door."

Her eyes widened.

"Then, he opens the door and stands there."

Hannah's hands shook. She bit her lip and trembled. Cutler could see that she *wanted* to pull the trigger but something prevented her from doing so.

"What do you do?" he asked softly.

Her hands shook even more. She shut her eyes and emitted an almost inaudible whimper. Then she suddenly exhaled loudly and put the gun on the desk. "I can't," she whispered.

Cutler was pleased. It was the reaction he had been hoping for. "You appeared to be in control until the very last second," he said.

"I didn't like it," she said. "I mean, yeah, you're right. It felt exciting at first, but when it came down to pulling the trigger, I just couldn't do it." She stood and stepped away from the desk. It was almost as if she didn't want to acknowledge what just occurred.

"That was very good, Hannah," Cutler said.

"What do you mean?"

"You did well. After what you said to Doctor Lazar, I wanted to see how far you would really go. I will bet that you'll sleep very well tonight."

She went back to her original chair. "I feel kinda shaky."

"That's to be expected. You used some adrenaline doing that exercise." Cutler looked at his watch and added, "Our time is up for today. But I think we've made a good start. I can see we have some things to work on, don't you?"

She shrugged. "I guess so."

"Let's meet again in a few days. In the meantime, if this detective that you said likes you tries to see you again, by all means, do something about it. Go for it. Will you try?"

She sighed heavily and said, "I guess so."

Chapter 13

Panther greeted Hannah at Cozzone's front door when she returned from seeing the therapist. The cat slithered around her legs as she shut and locked the door behind her.

"Did you miss me, boy?" she asked sweetly. "You've had your dinner, are you just looking for affection?"

She reached down and scratched his head, then walked into the apartment. She hadn't eaten yet, so she decided to cook some pasta and open a jar of sauce. Hannah put the water on to boil and rummaged in the fridge for some vegetables to throw into the mix. She found some broccoli that would do.

As she prepared the meal, Hannah reflected on the meeting with the new therapist. She had been surprised by how well it had gone. Normally she didn't put much stock in that sort of thing. She knew she had psychological problems. She knew that she was depressed, withdrawn, and paranoid. What did they expect? When someone is assaulted and nearly raped, hit on the head, and left with a mysterious and rare neurological condition that effected one's social capabilities, you can't very well expect them to come out completely normal.

The stuff with the toy gun was unnerving but the therapist had been correct – it had felt *great* until the deciding moment. For the first time in five years, Hannah felt empowered, as if she could transcend her little private world of fear, paranoia, and anxiety. She wondered how real these feelings were. Could she eventually get to where she could pull the trigger? Could she really kill the man who had assaulted her if she was given the chance? Her immediate intellectual response was that she could never do it, but an emotional contradiction was overpowering. In her heart of hearts, she knew that the hatred and rage she had lived with since the assault would override her rational side. She just might be able to do it.

But it was moot point, wasn't it? Timothy Edward Lane was in jail. He could never harm her again.

She opened the cupboard and pulled out the bottle of Jack Daniel's. Out of habit, she got a glass, plopped in a couple of ice cubes from the freezer, and poured herself a drink. She sat on one of the tall barstools that lined the kitchen counter and waited for the water to boil.

Dr. Tom Cagle. He seemed to be very understanding. There was something about him that was familiar, but Hannah had experienced that sort of feeling before. Since she often didn't know if she recognized someone or not, her mind played tricks on her. She would think that someone was familiar when in fact they weren't. Now she was never sure whom she knew and whom she didn't. It was all very confusing. At any rate, there was an air about him that seemed familiar. Maybe it was a smell or the way he held himself.

The therapist had brought up a lot of things that she didn't like thinking about, but she knew that they were important issues. Did she really isolate herself so much that she would eventually have no social skills whatsoever? Hannah really didn't see how she could improve the situation. The mere thought of going out in public to have *fun* terrified her. It was the quickest way to produce a panic attack. Hannah felt the anxiety begin to bubble up in her chest just by *imagining* a public situation. Sometimes it felt as if she were having cardiac arrest.

Forget it, she told herself. She wasn't about to go out to "meet people." No way. Better to stay at home, alone and safe. Safe from all those faces that meant nothing to her.

The phone rang. There was one in the kitchen and several more dispersed throughout the house. The answering machine, however, was in the office. She had forgotten to check it upon returning. She picked up the receiver.

"Hello? Cozzone residence."

"Hannah? Is that you?"

It was Cozzone.

"John! Hello!"

"Hi, how's it going?"

"Fine. No disasters to report," she said.

"Any calls for me?"

"Not that I know of. Actually I just walked in and haven't checked the machine upstairs yet. I'm in the kitchen."

"Well, don't worry about it. I can't imagine anyone trying to get hold of me this week."

"Where are you?"

"We're in Chicago. Having a great time."

"When will you be coming back?"

"Not sure yet. Hopefully sometime next week. You got big plans for the weekend? Have you invited the entire cast of Chippendale's over for a party on Saturday?"

"Eewww, John, please." She managed to laugh. "What would I do with a bunch of Chippendale's guys?"

"Hannah, if you don't know then I'm not going to tell you."

"John!"

"Listen, I gotta go. I was just checking in. Everything okay? You're not too lonesome?"

"I have Panther here with me. Tomorrow night my friend Liz is coming over for dinner. I'm fine, don't worry. Oh, and I'm nearly finished with the manuscript. I'll be able to start on the other things this weekend."

"That's great. Well, I'll talk to you at the end of the weekend, okay?"

"Okay. Bye!"

"See ya!"

He hung up and she replaced the receiver. The water was boiling so she moved off the stool and put the pasta in the pot. She then ran upstairs and into the office. Sure enough, the answering machine was blinking, indicating that there were three messages.

Hannah punched the button and listened. The first message was someone for Cozzone, having to do with a magazine article that he was writing. She made a note of the man's name and phone and listened to the next message. This one was from Cozzone himself. He had called earlier, while she was out, and simply said that he'd call back in a little while.

The third message caused her heart to skip a beat.

"Hey, baby. Howzit goin'? I know you're there, baby, there's no use hidin' from me. I'm comin' to get you real soon. There's a score to settle, know what I mean? Have a good evenin'. We'll talk soon."

My God, my God! She quickly ran through the first two messages again so that she could hear the third once more. As she listened, the dreadful anxiety gripped her ribcage with such force that she had to sit down.

It was him. It was the assailant. Her attacker. The man who had tried to rape her and who permanently disabled her. He was back. He was after her again.

No, it couldn't be! Timothy Lane was in jail! Or was he? Did he get out? Weren't they supposed to tell her if he got out on parole? She hadn't heard anything. She bolted from the chair and ran downstairs to get her purse that she had left on the kitchen counter. She grabbed it and skirted upstairs again, opening it and shuffled through her wallet as she did so. Detective Blaine's card was there where she had left it.

Hannah dialed the number on the card and got the detective's answering machine. Of course he wouldn't be there, it was too late in the evening. Didn't detectives work all hours, though? They certainly did on television.

She was about to leave a message at the beep but then she got another idea. What was she doing calling Blaine, anyway? He was no longer assigned to her. He was probably busy with other cases.

She had placed Detective Flannery's card in her wallet next to Blaine's. He's the one she should be calling, she thought. He had an interest in her, in her case, and was a very nice man. Her therapist's words also echoed in her mind. *Go for it.*

Hannah dialed the number. She winced when an answering machine picked up.

"Hi, you've reached Detective Sean Flannery of the 97th Precinct. I'm away from my desk, but if you leave a message at the beep I'll be sure to phone you back as soon as I can."

Hannah nearly left a message but instead she simply hung up. She didn't want to sound like a hysterical fool. The message on Cozzone's machine was probably a prank call, not even directed at her. It was probably nothing.

"Hey baby, howzit goin'?"

The words reverberated in her head. It was exactly what the assailant had said to her as she walked past him on First Avenue. The words were the same on the answering machine. The voice was the same. It was *him*! It was *him*!

She picked up the phone again and dialed Flannery's number. This time when she got the answering machine, she left a message.

"Uhm, Detective Flannery? This is Hannah McCleary. We, uhm, we met Tuesday in front of my apartment?" She made a face and shook her head. What the hell was she saying? Of course he would know they had met. He had sought her out!

"Uhm, I need you to call me when you get this message. I'm at my cousin's house, the writer. It's where I've been staying because I'm housesitting."

She recited the phone number and hung up abruptly. She thought that she must have sounded like a nervous schoolgirl. It would be a miracle if the man wanted to see her now.

Hannah sighed and looked at the answering machine. She erased the first two messages but left the one from the creep. She wanted Detective Flannery to hear it, *if* he called her back. It was harassment, wasn't it? Couldn't someone be arrested for that? Didn't they have ways to trace phone calls back to whoever had made them? She could make sure this creep didn't bother her.

What if he wanted to kill her?

Hannah shivered and got up from the desk. She went back downstairs and found that the water was boiling over. She quickly turned off the heat, stirred the pasta, and then looked in the cupboard for a colander. Hannah suddenly realized that she hadn't opened the jar of sauce to heat it. She let the pasta sit in the hot water while she found a small pot to pour the sauce into.

Five minutes later she was ready to sit and eat. The cat had perched on the counter next to her, taking in the aroma of the spaghetti sauce. Hannah found a bottle of red wine in the rack and opened it. She decided that she would get pleasantly plowed. She nearly laughed when she saw that she had a glass of Jack Daniel's as well as a glass of wine by her plate.

She started to eat and sip both drinks as she went. Her heart was still pumping fast, for the message upstairs had truly alarmed her. She couldn't get the voice out of her head.

The phone rang, causing her to jump. She reached for the receiver but froze. What if it was the creep again? What would she do?

She hesitated, listening to the ring… twice… three times…

What if it was Detective Flannery?

She grabbed the receiver. "Hello?"

"Hannah?"

"Yes?"

"It's Sean. Detective Flannery."

"Oh, yes, hi. Thank you for calling me back."

"What is it? Is anything wrong?" The voice was comforting.

"Uhm, there was a message on the answering machine. I think it's from him, the man who assaulted me."

"What? Really?"

"Yes, he sounds the same and everything."

"But Hannah, your assailant is, uhm, in jail."

Hannah detected a hesitation in the detective's voice. "Can you check on it? Confirm it? See if he got out on parole or something?"

"Uhm, sure, I can check. You want me to do that for you?"

"Yes, please, would you?" His concern gave her a little relief.

"Of course, but I probably won't be able to do much until tomorrow. What did this man on your answering machine say?"

"That he was coming to get me or something like that. That he had a score to settle."

"Sheesh," Flannery said. "Look, Hannah, I don't think this could be your assailant. How would he even know where to find you? You're not at home, right?"

"Right."

"Look, just lock the doors and try not to worry about it. I'll come over in the morning, how would that be? I'll have a listen and we can take it from there, all right?"

"Okay."

"Good. You gonna be all right now?"

"Yes. Thank you."

"You're welcome. And Hannah?"

"Yes?"

"I'm glad you called."

He hung up. She smiled for a moment, but the panic had not completely left her. No, she was not all right, but she would have to live with it until tomorrow.

Chapter 14

Dominic DeLauria sat in a navy blue '97 Chevy Malibu that was parked on East 63rd Street, across from and a little east of John Cozzone's townhouse. The used car was another one of the perks that Pontecorva provided him when DeLauria asked for a set of wheels. It wasn't a bad car, despite the 70,000 miles that was already on it. Whoever had owned it before had taken care of it. The tires were new and the engine purred as if it were refurbished. DeLauria guessed that Pontecorva figured it was better to loan out a car than to provide a driver and vehicle whenever DeLauria needed one. Parking was a bit of a hassle in lower Manhattan, but after cruising the blocks near his apartment for a little while he could usually find a space.

Locating Cozzone's house hadn't been difficult. The writer wasn't listed, but Pontecorva had ways of finding out addresses, especially for people who didn't want to be found. Once DeLauria had verified that the townhouse indeed belonged to the writer named John Cozzone, he had placed a phone call to the residence, directed at "Hannah." He had used the word "baby" a couple of times, since she had also used it when she gunned down Charlie Patrone and his bodyguard. It was just a little message to say that he was on to her. Of course, it was entirely probable that the woman had used an alias, and that her name wasn't really Hannah. After all, Cozzone had told the boys that his name was Vincent.

He had kept watch on the townhouse all night after the phone call. No one had left the place. There was obviously some activity inside, for lights went on and off on all of the floors. If the broad and Cozzone were in there, they would surely have to come out eventually.

DeLauria's plan was to slowly terrorize them, plant little hints that they were in big trouble. If he could catch them attempting to run, that would be sweet. He had no problem whacking a couple of thieves and murderers who went against the Pontecorva family, especially if they were trying to give him the slip.

As long as they didn't attempt to run, DeLauria hoped to finish the job in a couple of days. After he had primed them with fear, he would simply break down the door one night and shoot them in bed.

He yawned once and considered going into the little diner at the end of the block for something to eat. Pontecorva had offered some low-level help if DeLauria needed it. At first DeLauria had refused, citing the fact that he always worked alone. However, after a full night of staking out the townhouse, he realized that another set of eyes might be a good idea after all. A guy needed to get some sleep if he was to remain sharp and focused.

DeLauria picked up his cell phone and made a call. When the liaison answered, DeLauria gave the man his location and asked for backup. Anyone who might have been listening would have thought he was a cop. The liaison promised that someone would be there in an hour.

DeLauria stretched and then scanned the townhouse for some signs of life. It was very quiet but it was still early. People were just now getting out and about to go to work.

A red Toyota Corolla drove slowly down the street, the driver obviously looking for a place to park. DeLauria paid him little mind until the car parallel parked in a space not far from the townhouse. A man who appeared to be in his thirties got out of the car and walked up the steps of Cozzone's townhouse. He was wearing a gray trenchcoat. DeLauria thought he smelled like a cop even from this distance.

The man rang the doorbell and waited. DeLauria watched with interest as the door opened and the man greeted a woman. She was partially hidden by the open door, but DeLauria could see that she was blonde and probably in her twenties or thirties. Could this be the mysterious Hannah? Had she called the cops because of the message DeLauria had left on the answering machine the previous evening?

The cop stepped inside and the door closed. Fine, DeLauria thought. He could wait.

***

"Thank you for coming," Hannah said.

Cutler removed the trenchcoat and said, "I don't know why I wear this thing, the weather's beautiful. I guess it keeps me in character." He hung it over the bottom post of the stair banister. "Now, what seems to be the problem?"

"I want you to hear something." She led him up the stairs and into the office. The answering machine still displayed the "1" on the message indicator. Hannah pushed the button and looked at him.

Cutler listened to the creep's message and smiled inwardly. He hadn't counted on this but it was a fantastic stroke of luck. *This* he could use. Her delusions of paranoia might not be delusions after all.

"You really think this is the guy who attacked you?" he asked.

"It sounds like him."

"Hannah, is there anyone who might be playing a practical joke on you? Granted, it's in bad taste."

"No. I have no friends. I have no enemies either. Except maybe Timothy Lane. Did you find out if he's still in jail?"

"I haven't had the chance. I came straight over here this morning." Cutler wasn't sure how he was going to find out that information. "He was imprisoned at…?" He snapped his fingers as if he were having a temporary memory loss.

"Rikers Island," she answered.

"Right. I'll see what I can do when I get back to the precinct."

"What should I do about this? This guy knows where I am." She sat in the chair and pulled on her fingers, just as she had done in the therapist's office. She was obviously quite agitated.

"Can you go home?" Cutler asked.

"Not really," she said. "I've promised to house sit for my cousin. I have work to do here. It's my job. Besides, don't you think he'd know where I live, too? He was able to find me here."

Cutler rubbed his chin and gazed at her. She looked so helpless and fragile sitting in the chair, looking at him with her large blue eyes. She was an urchin, a creature from the fantasy paintings by Maxfield Parrish. The more he saw her, the more attractive she was to him.

"Look, Hannah, there's really nothing we can do at the moment. Let's wait and see if he calls again," he said.

"But can't you trace the call or something?"

He shook his head. "That's more complicated than it sounds. You need court orders and stuff." Cutler wasn't sure that was the truth, but she seemed to buy it.

She became quiet and reverted to the finger-pulling routine.

"Look," he said, "why don't we go out for some breakfast? Have you had breakfast?"

She looked up at him and almost smiled. "Really? You want to?"

"Of course. Let's go. We can find somewhere around here, can't we?"

"I think I know a coffee shop," she said. "Just give me a second." She stood, went out of the office, and trotted up the stairs to the next floor.

"I'll just wait downstairs," he called out.

***

DeLauria was about to place another call to the liaison when he saw the townhouse door open. The cop and the girl came out. The couple started walking east and they didn't appear to be in any kind of hurry. It was a leisurely stroll, as if they were going out for a bite to eat.

He watched them carefully, especially the girl. The description he had received on the hitter was that she was blonde, good-looking, and in her thirties. This woman walking with the cop fit the bill. She didn't look like much of a killer, but it had to be her. DeLauria knew that looks could be deceiving. No one was what he or she seemed.

He wanted to get out of the car and follow them, but he had to wait for his backup. DeLauria looked at his watch and saw the he had about twenty more minutes to wait.

Fuck it, he thought. He got out and trailed the couple, keeping a safe distance. When he got to the corner of Second Avenue, he saw them go into a coffee shop across the street. Perfect, he couldn't ask for more.

DeLauria turned around so that he could see all of 63rd Street. If the backup arrived, he'd be able to spot the guy. DeLauria bought a newspaper from the newsstand on the corner and stood against the wall, keeping his eyes in both directions.

Chapter 15

John Cozzone was ready to either strangle Sophia or run out on her. Once again she had scared the shit out of him and he didn't know how to handle it.

They were in Grant Park near the big fountain in the glorious Loop of downtown Chicago. The sun was bright and it was a hot day. Some kind of summer food festival was going on, and the place was jam-packed with humanity. They even called it the Summer Food Festival of Chicago, but all Cozzone could think about was that it should have been named the Summer Fool Festival of Chicago. It was impossible to move through the crowd without making unwanted contact with bodies and they were everywhere: families with little kids, strollers, vendors, hawkers, cops, bikers, people of all ages, races, and economic income. Someone would have to be nuts to voluntarily attend the thing.

What a place to meet a drug connection.

"Why did you have to suggest that we meet here?" he asked Sophia.

"I thought it would be fun," she said. "Are you hungry? That food looks pretty good."

Cozzone was too high on coke to think about food. The smells of the festival nearly nauseated him.

"I'm not hungry," he said.

"I guess I'm not either," Sophia said. "Where the fuck is he? He said by the fountain, right?"

"By the fountain."

When they arrived in Chicago, Sophia had insisted that they stay at the Drake, one of most expensive hotels in town. Cozzone could use a credit card but he hoped that they wouldn't hang around the city too long. Until they got rid of the cocaine, he was living on the dregs of what little income he had made writing articles for magazines that paid little more than cab fare. The money he had put up to pay for the cocaine in New York had to go back into his safe and he didn't like carrying it around. Once they were settled in the room, Sophia then proceeded to snort some of the coke that they had brought across the country to sell, ordered room service, and then wasn't able to eat.

The sex had been good, the first time they had done it since they had hit the road, but the next morning she was giving orders again. Cozzone finally figured that he really didn't like Sophia. She was a stereotypical mafia princess. She thought she was the female equivalent of Tony Soprano. When she was high she believed that she was invincible, that she could do anything and get away with it.

The scary thing happened when they tried to sell the stuff. She had pulled the gun on Ramon in the hotel room. Cozzone's connection, a Puerto Rican and his *compadre* had balked at the price. Sophia had upped the ante without telling Cozzone she was going to do so. When Ramon complained that the price wasn't what he had been led to believe it would be, she drew the Colt and pointed it at him.

"Listen, *amigo*, our costs were a little higher than *we* were led to believe," she said. "Now you've had a chance to sample it and you said it was some of the best shit you've ever had. So, baby, you either walk the walk or get the fuck out of here."

When he heard that, Cozzone had nearly choked on his own saliva. He froze, expecting Ramon's friend to pull out a sub-machinegun and blast them both to hell.

Instead, Ramon raised his hands and stood from the dining room table.

"Fine," he said. "We leave." He looked at his pal, nodded, and they both left the room.

After a minute, Cozzone spat, "What the *fuck* are you doing?"

"We can do better than them," she said, placing the gun back in her purse.

"What are you talking about? Why did you raise the price? That's not what we had promised them!" Cozzone was exasperated.

"Would you chill out? We need to find a more upscale buyer. We can get at least a third more if we find the right people."

"Are you mad? Do you realize you pulled a gun at a drug exchange? That's how people get shot and killed! What if his pal had drawn a gun and shot us both?"

"Well, he didn't, did he? I don't know, John, sometimes I think you don't have the stomach for this. I might need to get me a new partner."

"Fine! Get yourself a goddamned new partner!" Cozzone stood and left the room. He had then spent two hours downstairs in the bar before she came down and joined him. By then she had mellowed out and apologized.

The next morning Cozzone had phoned another contact, someone more "upscale." The man called himself George and he had agreed to meet them on Friday at the fountain in Grant Park at Sophia's suggestion.

Now Cozzone was strung out, hot, and nervous. He rubbed the sweat off his forehead and turned to Sophia. "I don't think he's coming. Let's go."

"Shit, John, he was your contact."

"I know. We should have just sold the stuff to Ramon."

She ignored the comment and then squinted, looking past John. "I think he's coming," she said.

Cozzone turned and saw George – a big white guy with long blonde hair tied in a ponytail. Cozzone had known him from years ago but they weren't particularly friends. Nevertheless, Cozzone pretended that they were bosom buddies.

"George! How are you?" Cozzone said, sticking out his hand.

The big man clasped it and said, "Long time no see, you mangy Italian. Who's the beauty queen you got here?"

Sophia put on the charm. "I'm Sophia, baby."

"I'm George. What say we get out of this crowd and go somewhere to talk?"

"That's a *goddamned* good idea, George," Cozzone said.

***

They ended up back at the Drake. George wanted to see the product before committing to anything. Sophia wanted to see the money before revealing the product. George shrugged and said that he could get it within an hour.

"I'm not going to carry a half-million bucks around with me," he said. "You think I'm nuts?"

Sophia played hardball. "Then we'll take a down payment for sampling. Say, five hundred dollars?"

"What? First time I've ever heard that," the man said. He looked at Cozzone. "What kind of bullshit game are you playing, John?"

"I'm just the driver, George," Cozzone said. "Sophia here is in charge. It's her show."

"All right," Sophia said. "I'll be fair. If you don't like what you sample, then I'll give back the five hundred bucks."

George squinted at her.

She batted her eyes. "You have my personal guarantee, baby."

George smiled. "All right." He reached into his pocket and removed a wallet. He counted five one hundred-dollar bills and slid them across the table to Sophia. She picked up the money and deposited it in her own pocket, then opened the gym bag to extract the sample cocaine. She placed the mirror on the table and poured two lines. Sophia handed a straw to George and said, "Knock yourself out, baby."

George snorted the coke, then used his finger to clean off the mirror. He licked his finger and then shook his head. "Wow, man. That's powerful shit!" he said.

"You can imagine how you could cut it," she said. "One million. Cash. Today or forget it."

"One million?" George said. "John told me half that on the phone."

"It's gonna be two million tomorrow," Sophia said. "The longer you wait, the more expensive it gets."

George stood and said, "Give me a couple of hours. I'll be back. Don't sell it to anyone else, y'hear? Damn, that's good shit!"

After he had left the room, Cozzone just shook his head.

"What did I tell you?" she asked, smug as a bug.

George was back in an hour and a half. He carried a metal Samsonite suitcase into the room, picked it up and put it on the table, then unlocked three padlocks. Stacks of clean, crisp one hundred-dollar bills were neatly packed inside.

"You want to count it?" George asked.

"Yes," Sophia said. "Go over there and watch TV or read a magazine, okay? I don't like people watching me while I count."

"Come on, George," Cozzone said, gesturing him to move over to the sofa. George pulled out a joint and lit it.

"Put that out," Sophia said.

"Why?" George asked.

"I don't want to attract any attention. Someone might smell it in the hallway."

George shrugged, put it out, and stuck the joint back in his pocket. Cozzone turned on the television and started flipping channels with the remote. He finally settled on an old Three Stooges short.

"Does it have Curly in it?" George asked. "I only like the ones with Curly."

"I think so," Cozzone said. Sure enough, Curly Howard appeared on the screen, being chased by a man in a gorilla suit.

Twenty minutes later, Sophia closed the suitcase and said, "Fine. Here you go." She put the gym bag and the man's five hundred-dollar deposit on the table. "Don't snort it all in one place."

George stood and walked to the table. He picked up the gym bag, looked inside, and said, "It was a pleasure doing business with you."

"Yeah, it was, now get lost, baby," Sophia said.

George turned to Cozzone and said, "You've got yourself a real charmer there, John."

Cozzone laughed nervously and then held out his hand. "Good luck, George."

But before the man could shake hands with Cozzone, a gun blast blew a hole in the side of his head. A mass of red and grey matter splattered over the entry hall wall. George's body slammed against the wall and slid down, leaving a trail of bloody mess.

Sophia stood with the Colt in both hands. After a few seconds, she lowered her arms and put away the gun.

"Now we gotta get rid of him," she said nonchalantly. "And we get to keep the stuff *and* the money!"

"Sophia!" Cozzone was trembling. His mouth was open but he couldn't find the words to speak. "What... what...?"

"Come on, John, you gotta be ruthless in this business if you want to get anywhere. I'm not a Castellano for nothing."

Cozzone was in shock. He stumbled back into the living room and fell onto one of the easy chairs.

"Don't worry, John, I'll take care of it," she said. "But you can't wimp out on me. You gotta help me."

Cozzone raised his voice. "Jesus, Sophia, what's *with* you?"

"Just doing what we have to do."

"Christ! You're crazy! You're not the same person I met in Tribeca a month ago."

"It's an act, John, don't you get it?" she said, patting the suitcase. "Hey, we're rich, baby!"

"Yeah, yeah. Well, I don't particularly like the act, Sophia. I didn't particularly want to be the next Bonnie and Clyde. Fuck you, Sophia! *Fuck you!*"

"John, we all put on false faces. Everything will be back to normal when we get back to New York."

"You think I'm gonna get in a car with you?"

"You want your half of the money, don't you?"

Cozzone's mind was dashing all over the place. He wasn't sure what to do.

"Now come on and help me clean this place up," she said. Cozzone was amazed at how calm she was. "We can dump the body in the garbage chute, check out, and be on the road in an hour. Would you like that?"

Cozzone whispered. "Yes."

"Good. Then let's get moving. Oh, and fuck you, too, baby."

Chapter 16

Hannah and Cutler grabbed the only free table in the coffee shop, which happened to be next to the window. A middle-aged waitress with a thick Brooklyn accent said, "How ya doin'," (it wasn't a question) and tossed a couple of menus on the table. "Coffee?"

"Please," Cutler said. He looked at Hannah inquisitively.

"Yes, coffee," she replied.

The waitress quickly filled two small glasses of water on autopilot, spilling a little and ignoring it, and then walked away.

Cutler spoke in a falsetto, imitating the woman. "Certainly, it will be my pleasure to serve you, comin' right up!" This caused Hannah to smile. "You can tell that she loves *her* job," Cutler said, resuming his normal voice.

"What are you going to have?" she asked.

"Eggs. Maybe pancakes. What about you?"

"I don't know." She looked at the menu but seemed distracted.

"Try to relax," Cutler said.

"Sorry, I'm just a little nervous."

"Don't worry about the guy on the phone."

"That's not what I'm nervous about."

"What are you nervous about?"

"The fact that I haven't been to breakfast with a man in several years." She continued to look at the menu as she said it, but then looked up to note his reaction. "Detective Flannery" was looking at her with a warm smile on his face. She could see that. She was able to discern when someone was smiling or frowning, it's just that she could never put all the parts of a face together into a coherent picture. She could focus on the eyes alone, or the nose, or the mouth, as if they were separate pieces of a puzzle. She had to use her imagination to assemble it and create a sum of all the parts. Considering the individual pieces, Hannah could see that the detective was very handsome.

The waitress came back with the coffee. She poured two cups and pointed at the little tin and said, "There's the cream. You know what you're havin'?"

"Go ahead," Hannah prompted Cutler.

"I'll have three scrambled eggs, bacon, and wheat toast."

Hannah was flustered. "Oh, I'll have the same."

The waitress nodded, scribbled on her pad, and walked away.

"So, here we are," Cutler said.

She laughed nervously. "Yeah, here we are."

"Tell me about your work."

Hannah shrugged. "It's nothing much. I type my cousin's manuscripts. He's a writer. I do personal assistant stuff for him. I like it. I have a lot of freedom."

"Sounds idyllic. I hardly have an hour to myself."

"Oh, am I keeping you from work?"

"No, no, I didn't mean that. I'm allowed to go have breakfast. I, uhm, I called the precinct and told them I'd be a little late this morning."

"How long have you been a detective?" she asked.

"Actually not long. I was a street cop for a few years and worked my way up. I've been a detective for two years."

"I see. Are you from New York?"

"Me? Nah, I'm from Virginia. Ever been there?"

"No, I'm afraid not. I haven't been anywhere. I'm pretty boring."

"Oh, come on. You know, Hannah, you don't have a very high self-esteem. I hope you don't mind me saying that."

"No, I don't mind, because you're absolutely right. I'm, well, I'm a very shy person." She lowered her head.

"I didn't mean to embarrass you."

"That's okay. I get embarrassed easily."

"Well, I think you're cute when you're embarrassed." This caused her to blush even more.

The waitress brought the food. "That was fast," Cutler commented. The waitress didn't acknowledge him, just set down the plates and walked away.

Cutler tasted the eggs and said, "Well, the food is certainly better than the service."

"I guess that counts for something," Hannah replied.

They ate in silence for a few minutes. Finally, Cutler broke the awkwardness by asking, "What do you do for fun?"

She laughed a bit. "Oh, I don't have fun. None at all."

"Come on!"

"No, really. I said I'm boring and I meant it. I go to work and I go home. I read. I listen to music. That's about it."

"What about friends? Don't you have friends?"

"Not really. I have a neighbor that I guess I'm friends with. That's about it."

"Didn't you have friends in Albany?" he asked.

"Well, sure, back in high school, but…" She stopped and looked at him curiously. "How did you know I was from Albany?"

Oh, shit, Cutler thought. She had told *Dr. Tom Cagle* about being from Albany, not Detective Flannery.

"It was, uhm, you know, in your file," he answered, not missing a beat.

"Oh," she said. "What else do you know about me?"

He laughed. "That you like to dress up in black leather and crack a whip."

Her brow creased. She didn't get it.

"Never mind," he said. "Bad joke. I'm a cop. We all have weird senses of humor."

They ate some more in silence. Hannah looked out the window and frowned.

"There's a man across the street that's been looking at us," she said.

Cutler turned to look. "Where?"

"That guy with the newspaper, on the corner."

"How do you know he's looking at us? Looks to me like he's reading his paper."

"He keeps looking over this way," she said.

"Hannah, you're paranoid. He's probably waiting for someone or for a bus. Look, he's near the bus stop."

"But he's not standing *in* the bus stop. I'd swear he's watching us. He can see us through the window."

Cutler turned back to her and said, "I think you're imagining things. That phone call really has you spooked."

She went back to eating without replying.

"Would you like me to come see you tonight?" he asked.

"Oh, I can't. My friend Liz is coming over for dinner this evening."

"I thought you said you didn't have any friends."

"I don't. She's my neighbor. She lives on the floor below. I guess we're friends, but we don't really hang out together."

Cutler finished his meal and looked out the window. The man was still there, but he didn't appear suspicious to Cutler.

"Detective Flannery?" Hannah asked.

"Yes? Hey, call me Sean."

"Sean?"

"Yes, Hannah?"

"Would you mind walking me to my apartment? I'd like to get a book and bring it back to my cousin's. Do you have time?"

"Sure. No problem."

Hannah put down her fork, her food half-eaten.

"Is that all you want?" Cutler asked.

"Yeah. I really don't eat much."

"You eat like a bird. No wonder you're so thin."

"Am I too thin?"

"You're thin, but I like thin women."

The waitress came by and Cutler asked for the check. Hannah started to look in her purse but Cutler stopped her. "I'll get this."

"Are you sure?" she asked.

"Absolutely." He counted out the money and left it on the table. "Ready?"

She nodded but looked out the window with trepidation.

"Don't worry about him, he's nobody," Cutler said.

"If you say so."

They got up, left the coffee shop, and began to walk north. They went east on 72nd Street to First Avenue and then continued uptown. Eventually they arrived at Hannah's building.

"Do you want me to walk you back to your cousin's?" Cutler asked.

"No, that's all right," she answered. "I need to do a few things here before going back. Thank you, though."

"You're quite welcome."

He hesitated a moment and then leaned in to kiss Hannah on the cheek. She instinctively jerked away and said, "Oh!"

"I'm sorry," he said. "I didn't..."

"No, it's all right. I... I mean, you surprised me..." She was flustered again.

Instead, Cutler held out his hand. "I'll see you soon?"

She tentatively took his hand and said, "Yes."

"Bye, then." He smiled at her and then proceeded to walk south. She watched him for a moment, then went inside her building.

Cutler felt pretty good about the morning. He felt that he was gaining her trust. He would have her wrapped around his finger in no time.

Movement up ahead caught Cutler's attention and he could have sworn that he saw the man who had been across the street from the coffee shop duck into a building. Cutler walked a little faster. When he reached the building, he saw that it was a drug store. Cutler looked through the glass door but did not see the man. He shrugged. Must have been his imagination. He went on back toward where Hannah's cousin lived so that he could pick up his car.

***

Dominic DeLauria waited until the cop had gone past the drug store before he looked outside. He peered in both directions and didn't see him. DeLauria was afraid he had been made but apparently he was safe. He left the drug store and walked north, toward the building where the woman had entered. Odd that she had done that. DeLauria wondered if perhaps she didn't live with Cozzone and maybe had her own place.

When he got to the building he saw that it was a simple brownstone with several apartments. He stepped inside the inner foyer and scanned the mailboxes.

One name stood out, causing DeLauria to raise his eyebrows.

Hannah McCleary.

Well, I'll be damned, he thought. She really *was* the shooter!

Chapter 17

Hannah had gone back to Cozzone's townhouse around noon so that she could get some work done. She left a message for Liz to come over at seven o'clock and then proceeded to type the new material her cousin had left. Her mind kept wandering, though, replaying the scene at breakfast. She kept thinking about Detective Sean Flannery.

He was such a nice man. Hannah had never known someone like him and she was truly beginning to like the guy. Unfortunately, as hard as she tried to do so, she was unable to recall anything about his face. This was often the case since the assault. Not only could she never recognize people when she saw them, she couldn't recall faces she had known before the bump on the head, not even her own mother and father. Of course, they had both died when she had been much younger. Could orphans with normal facial recognition conjure up images of their parents' faces? She didn't know.

Her thoughts also invariably slipped over to the strange man she had seen across the street from the coffee shop. Despite what Sean had told her, Hannah had a very bad feeling about the man reading the newspaper. His build was very similar to the man that assaulted her. What if it was Timothy Lane? She had come to trust her instincts in the past five years and this was one instance in which her instincts were shouting a warning.

But what if Timothy Lane wasn't the true assailant? What if this man she had seen in the street was the genuine rapist who had accosted her that night? What if he had returned to finish the job? He had somehow found her again and was watching her every move. He had left that threatening phone message. He was stalking her as she traveled between her apartment and Cozzone's townhouse. He knew where she lived and worked and was formulating a plan that would offer the best opportunity for him to strike again, this time with complete success.

Stop it! she commanded herself. She was mind-racing again, creating scenarios in her head that were simply not based in any kind of rational thinking. Hannah knew that she had become paranoid and fearful since the assault and that it sometimes took a great mental effort to keep her from working herself into a panic.

She looked at her watch and saw that it was two o'clock. She decided that it wouldn't hurt to have a small drink. Hannah left the desk, went downstairs, opened the cupboard, and found her old friend Jack Daniel's. The sound of the ice cubes dropping into the glass was comforting and she already felt better before she had taken her first sip. She brought the drink back upstairs and nursed it as she continued to work. The alcohol spread throughout her body, dampening the hard-edged anxiety.

The afternoon passed quickly and before she knew it the time had come for her to prepare dinner. She had bought a whole chicken, some potatoes, lettuce, carrots, and tomatoes. Using a recipe she had plucked from a magazine, Hannah proceeded to bake the chicken and potatoes in the oven and then made a salad. She hoped that Liz would bring a bottle of wine. If not, they would have to settle for fruit juice, soda, or Jack Daniel's.

Liz arrived late, closer to the seven-thirty. When she walked in the door, Hannah smelled liquor on her breath.

"Hi, Hannah," Liz said, slurring her words.

"Hi, Liz," Hannah said. "Are you all right?"

"I'm a little drunk, but I'm okay," she said as she stumbled through the door. She bumped into Hannah as she did so. "Oops, sorry."

"Gee, it's awfully early to be drunk!" Hannah laughed.

"Don't laugh. It's better than cutting my wrists."

"What are you talking about?"

"You remember me telling you about Sylvia, one of the waitresses at the bar?"

"Uhm, no. I don't think you mentioned her."

"I didn't? Oh, I thought I did. Anyway, she dumped me."

"Liz, I didn't even know you were in a relationship."

"I wasn't. She dumped me before we could get into a relationship."

Hannah shook her head. "Come in and sit down. I'd offer you a drink but I think you've probably had enough."

Liz held up a bag. "I brought wine!"

Hannah took it from her and said, "Thanks. You sit down and I'll finish in the kitchen."

"I don't wanna sit down. I wanna help."

"Well, you can sit there on the stool, but there's really nothing for you to do. Just relax and tell me about Sylvia."

Hannah continued to prepare things and set the dining table while Liz dominated the conversation. She played with the *chai* around her neck as she spoke.

"She was so cute!" she said. "Not as cute as you, but pretty damn cute." This made Hannah blush but she continued to work without acknowledging the compliment.

"How long have you known her?"

"She started working at the bar a month ago. We messed around in the storage room once during a break and I thought there might be something happening. It was, you know, kinda hot. We had one date not long after that. Went out to dinner, went to a movie, ended up back at her place. But ever since then, any time I tried to move things along she just gave me the cold shoulder. Finally, today, she told me to fuck off."

"She used those words?"

"More or less. No, not really, but that was the subtext."

"What did you do to deserve that?"

"I dunno." Liz hiccuped. "'Scuse me. Gee, I better have something to drink. I have the hiccups. Open that goddamned wine."

"I don't know, Liz, you're already pretty wasted," Hannah said, smiling and shaking her head.

"Open it, goddamn it!"

"All right, but if you pass out on me, I'll…"

"You'll what?"

"I don't know. Just don't!"

She found a corkscrew in the kitchen and opened the wine, a surprisingly good Chilean cabernet. They clinked glasses and Hannah sat on the stool next to Liz.

"Dinner will be ready soon," Hannah said.

"Good, I'm starving," Liz replied. Then she saw the bottle of Jack Daniel's on the counter. "Hey, I see dessert."

"Liz, gee," Hannah said, rolling her eyes.

"I hope you don't mind, but I plan on getting totally sloshed tonight."

"I think you already are."

"Nah, I've got a long way to go. So what's up with you? How's work?"

Hannah shrugged. "Oh, you know. Same as always."

"Have you heard from your cousin?"

"He called once."

"He's pretty good looking, isn't he?"

Hannah thought that he might be, but she wasn't sure. "I guess so."

Liz snorted. "Not that *I* care."

"Did you ever date men?" Hannah asked.

"Sure, I had my share of dick."

"Liz!"

"Come on, Hannah, don't act like you've never heard that word before."

Hannah just shook her head and smiled, indicating that it was useless trying to steer the conversation away from the subject.

"Yeah, I dated men," Liz continued. "It wasn't what I had been led to believe it would be, you know? You know how we're preconditioned to fall in love with some man and get married and live happily ever after? That Prince Charming bullshit, a white wedding, a nice house in the suburbs… what a load of crap. I think I knew something was different about me when I was eight years old, but I didn't do anything about it. It wasn't until after college, when I realized that I never felt any kind of buzz when I was with a man. Now women – that was a different story. I had my first lesbian experience my junior year in college and it was like the Fourth of July. Still, I ignored it and chalked it up to just one of those things, you know, experimentation and all that. Then there was Julia, this lady I met after I graduated. Wow, she convinced me. Boy, did she ever. Now I'm Liz the Lez and proud of it."

Hannah didn't know how to respond. She wasn't comfortable talking about sex, be it Liz's preferences and history, or her own. There wasn't much to talk about with regard to her past anyway.

"What about you, Hannah?" Liz asked. "How come you don't have a boyfriend?"

Hannah shrugged. "I don't know. I'm not the type of girl boyfriends have."

"Bullshit. You're pretty. You're a little shy and quiet, but there are plenty of guys that like that. You're not gay are you?"

"No," Hannah said, laughing.

"You're not bisexual, just waiting for me to make a move and see if there are sparks?"

"'Fraid not, Liz," Hannah said, still laughing.

"Darn," Liz said. She took a drink and said, "Hey, I'm just teasing you, you know that."

"I know."

"I don't want you to feel uncomfortable."

"I'm not."

The bell on the timer rang. Hannah said, "Oh!" and jumped off the stool. "Why don't you go have a seat at the dining table and I'll be right in."

"Nonsense, let me help you carry stuff. You're not the goddamned maid."

The two women eventually placed themselves at the table and began to eat. The chicken had come out nicely and Liz said so. The wine flowed freely as they spoke about their respective childhoods and the trials of junior high and high school. Liz revealed more about her love life but failed to draw out Hannah on any of hers.

"Come on, Hannah. You *have* had sex, haven't you?" she asked, none too tactfully.

"Yes, Liz, I have. It wasn't very memorable."

"How long ago?"

"Must we talk about this? It was years ago."

"*Years*? Honey, we need to get you laid. That's your problem, you need to get naked with another body."

"Liz!"

"I'm serious, sweetie. You're way too withdrawn. I see you up there in your little apartment, all alone, and I feel for you," Liz said. "You never go out, you don't do anything to get yourself a lover."

"That's not quite true," Hannah replied, a little offended. "I may be seeing someone now."

Liz raised her eyebrows. "What did you say?"

Hannah laughed at her reaction. "There might be someone. I don't know yet."

"Really? Who is it?"

"He's a cop."

"A *cop*!"

"Remember the guy that was outside the building. The one you told me about?"

"Yeah. *Him*?"

Hannah nodded. "He's a detective."

Liz frowned and took a sip of wine. "He was good looking," she said. "But he didn't strike me as being a cop."

"How so?"

"I dunno. He didn't have the right attitude. If he was a cop he seemed too… inexperienced, or something. You know what I mean?"

"No."

"Well, neither do I." She raised her glass. "To hell with it. Congratulations. Tell me more."

"There's nothing to tell. We've had one date, if you can call it that. We went out to breakfast this morning."

"Hey, that's a start! What's his name?"

"Sean."

Liz nodded with approval.

They finished the meal and cleared the table together. Hannah insisted on leaving the dirty dishes until later. Liz grabbed the bottle of Jack Daniel's and two new glasses before they headed for the living room to sit in front of the television. Instead of turning it on, though, Hannah put on a jazz CD and then sat on the sofa next to Liz.

"How come you never wear makeup?" Liz asked.

Hannah shrugged. "I've never had much use for it."

"It would do wonders for you," Liz said, brushing back the wave of blonde hair that hung over Hannah's forehead. "You're very pretty, naturally pretty, but makeup would just, you know, sharpen up things. It would accent your eyes. And your mouth. Make it real kissable."

Hannah looked down and blushed. The alcohol was certainly getting to her, too. She didn't understand how Liz was still conscious.

Liz then took Hannah's free hand and gently said, "Something happened to you, didn't it? In the past, I mean. Something bad."

Hannah was quiet for a moment but didn't take her hand away. Eventually she nodded.

"What was it?"

Hannah didn't say anything.

"You can tell me. I'm your friend," Liz said.

"It's hard to talk about," Hannah finally muttered.

"That's okay. Pretend I'm a shrink."

Hannah laughed. "I have a shrink, did you know that?"

"No, really? What for?"

"For everything you've said. Depression, shyness, paranoia..."

"Wow. How often do you see her?"

"It's a him. Doctor Cagle is his name. I've seen him only once so far, but I'm going again next week."

"Is he good?"

Hannah nodded. "Yeah, I was surprised. I normally don't put much faith in that stuff, but he was good at nailing down the things I've been having trouble with."

"So what is it, Hannah? Were you abused by your father or something like that?"

"No, nothing like that."

"Well, what?"

"I was almost raped. Some guy assaulted me. In the little inner alcove of our building, where the mailboxes are."

Liz's eyes went wide. "Oh my God, Hannah! Really? Jesus, where was I?"

"It was before you moved in. Five years ago."

"What happened?"

"I was coming home late from the bank where I used to work. I had stayed after hours to finish an auditing project. I decided to walk because the bus just never came. I was walking up First Avenue and this guy appeared out of the dark and started following me. He was saying things to me, trying to get me to stop. I just kept on walking. No one else was around. It was very strange. It was around eleven o'clock and hardly anyone was on the streets. Well, he caught up with me at our building. I was trying to unlock the door to get inside when he got me. I… I got hit on the head. The next thing I knew, I was in the hospital."

"But he didn't, you know, rape you?"

"Apparently not. Somebody came in time. I think someone had heard me scream and they had called the police. The guy ran away. The police really took their time getting there. I don't know how long it was but I was angry about it afterwards, when I found out. But they did grab him a few blocks away. I was unconscious, but that's what I was told."

"So they caught him?"

Hannah nodded. "Yeah. They picked him up a couple of avenues over. The guy kept insisting that they had the wrong man, but apparently he had done it before. He had been accused of a sexual assault before but had gotten off, or maybe he did a little time, I can't remember. Anyway, he went to prison, to Rikers Island. He got seven years and I hope he's still there. I'm trying to get that confirmed."

"You poor baby," Liz said. She leaned over and embraced Hannah, who allowed her to do so. The cloud of alcohol had completely dulled her senses. Normally she would have gently pulled away, but it felt good to have someone give her a hug. Before she knew it, she was hugging Liz back. They sat there together, arms entwined, until Liz slowly turned her head to Hannah's and looked into her eyes.

Hannah studied the woman's face. Up close like that it was almost a complete thing. Hannah had never gleaned a person's face in that close proximity since the assault and thus never knew what effect it might have on her visual recognition faculties. While the face was still broken up in sections, there was much more cohesiveness. Hannah could accurately say that she was looking at a face.

"You're very pretty," Liz whispered.

"Thank you," Hannah said. "So are you."

Liz leaned in and touched her lips against Hannah's. Hannah was too intoxicated to resist, and besides, it felt nice. Feeling the lack of resistance, Liz pressed her mouth harder against Hannah's lips and held it there. Hannah opened her mouth and invited Liz's tongue to work its way in. Hannah did the same with her own tongue, and for several seconds the two women carefully explored and probed each other. The kiss surprised Hannah but it didn't repulse her. She went with the flow, not thinking about where it might end up.

Surprisingly, it was Liz who broke away and said, "Oh, shit. Where's the bathroom?"

Hannah pointed. "Down that way, to the left. You okay?"

Liz looked a little green. She shook her head and took off toward the hallway, crashing into a table as she went. Hannah got up and followed her, but Liz slammed the bathroom door shut. Within seconds, Hannah heard Liz vomiting. She shuddered and moved back into the living room, not sure what to do. The retching went on for several minutes. Just when Hannah thought it was finished, Liz heaved some more.

When it was finally quiet, Hannah crept back into the hallway and knocked on the bathroom door.

"Liz? You all right?"

She heard a muffled affirmative.

"You need help? Should I come in?"

This time, a muffled negative.

"There should be washcloths in the cupboard. And a towel. Can I get you anything?"

"No, thanks. I'm sorry."

"Don't be sorry. I *told* you that you had way too much to drink."

Hannah went back into the living room and picked up the glasses and empty bottle. She was pretty tipsy herself, but nowhere near the extent that Liz was. Hannah went into the kitchen, threw the bottle in the garbage, set the glasses by the dirty dishes, and then went back to the hallway.

"How are you now?" she called out. The bathroom door opened and Liz slowly emerged. Hannah could see that her skin was pale.

"I feel awful," Liz said.

"You want to lie down?"

Liz nodded.

"Let's go upstairs," Hannah said.

"I'll just lie on the couch."

"Nonsense, I'll take you to a nice big bed." She put her arm around Liz and helped her up the flight of stairs. Liz was shaky and leaned on Hannah.

"I'm sorry," she said again.

"Stop it, it's all right." They made it to the second floor. Hannah decided to take her up to the master bedroom, where the bed was huge. "One more flight, you can do it."

Liz groaned and they continued the ascent. When they got to the third floor, Liz nearly fell but Hannah managed to brace her against the wall.

"Okay, here we go," she said, attempting to support Liz on her back. They entered Cozzone's bedroom and Liz dropped onto the bed. Before Hannah could say anything, Liz was asleep. Hannah wondered what she should do next.

"What the hell," she muttered. She removed Liz's shoes and then unbuckled the woman's belt. She pulled off the blue jeans and then managed to tug Liz's sweatshirt over her head. Liz was now wearing just panties and a bra. Hannah considered removing the gold *chai* and chain from around Liz's neck but decided to leave it.

Hannah covered her with a sheet and blanket, then went to the bathroom to have a pee. When she got back to the bedroom, Liz was snoring lightly. Hannah removed her own clothes down to underwear, then got into bed on the other side of Liz.

Before long, she too was fast asleep.

Chapter 18

They had to stop in South Bend, Indiana, because Sophia felt ill. Cozzone looked at his watch and saw that it was approximately 9:30. He wanted to keep driving until they reached Ohio, but she insisted that they stop. Cozzone pulled over at a Mobil station and let her out of the car. She ran to the Ladies room with her hand over her mouth.

Cozzone shook his head in disgust. She had consumed a lot of vodka from a bottle she had bought upon leaving Chicago. On top of all the cocaine she had ingested, that had made her one unhappy camper. He picked the bottle off the floorboard and saw that it was still half full. He decided to get rid of it. She wouldn't know the difference at this point.

He got out of the car and tossed the bottle into the garbage. He went ahead and filled up with gas, paid for it with a credit card, and then drove the BMW over to the side of the station to wait for her. When she finally emerged, she looked terrible. She slumped in the doorway of the Ladies room and remained there, totally out of it.

"Aww, Jesus," Cozzone said as he got out of the car again. He went to her and helped her to the BMW. "Sophia, are you gonna make it?"

"No," she moaned. "Listen, can we stop at a hotel for a little while? I just wanna sleep." She was slurring her words badly.

"Can't you sleep in the car? We can keep going."

She shook her head. "It's making me car sick. Really. I gotta lie down and be motionless for a while."

Cozzone shut the car door, went around, and got in the driver's seat. He backed out and drove a ways, considering the situation. Sophia hunched against the passenger door and groaned loudly.

"Are you gonna throw up again?" he asked.

"I might," she murmured.

"Aww, hell." He saw a Best Western up ahead and pulled into it.

***

An hour later, Sophia was passed out on one of the queen beds, dead to the world.

Cozzone sat in the hotel room, anxious and agitated. He was so afraid that there would be a knock on the door at any moment. *"Open up, it's the police!"* Cozzone imagined his whole life going down the drain, all because of a psychopathic mafia princess.

He replayed the events of the last several days in his mind and attempted to make sense of it.

The woman was a murderer. How could he have gotten mixed up with her? What did he see in her? How was he going to get out of this? He was tempted to just pick up and leave her in the hotel. He could get in his car and drive home without her. But, knowing her, she'd probably place a *vendetta* on his head. He wouldn't last a week.

Then there was all that money and cocaine they were sitting on. He couldn't just walk away from that.

Cozzone stared at the metal suitcase that contained a million dollars. Actually, it was a little less now. Cozzone's original thirty grand had been added to the sum and then he and Sophia had each removed a handful of stacks for "spending money." She hadn't wasted any time spending some of it, either. On the way out of Chicago, she made him stop at a liquor store for the bottle of vodka and a jewelry store for a fancy diamond watch that she paid cash for. It had made the jeweler's day.

Cozzone suspected that it wasn't a very good idea for them to be throwing a lot of money around. Somebody was going to talk.

And what about George Williams, the poor schmuck who got shot at the Drake Hotel? What are the authorities going to do when they find his body? Sophia kept insisting that there was nothing to tie him to them, but Cozzone wasn't convinced. Who knows what George might have told someone before coming over to close the deal? Surely he had partners.

The more Cozzone thought about it all, the more nervous and frightened he got. It wasn't safe to be traveling with all that money and all that dope.

Suppose he hid it? Sophia would never know. She was out cold.

He looked at his watch again. Impulsively making a decision, Cozzone stood, took hold of the metal suitcase and the gym bag, and quietly went out the door. He took the elevator downstairs and found the night manager – a college-aged kid who looked as if he could use some extra dough.

First, Cozzone asked the kid if there were any empty boxes in the hotel. The boy produced some shipping boxes that were used for various purposes. Cozzone took the boxes and some packing tape, disappeared into the Men's room, and returned a few minutes later. He then paid the night manager a thousand dollars to do a favor for him come Monday morning.

Chapter 19

The sun's rays streamed in through the blinds and woke Hannah. She opened her eyes and immediately felt a presence beside her in the bed. She gasped, turned to look and then realized it was only Liz. They had slept in the same bed all night.

Hannah glanced at the digital clock on the nightstand and saw that it was after eight. She quietly slipped her legs out from under the sheets and stood. She tiptoed around the bed toward the bathroom as Liz began to stir. The woman groaned and opened her eyes.

"Good morning," Hannah said.

"Where the fuck am I?" Liz asked hoarsely.

"You're in my cousin's townhouse. Remember last night? We had dinner together and you had a little too much to drink."

"Oh yeah," Liz said. "For a minute I thought I was at my mother's house, and that would have really been a nightmare." She sat up and saw that she was dressed in her underwear. She then looked at the empty other half of the bed and back at Hannah, who was also scantily dressed. Liz's brow creased as she tried to put it together.

"Don't worry," Hannah said. "Nothing happened."

"No? Oh, well, I guess that's good," Liz replied. "Not that I wouldn't mind if it had, but I would have liked to remember it if it did."

"You got pretty sick. I had to help you to bed and I just figured that there was enough room. I should have gone to one of the guest rooms but I'm used to it in here."

"Sorry. I hope I wasn't much trouble."

Hannah gave her a wave and went into the bathroom. When she returned, Liz was up and getting dressed.

"I better go," she said.

"You don't have to rush off. How do you feel?"

"Like a truck ran over me. Listen, I feel kinda weird, I should just go."

"You're welcome to stay. You want coffee?" Hannah pulled on her jeans and put on a fresh blouse.

Liz shook her head. "I'm really embarrassed. Parts of the evening are coming back to me. Look, Hannah, if I made a pass at you or something and it made you uncomfortable…"

"Liz, don't worry about it. Now please don't feel bad and come downstairs. Let's have coffee. I'm going to go make it." She left Liz in the room and descended the stairs to the first floor. She put on water to boil and got two cups out of the pantry. As she prepared the Mr. Coffee machine, Liz came down.

"I'm going," she said. "Thanks for last night."

"You sure? Liz, you have no reason to feel embarrassed."

"I don't, I just want to be alone. Thanks for everything. I'll see you at home."

"Okay, if you really want. Thanks for coming over last night."

Liz walked to the front door and noticed an envelope on the floor. "Hey, there's a letter here. Someone must have put it through the mail slot." She picked it up and the name "Hannah" was written on it.

"Bring it here, would you?" Hannah asked. "Who's it from?"

"It doesn't say. It has your name on it." Liz walked back to the kitchen and handed it to her.

"Hmmm." She took the letter. "Well, thanks."

"See ya." Liz retraced her steps to the front door and left.

Hannah stared at the letter. What on earth could this be? She turned it over in search of some clue as to its origin but found none. She then tore it open and found a small piece of white paper with a short typed message on it.

HEY BABY, GUESS WHAT? YOU CAN'T RUN AWAY.
THE GAME IS ALMOST OVER.
THIS TIME I'LL FINISH THE JOB.

Hannah dropped the letter as if it were on fire. She was suddenly stricken with a searing pain that originated in her chest and spread to her extremities. She felt her heart rate increase and could hear its thumping in her head. She broke out in a sweat and began to shake uncontrollably. She wanted to scream but found that she couldn't make her vocal cords obey the command.

He was out of jail. The creep was free. And he knew where she was.

***

Dominic DeLauria sat in the Malibu with the lookout they had sent him – the young punk named Favio who had been his driver earlier – watching the Cozzone residence from across the street. He had stuck the letter through the mail slot during the night and was now waiting for the trigger woman to make a move. Surely she would try to run for it. DeLauria kept waiting for her to emerge from the house with a suitcase, ready to flag down a taxicab to take her to the airport or a train station. The woman had to be smart, otherwise she never could have pulled off the double hit on Patrone and his man. If she was that smart, then she would understand what all the messages were supposed to mean. Surely she had figured out by now that the Pontecorvas were on to her and Cozzone.

And what about Cozzone? DeLauria hadn't seen him. Where was he? Had he already disappeared? Why would he leave his girlfriend alone in his house? The only answer to that was that he took the cocaine out of town to sell it. That meant he'd be back soon. DeLauria figured he'd wait until the guy was back home, and then he'd kill them both.

Favio opened a brown bag and pulled out a thick salami sandwich on rye. It was full of mustard and oil, and it dripped all over him as he took a bite.

"Christ, that's disgusting," DeLauria said, his stomach turning.

"Yeah, but it's good," Favio said, his mouth full of food. The words came out as "Yehmf, buh essh gumph."

"How old are you, kid?"

Favio swallowed the bite and answered, "Twenty-three."

DeLauria was surprised. He had thought the kid was still in his teens. "Are you related to Pontecorva?"

Favio shook his head. "Nah, but my uncle works for Jimmy Fontana."

That explained it. Fontana was one of Pontecorva's lieutenants, what they called a *caporegime.*

"What kind of piece you carrying?" DeLauria asked.

Favio took another bite and said, "Smumf ann Weshum."

"What?"

Favio swallowed. "Smith and Wesson."

DeLauria nodded. Enough small talk. He didn't want to get too friendly with the kid.

"Stay here," he ordered. "I'm gonna find someplace to take a leak and get some breakfast for myself. You keep watch."

He started to get out but Favio pointed and said, "Look, the door's opening." DeLauria turned to see a heavy-set woman come out of the front door and start walking toward Second Avenue.

"Who's she?" Favio asked.

"I don't know," DeLauria said. "She showed up last night when you were gettin' the pizza."

"She was there all night?"

"Yeah." DeLauria watched the woman. She looked a little out of it. He wondered if she and Hannah McCleary had been up all night snorting coke. Enjoying the fruits of her and Cozzone's labors. Then he thought of something else. What if she was a mule? What if she was helping to distribute the product?

"Stay here," he ordered Favio. "Ring my cell phone if anyone else comes or goes."

"Where you going?"

"I'm gonna follow her, see what's up."

He got out of the car and walked east, staying on the other side of the street from the woman. When she turned to walk north on Second Avenue, he did the same. He followed her up to 71st Street, and then she turned east again. She stopped briefly at a convenience store to buy a newspaper and what appeared to be a half-quart of orange juice. DeLauria loitered in front of a bakery until she got moving again. He then followed her to First Avenue, where she turned and headed north.

She's going to McCleary's apartment, DeLauria thought. That was it. Hannah McCleary sent her to her apartment to pick up some things because Hannah was too scared to come out. She knew she was being watched. This woman had to be in on everything.

He picked up the pace until he was just a few feet behind his prey. As he predicted, she stopped in front of Hannah McCleary's building and went inside.

DeLauria froze when he saw the trenchcoat. The cop he had seen at the Cozzone residence was in front of the building, too. The woman stopped to talk to him.

What the fuck was going on? he wondered. Was the woman working for the police? Maybe they were already on to McCleary and Cozzone. That had to be it.

This changed things. DeLauria turned around and walked back

toward 63rd Street, pondering the situation and what he was going to do about it.

His mission was to retrieve the Pontecorva's cocaine or, failing that, the money that was paid for it. He aimed to do just that. If the police got in the way, he'd never get close. The big lady could be a big problem.

DeLauria's specialty was getting rid of big problems.

***

Bill Cutler adjusted his fake glasses and spoke to the woman that approached the building.

"Excuse me, but are you Liz?" he asked in his Virginia accent.

"Yes. And I think I know who you are," the woman said. "You're Sean, aren't you?"

"That's right," Cutler said, smiling. "Has someone been talking about me?"

Liz smiled. "I'm not telling. Are you looking for her?"

"Yeah, is she around?"

"She's not at home. She's at her cousin's place."

"Oh, right, I know where that is," he said.

Liz looked at him curiously. Cutler could see that she was wondering why he wouldn't have known that. Couldn't he have called before coming over?

"I was in the neighborhood on a case," he said, attempting to preempt her suspicions. "I thought I'd see if she was here."

"I see," Liz said. "Well, nice to meet you." She started to go inside, then stopped to say, "I hope you're a nice guy. I'd hate to see that little girl hurt. She's pretty fragile."

Cutler feigned shock. "Do I look like the kind of guy who would do that?"

Liz answered, "Yeah. Any guy is capable of doing that."

Cutler looked the woman up and down. He remembered what Hannah had told "Dr. Cagle" about her neighbor.

"Oh, I see," he said, "you have a problem with men."

Liz apparently didn't like the tone of his voice and frowned. "Look, I gotta go inside and put this stuff down. Have a nice day."

"You know, things might be different for you if you had a real man," Cutler said. He was angry and knew that he was about to lose control. When that happened, the tunnel vision set in. When he lost sight of peripheral objects, he knew that he was headed for trouble.

The woman gaped at him with an open mouth. She finally said, "Fuck you, mister," and then started inside the building. She opened the inner door, stepped inside, turned to him, and said, "I don't believe you're a cop, and I'm gonna tell Hannah that."

"Hey!" he shouted, but she had already shut and locked the door behind her.

Cutler whirled around and walked south. He was fuming. He wanted to punch something. He was experiencing the feelings that he had been trying to suppress for the last few years.

He thought of what the ensuing conversation with his brother might be like.

"Have you been taking your medication, Bill?"

"No, Patrick, I haven't."

"You idiot! You want to go to jail? Is that what you want?"

"Go dig a hole and climb into it, Patrick."

Cutler rounded a corner and got into his Toyota. Perhaps a good stiff drink would calm him down. He started the car, pulled out of the space, and drove toward his home in Queens.

Chapter 20

Hannah spent Saturday in the same condition that Liz had been in the night before. After seeing the note that had been dropped in Cozzone's mail slot, she had attempted to phone Sean Flannery several times but he never returned her calls. Calling the police was another option but she ultimately figured it would do no good. What could they do about a nasty note? She finally surrendered to the Jack Daniel's, sat with it while she watched television, and eventually fell asleep.

When she awoke, night had fallen. She felt awful and wasn't sure where she was. After a moment she realized that she was on the couch in the townhouse living room with Panther lying at her feet. The open Jack Daniel's bottle was a little less than half-full and was sitting on the coffee table. She managed to pull herself up, screw the lid on the bottle, and face forward.

The digital clock on the TV read 9:20. Hannah couldn't believe she had slept away the day. She still felt drunk.

Panther stretched and meowed. He had missed dinner.

"All right, Panther," she said, but her voice came out cracked. She used one of the arms on the couch for leverage and pushed herself to her feet. She slowly walked into the kitchen, poured the cat's dry food into his bowl, and went into the bathroom.

When she came out she decided that she'd better go back to sleep. She carefully went up the stairs and went into the office. The answering machine still displayed the "1" that was Timothy Lane's horrid message.

"To hell with you," she said. She punched the Erase button.

Hannah turned off the light and went upstairs to the master bedroom. She removed her clothes, dropped them on the floor, and crawled between the sheets.

***

Liz Rosenthal was late for work on Saturday night.

The altercation with the asshole named Sean had left her in a foul mood and she was dreadfully hung over, so she had napped most of the day. When she got up, she wanted to call Hannah to let her know that she was making a terrible mistake with her new boyfriend. The guy was not what he appeared to be. Liz thought that Hannah should know the terrible things Sean had said to her, but she didn't have the Cozzone phone number. She tried to get it from Directory Assistance but learned that it was unlisted.

Liz thought she might run by the townhouse on her way to work to tell Hannah what she thought, but she was running out of time. It would have to wait.

She ran out of the apartment and walked west toward Lexington Avenue and the Number 6 subway line. She would just make it if the trains were on time. She had to be at work at 10:00 and stay until 4:00. It was now 9:35.

As she walked the stretch between Third Avenue and Lexington, Liz felt as if she were being watched. It was an odd tingling sensation on the back of her neck. She turned around and saw a man at the far end of the street walking toward her. Because of his distance and the darkness, she couldn't tell who he was.

Big deal, she thought. There were plenty of people out.

She kept walking, got to the subway entrance, and went down the steps. Luckily, she could hear the train and see the approaching headlights. She swiped her Metro card and went through the turnstile.

The trip to Lower Manhattan took fifteen minutes. She then had to walk east to Avenue A where Alice's was located. It was a funky bar in a hip neighborhood. Most of the gay bars were on the West Side, but Alice's had found its niche on the opposite side of the island. Named for Alice B. Toklas, the bar catered to both genders, but its main clientele were lesbians over the age of thirty. Younger women came in occasionally, but they tended to go to the more fashionable places on the West Side. That suited Liz just fine. She liked her job and found camaraderie there.

As she crossed Second Avenue, the back of her neck tingled again. She turned and saw the figure again, a block away, walking in her direction. Was it the same guy? She was pretty sure it was.

Down on the Lower East Side it was darker and not as populated. Twenty years ago it would have been considered a dangerous area, but these days it wasn't so bad. She wished that there were more pedestrians out and about, though.

Liz made it to Alice's safely. As she entered, she was deluged by k. d. Lang's voice blaring through the quad speakers that hung in the four corners of the space. The bar was fairly small and seemed crowded when twenty people occupied it. There appeared to be many more than that tonight. All women. Virginia was bartending and Sally was the only waitress. Besides the typical selection of alcohol and soft drinks, the bar served nibbles and sandwiches but nothing that had to be cooked. Liz was thankful for that.

"God, I'm glad you showed up," Sally said.

"I'm not late am I?" Liz asked.

"No, it's just that we're busy."

"Let me go in the back for a second and I'll be right out. And hey…"

"What?"

Liz had to lean in close to be heard over the music. "I think some guy was following me from the subway. I don't know if he'll come in here or not, but keep an eye out. He was creepy."

"Sure thing," Sally said.

Liz went behind the bar and said hello to Virginia.

"Liz, I need some ice. Sally's been too busy to go out back and get some. Can you be a sweetie and do it?" Virginia asked.

Liz balked. She didn't want to go outside again.

"What's wrong?" Virginia asked.

Liz decided to play it cool. Virginia was the boss. "Oh, nothing. I'll do it," she said, taking the big plastic bucket that was used to carry the ice in.

She went through the Employees Only door into what was essentially the clean-up area. Dirty glasses and plates piled up around the sink until the bar closed at four, when someone finally got around to cleaning them. A small office was off to the right and the back door was straight ahead.

Liz didn't like it that the ice machine was outside in the storeroom. Behind the bar was an unheated, attached storeroom. The ice machine was in there, along with unused furniture and other odds and ends. The problem was that one couldn't enter it from the bar. It was necessary to go outside through the back door, walk twelve feet through a dark alleyway, and unlock the storeroom door to get inside. It was a major pain in the butt, especially in the winter.

Liz took the key from the ring on the wall and went outside with the bucket. The music followed her, and she was always amazed that they never got complaints from the neighbors regarding the noise. The alley was quite dark, as expected. Liz had asked Virginia to put in a light but it had never been done.

She walked to the storeroom door and unlocked it. As soon as she opened it, she felt the presence beside her.

No one inside the bar heard her scream.

***

"So what are we gonna do with the stuff?" Sophia asked as the BMW sped toward Toledo at seventy-five miles per hour. The illuminated clock on the dash read 1:12. There wasn't much traffic on the Turnpike at that hour. The landscape was very dark and wide-open.

"What stuff?" Cozzone asked. He had a headache and was tired of driving.

"The coke, dummy," Sophia said. "What we didn't sell in Chicago."

"Oh. That."

"Well?"

"We'll sell it. What do you think?"

"Yeah, but when?"

"Geez, Sophia, we're sitting on a million dollars. What's the rush?"

"Best to get rid of it as soon as possible. You never know." She looked back behind them as if to make sure that the trunk was still closed. "You sure the money's safe back there?"

"Sophia, it's in the trunk. In the suitcase, and it's locked."

"I know, I know. I guess I just want to play with it," she said, laughing. "I want to take a handful of it and shuffle it like a deck of cards. I want to rub it all over my body. Hey, let's stop and get a hotel. We can fuck on a bed of money."

"Jesus, Sophia, you slept until noon today. We barely got out of that hotel in Indiana before checkout time. Almost cost us another night's stay."

"What's the big deal? Like you said, we're sitting on a million dollars!"

Cozzone sighed. "We haven't been driving that long. You wanted to go see a *movie,* for Chrissakes, and then have a fancy dinner in fucking South Bend. We wasted a lot of time! Now you want to stop at another hotel? Let's see if we can get to Cleveland before we stop, okay?"

"I dunno, it's pretty late," she said. "Don't you want to fuck me again?"

Cozzone said, "Nice idea, but my head's about to split."

The truth of the matter was that he was scared to death of Sophia. He had kept one eye on the road as he drove, but the other eye he had placed squarely on his passenger. Her behavior since leaving Chicago had been erratic, confounding, and bizarre. The sooner he got back to New York, the better.

"I have a cure for that," she said, pulling out a vial of cocaine.

"No thanks. I think that's why my head hurts so. I've been doing way too much of that shit."

"Well, find a place to stop. I think we can do better than a Motel 6, too." She put the spoon up to her nose and snorted.

"Sophia, you're gonna irrigate a hole in your septum if you keep that up," Cozzone said. "Didn't you have enough yesterday? You were so sick last night you couldn't stand up."

"Oh, shut up." She put her head back and closed her eyes, enjoying the rush.

Cozzone shook his head and continued to drive, pushing the car to eighty. How was he going to get rid of her? He had got in over his head with this one. She was beautiful and a tiger in bed, but she was *insane.* Eventually he would have to settle up with her, give her half the money and cocaine, and tell her he couldn't see her anymore. That was the best way to handle it. Best to make a clean break.

"You know they're going to be looking for us," Cozzone said.

"So? They're not going to know who they're looking for, and they're not going to find us."

"What makes you so sure?"

"Because the police are inherently stupid."

He didn't reply to that.

They drove a little while in silence. She was enjoying the high and he concentrated on getting to Toledo. Surely the Chicago police would be looking for a BMW. Nobody ever got away with murder the way Sophia thought.

"John?" she asked, dreamily.

"Yeah?"

"Let's get married."

Cozzone winced. "You're kidding, right?"

"No, let's do. We make a good team."

He didn't say anything.

She opened her eyes and raised her head. "What, you don't want to?"

"Sophia, we've known each other, what, not even a month?"

She snuggled closer to him and put her mouth on his ear. She whispered, "Yeah, but look how well you've gotten to know me." She licked his ear and he recoiled.

"Hey, cut it out, I'm trying to drive here."

She reached down and put her hand on his crotch. "Maybe I can convince you we're a good team." She unzipped his pants.

"Sophia, stop. I'm not really in the mood."

She fumbled for his penis and he pushed her away, a little too forcibly.

"Hey!" she yelled. She looked at him with fury in her eyes. "You shit!" She started to hit him with her fists.

"Sophia! Stop!" He shoved her away again but she kept coming at him. The BMW swerved as Cozzone temporarily lost control of the car. He got it back in the lane just as her fist smashed into his ear, sending a jolt of pain into his brain.

"Aggghh!" he yelled. He immediately grabbed the side of his head and cowered. He thought that she must have damaged his eardrum or something, for all he could hear was a terrible ringing as a tremendous pain bore into the side of his head.

"John, look out!" she cried.

The BMW swerved again and hit the median that divided the Interstate into east and westbound traffic. The car ricocheted, careened back across the lane, and soared off the road to the right. It broke through a barbed wire fence doing at least eighty, then crashed head-on into a bank of dirt. The BMW did a spectacular flip over the bank, somersaulted twice, and finally came to a rest in the darkness, upside down.

One headlight cast a beam of illumination across the field away from the highway. The other lamp was smashed. The motor was still running but coughed sporadically, breaking up the otherwise silent and eerie stillness of the night.

After what seemed to be an eternity inside the disabled vehicle, Sophia opened her eyes. The first thing she felt was the wetness on her face. She wiped it with her right hand and looked. Red. Blood. Then next thing that she was aware of was the pain in her back and stomach. The seat belt had kept her from flying through the windshield, but she had slammed her head against the passenger window, across which a huge spider-web crack had spread.

Where was she? Everything was so hazy.

There was a man slumped over the steering wheel, twisted at a grotesque angle. Who was he? Did she know him? She reached over and lifted his head. The guy didn't look familiar, and he was not in good shape. He might even be dead.

"Hey," she tried to say, but it came out as a whisper. "Hey, you. Wake up."

The man didn't move. Sophia noticed that his neck was bent strangely. A lump that looked like his Adam's Apple was actually on the right side, below his ear.

"Hey!"

She knew he was dead. She didn't know who the fuck he was, but she could clearly see that he wasn't going to be breathing again any time soon.

Sophia peered through the windshield and realized that the car was upside down. She had to get out. She struggled with the seatbelt, trying to figure out how it worked until finally it unclasped. She dropped from the seat to the roof of the car and lay there, the world completely topsy-turvy. The strange man resembled a limp, broken puppet, hanging from the driver's seat by his seatbelt.

Now completely freaked out, Sophia screamed and panicked. She lunged for the door and searched frantically for the latch. She eventually found it and managed to open the door a little, but it was stuck against something. She shoved and she pushed, inching the door open just enough so that she could slither out. The pain in her back was unbearable as she did so, and then she felt something wrong with her left leg, too. Nevertheless, she kept up the effort and eventually crawled out. She felt cold ground. Grass. Dirt.

She moved on her belly, snaking away from the overturned car until she was able to lie flat and catch her breath. The pain in her back wasn't as bad as long as she stayed straight. Her leg hurt, though. She caught her breath, willing herself to take one moment at a time. Up above her, a three-quarter moon illuminated the world around her well enough that she could see. After a few minutes, she raised her torso to look at her leg and saw that there was a gash in her thigh, all the way through the blue jeans. There was blood all over her.

Slowly, carefully, she stood. Could she walk? Sophia gingerly put one foot in front of the other and took baby steps away from the car. Her leg hurt like hell, but she could do it.

Where was she? What was she doing in that car? Who was the driver?

She didn't know.

She had heard of things like amnesia, but never thought it could really happen. What was her name?

"Sophia Cabrini," she said aloud.

Good. She knew her name. Where did she live?

"New York City," she muttered.

Excellent. All was not lost.

Now if she could just find a place to lie down a while. Maybe she could get a ride. Maybe she could call someone for help. The police. She should call the police. No, wait. She couldn't call the police. There was something wrong with that, but she wasn't sure what it was. She knew that she had to avoid the police for some reason. Maybe she would remember after she got some sleep.

Sophia made her way back to the car, crouched in pain, and peered through the open door. A purse was lying on the bottom of the roof. Was it hers? She took it and opened it. There was a wallet stuffed with a several hundred-dollar bills, a New York driver's license with her name and picture on it, and a handgun. Curious, she removed the Colt and examined it. Was this hers? She seemed to remember owning a gun, but what did she need it for? Sophia shrugged and put it back in the purse. At the bottom of the handbag was a mobile phone. She took it and flipped it open. She attempted to turn it on so that she could dial "911," but the thing wouldn't work. It must have been damaged in the wreck.

Sophia stood, stumbled forty feet to the highway, and looked back. The car was not visible from the road, although the beam from the headlight could be seen shining across the field. Surely someone would see that and stop. She began to walk on the shoulder in the same direction that the car would have been traveling.

A truck roared past her, its horn bellowing. It didn't slow down, much less stop. She turned to look back to see if any more vehicles were coming. She saw a pair of headlights approaching in the distance. Sophia held out her hand as if she were hailing a taxi in the city.

The car zoomed past her. She might as well have been invisible.

After ten minutes and three more cars that passed her but didn't stop, Sophia saw an exit sign and the words "Wauseon – 3 Miles."

She said, "Fuck it," and walked down the exit ramp. She continued to walk in a daze toward Wauseon, completely forgetting that she had left almost a million dollars with a dead stranger.

Chapter 21

Even though it was Sunday, Bill Cutler went into MedScript to use the company's facilities for making copies of his acting resume. He was never beyond stealing office supplies and taking advantage of what perks the job might have to offer. He had slept late and driven into the city around 11:00. The building was relatively empty – the doctors' offices were closed and only the workaholics in various other businesses would be coming in on a Sunday. Cutler greeted the security watchman downstairs and took the elevator up to the MedScript floor. He went straight to his office, where he found his message light blinking. He picked up the phone and listened.

The first one was from Patrick. Something about looking at a townhouse in Manhattan that turned out to be no good. He asked Bill to keep watch for available properties, preferably on the Upper East Side.

Yeah, right, Bill thought. He was *happy* to do that for him.

The next message, from sometime on Saturday, was from Hannah McCleary, who sounded hysterical. It had been put through to the line he had set up for Detective Sean Flannery. It hadn't been difficult. The numbers he gave Hannah for both Flannery and Dr. Cagle went to his cell phone or were re-routed to the voice mail at MedScript.

"Sean, it's Hannah," she said. "I heard from Timothy Lane. He's out of prison. He sent me a letter at my cousin's house, so he knows where I am. He threatened to kill me. Please call me."

What? What could she possibly mean? Was she totally nuts? The woman had *serious* mental problems.

She had left three more messages for Flannery during the day.

Cutler hung up the phone and rubbed his chin. In one way, this development would only help him in his seduction of her. But in another way, it could mean that he was going in over his head. The woman obviously had delusions. She was truly paranoid and had every reason to be seeing a shrink.

He picked up the phone and dialed the number of Cozzone's residence. Hannah answered after two rings.

"Hello?"

"Hannah, it's Sean," Cutler said, adapting the subtle southern accent of a man from Virginia.

"Oh, Sean, thank God you called. I'm so frightened. Where were you yesterday?"

"There, there, take it easy. I was out on a case all day yesterday. I'm sorry. What's the matter?"

"It's Timothy Lane. He's after me again! He put a letter in the mail slot here. He wants to kill me!" She was near hysterics.

"Now hold on. Take a deep breath."

"Did you find out anything about him? When did he get out of prison?"

Cutler decided to let her believe it. He figured that if he could play the white knight in shining armor, he would get her into bed that much more quickly. "Apparently he got out a week ago," he said. "Parole. It happens. They serve their time and they get out."

"Why didn't someone tell me?"

"The court is not obligated to do that, Hannah. He paid his debt to society."

"But he's *dangerous*! He's making threats!"

"Look, Hannah, I'll try to come see you tonight, all right? In the meantime, I think you should call your therapist. Try to see him today and maybe he can give you something to calm you down."

"On a Sunday?"

"Call him. Who knows, maybe he can see you. Wouldn't hurt to try."

"I'm afraid to go outside."

"Hannah, it's broad daylight. I seriously doubt that Lane is standing outside your door. It will be all right. I promise you. Look, I'll have a squad car sent over to circle the block a few times and look for anything suspicious, okay?"

"Okay."

"Listen, Hannah. Do you have a gun?" Dr. Tom Cagle knew the answer to that question, but Sean Flannery didn't.

"Uhm, my cousin does."

"Do you know how to use it?"

"I think so. You just aim and pull the trigger, don't you?"

"Yeah, that basically does the trick. Keep it near you. If someone tries to break into the house, shoot him. Simple as that." Cutler wanted to laugh at his own performance. What cop would blatantly encourage a civilian to use a gun against an intruder? She actually bought it.

"Are you serious?"

"Of course. People have a right to protect themselves. Now, call your therapist, all right? I'll phone you a little later."

"All right."

"You gonna be okay?"

"I guess. I miss you."

Cutler smiled. She really was falling for him. "I miss you too. I'll talk to you later," he said and hung up. What a gullible, whacked-out woman, he thought. She was playing right into his hands.

Three minutes later, the phone rang. He checked the line and was pleased to see that it was for Dr. Cagle. Adapting the Bostonian accent, he answered, "Dr. Cagle."

"Doctor Cagle? It's Hannah McCleary."

"Yes, Miss McCleary! How are you?"

"Not so good. I think I need to see you. I'm a mess."

"Why, what's wrong?"

"The man who assaulted me. He's out of prison and I believe he's after me."

"After you? Whatever for?"

"I don't know, to get revenge for me sending him to prison, I guess."

"Hmm. Well, it *is* Sunday… but I think I can meet you at my office. I have to go in and do some paperwork anyway. Can you come to the office right now?"

"I think so."

"Fine. I'll be expecting you. Say, thirty minutes?"

"All right."

After he hung up, Cutler left MedScript and took the elevator to the floor above. No one was around to see him stick the "Tom Cagle" sign on the storeroom door, unlock it, and go inside.

***

Sophia Cabrini awoke to the sound of a truck, its horn blaring as it soared across the sky.

The sky?

She opened her eyes and focused them on what appeared to be a blackened cave ceiling. Panic threatened to overtake her until she remembered where she was.

It was an abandoned piece of large pipeline, one of several sections that were behind a truck stop. She had crawled inside one of them during the night and fallen asleep. This was after she had walked into the truck stop like a zombie, attracting stares and unwanted questions. A gum-chewing waitress took one look at her and asked if she needed some help. Sophia had simply shaken her head and said, "Just show me where the bathroom is."

When she got a look at herself in the mirror, Sophia almost fainted. Dried, matted blood covered one side of her head and her blouse. She examined the cut on her forehead and determined that it wasn't too bad. It had coagulated and didn't appear to be anything that needed stitches. Her head hurt but she figured it was nothing that a couple of aspirin wouldn't cure. The gash on her thigh was worse but the makeshift bandage she had used hours earlier to soak up the blood had intitiated the healing process. She could live with it.

She carefully washed her hair in the sink and managed to get all the blood out. She opened her handbag and found lipstick and eyeliner. She applied the makeup and it made her look ten times better.

She had gone back out into the diner and gift shop with her hair soaking wet, picked out a T-shirt that said "Welcome to Ohio!" and a bottle of painkillers, and went to the counter to pay. The waitress asked, "Are you in some kind of trouble, honey?"

"No," Sophia replied. She just wanted to get out of there and stop attracting attention. She couldn't help feeling that she had done something terribly wrong and that the police would be after her. The sooner she could get somewhere safe where she could sleep and not be bothered, the better. She needed the time to try and recall what had happened to her.

Sophia left the truck stop and started to walk further along the highway toward Wauseon when she noticed the sections of pipeline. Each one was around five feet diameter and eight feet long. As it was summer, the night air was pleasant and conducive to camping out. She decided that she was way too tired to keep walking, so she looked around to determine that she wasn't being watched, then crawled into one of the pipe pieces that lay furthest away from the truck stop. She opened the bottle of aspirin and swallowed two tablets without water, nearly choking as she did so. Finally, she had curled into a ball and immediately fallen asleep.

Now that the sun was up, Sophia looked at her watch and saw that it was 10:35. She had slept about six hours.

Then she remembered. John. The car. A wreck.

The money.

"Oh my God," she said to no one.

She ran back to the truck stop and looked inside. There were five men having coffee and a different waitress from the one she had spoken to the night before.

"Uhm, excuse me?" she called.

They all looked up and stared at her.

"I, uhm, need a ride just a few miles back up the road toward Indiana. I think I left something on the side of the highway. Can somebody help me?"

No one said a word.

"Really, it's just a few miles. I was, uhm, I was in a wreck and I need to see if the car is still there. I have to get something out of it."

"Was it a BMW?" one of the drivers asked.

"Yeah."

"They towed it into Wauseon this morning," he said. "You say you were in the wreck?"

"They *towed it?*" she asked, incredulous. How was she going to get her money? "Where can I find it?"

"I guess you need to contact the sheriff's office. They probably want to talk to you. I understand someone was killed."

Sophia suddenly felt lightheaded. Then it was true. John was dead.

"Miss?" the driver asked. "You want me to call the sheriff for you?"

"Never mind," she answered and quickly went out the door. She ran around the building to the back before anyone could follow her outside. Someone would probably call the cops and they'd be looking for her. She had left the scene of an accident where someone had died. What if they'd found the money? Or the cocaine! A million dollars in cash and a few pounds of coke in the trunk of a dead guy's BMW was bound to attract attention.

The cops would most certainly want to talk to her.

She waited a few minutes until one guy came out of the truck stop and started walking toward his rig. He was not the one who had spoken to her. He was young, not bad looking. Sophia decided to give it a go.

She scooted around the building and called, "Hey."

The man turned.

"You wouldn't be going to Wauseon, would you?"

"No, I'm on my way to Toledo."

"Well, isn't Wauseon pretty close?"

"It's just a couple of miles down the road."

"Can I have a ride?" She said it with as much sex-kitten-overflow as she could muster.

The guy looked her up and down, trying to determine if she was trouble or not. She looked like she'd been through some kind of hell, and from what he had heard inside the cops were probably searching for her. Probably not a wise idea to get involved. Yet, she was pretty. And she had a hell of a body.

"All right," he said. "Come on."

Sophia smiled and followed him into his truck.

Chapter 22

Leaving the Cozzone residence had been another anxiety-producing moment. Hannah had gathered her handbag and descended the stairs when she stopped and thought for a moment. Sean had told her to keep the gun at hand. She should be protected. How else would she defend herself if Timothy Lane were outside? Hannah turned around and went back to the master bedroom. Without hesitation, she opened that bottom drawer and removed the case. She put it on the bed, opened it, and lifted the gun. It was heavy. The word "Browning" was engraved on the side. Did she know how to use it? She had seen enough movies and television programs that featured policemen and crooks loading their weapons. She knew that there was a clip that held the bullets that slipped into the grip. Hannah fiddled with the mechanism and released the cartridge. She counted several rounds of ammunition already in place and then shoved the clip back inside. Hannah felt empowered as she held the gun steady and looked through the sight. She knew that there was supposed to be a safety button somewhere, so she examined the gun more closely and found it. She made sure that the safety was on and then put the gun in her handbag.

Hannah didn't see anything out of the ordinary on the street outside. There were several cars parked along the curb, of course, but they all appeared to be empty. She locked the door behind her and walked rapidly to Second Avenue. She figured that she would forego catching a bus and splurge on a taxi.

It was when she got within thirty feet of the corner that she noticed two men sitting in a car parked on the other side of the street. They were looking at her. Hannah did what all women do in the city – she held her head up, looked forward, and continued walking. Nevertheless, she felt their gazes boring holes into her. She wanted to glance back to see if she might recognize them, but she knew that would be a fruitless exercise. Not only were they too far away, but her wretched prosopagnosia would make the task impossible.

She made it to the corner and held up her hand just as an empty taxicab drove by. It pulled over and she ran to get inside.

***

"What do you want to do?" Favio asked.

"Nothing yet," DeLauria replied. "Let her go for now. She'll be back."

"How do you know?"

"She doesn't have a suitcase. Besides, I want to catch her with Cozzone."

"We don't even know what he looks like."

"I've seen a picture of him. He'll come home."

DeLauria and his young partner sat in the Malibu and watched the blonde woman reach the end of the street and hail a taxi. She did seem to be in a hurry. What if she was going someplace to meet Cozzone? She could have warned him by phone that they were being watched. Maybe she was going to meet her boss, if she had one.

"Yeah, maybe we should follow her," DeLauria said.

DeLauria started the car, inched it in reverse within the small parking space, turned the wheel sharply, and pulled out into the street. The wheels screeching, the car sped to the corner and then turned down Second Avenue.

***

Hannah arrived at Dr. Tom Cagle's building twenty-five minutes after she had hung up the phone with him. As she ran inside, she didn't notice the Chevy Malibu idling against curb, some forty feet behind the taxicab that delivered her there.

She signed in downstairs and took the elevator to the appropriate floor. All along the hallway were other types of offices, but nothing resembling a doctor's suite. Once again, Hannah thought it odd that her therapist had a lone office so high above the other doctors' offices. But who was she to question the workings of the medical establishment?

She found the sign with the doctor's name and knocked on the door.

"Come in."

When she opened the door, Dr. Cagle was fiddling with a life-sized cardboard cut-out of what appeared to be a man in a business suit. She wasn't sure if the figure was an actor or a politician. Cagle stood it in front of his bookshelf.

"Ah, hello Hannah," he said. "Come in, have a seat."

She closed the door behind her and sat down. "What are you doing?"

Cutler laughed a little and said, "Oh, I'm a big supporter of President Bush. I thought this stand-up was funny."

"Is that who that is?"

"Yeah. Oh, I'm sorry. You don't recognize him, do you? It's George W. Bush. Isn't he something? I picked him up at a Times Square novelty shop. I couldn't resist."

The doctor finished setting the figure up. Hannah thought it was certainly incongruous, this tall man with a goofy grin standing in her therapist's office.

"Now then," Cagle said, sitting behind his desk. "What seems to be the problem?"

Hannah sat forward and whispered, her eyes wide with fear. "He's back, Doctor Cagle. Timothy Lane. He wants to kill me."

"And how do you know this?"

"He sent me a letter. He signed it and everything. He said he was watching me and that he would get me when I least expected it."

Cutler frowned and wrote something in the patient's "chart." He scribbled the message: "This woman is completely nuts!"

"Are you sure?" he asked.

"Of course I'm sure!"

"Do you have the note?"

Hannah winced. "Oh, I should have brought it. I meant to. I left it at home. Or rather, I left it at my cousin's house, where I've been staying the past few days."

Cutler nodded. He thought to himself that she had hallucinated the whole thing. It was entirely her imagination. There was no note, no mad rapist out to get revenge on her. Still, there was the phone message he had heard. It had to be a prank of some kind.

"All right, look, I want you to take one of these now and another at bedtime." He opened the drawer of his desk and removed a bottle of Vitamin C that he had disguised, replacing the label with one of his own. He dropped two tablets inside an envelope and handed it to her.

"What is it?" she asked.

"It's a mild sedative. It should relax you."

"I don't want to relax! I want to do something about this!"

"Well, Hannah, what do you want to do?"

"I want to tell this man to get out of my life! I want to break his neck for what he did to me last time! I want to shoot holes into him! He doesn't deserve to be let out of prison, much less be alive!"

My Lord, Cutler thought. The woman was straddling the edge of sanity. She was nearly where he wanted her.

"Do you remember what we worked on the last time you were here?" he asked.

"Yes."

"How did it make you feel?"

"It made me feel wonderful. I felt great afterwards. Can we do that again?"

"Certainly. Why don't we practice with President Bush there? He will make an excellent stand-in for your would-be rapist."

She stood and went to the other side of the room. Cutler opened the drawer and removed the toy gun, but she had already dug into her purse and found the Browning.

"Hannah, what is that?"

"It's my gun," she said. "It's for protection."

"My Lord, it's not loaded, is it?"

"No."

She aimed the gun at the George Bush cut-out. Cutler suddenly felt his palms begin to sweat. He hoped he had not gone too far with her. He was dealing with a severely disturbed woman. He now knew that she was capable of anything and he really didn't want her carrying a loaded gun. He would just have to make sure that she put all of her trust in Sean Flannery.

Cutler, as her trusted therapist Dr. Cagle, began to speak. "Very well. Close your eyes." She did so. "You're all alone. You're in your house. Maybe you're in your cousin's place. Whatever, you're all alone. You hear something outside, something at the door. Someone is there. You hear the doorbell. You don't want to answer it, because you know it's him. You know it's this man who is out of prison and who wants to hurt you again. What do you do?"

Standing there with her eyes closed, Hannah drifted into the fantasy of the situation. It was so real inside her mind that she could imagine the sounds and smells of the master bedroom in her cousin's house. She could see Panther curled up on the bed. John's underwear was still lying on the floor in the corner.

"I pick up the gun," she answered. As she said this, Hannah lifted the weapon and held it straight in front of her.

"Open your eyes."

She did.

"The man standing at the other end of the room is your nemesis. He is the man who tried to rape you. He is the man who gave you this terrible affliction that disallows you to recognize people. It's his fault, Hannah. He's the one who must pay. As you stand there with your weapon, he comes into the room. He's there with you."

Cutler noticed that she started breathing heavily. Her eyes glinted with a madness that he had never seen before.

Then it began to happen to him again. The tunnel vision. The disorientation and confusion.

No, not here! Not now! Not yet!

He watched her as if he wasn't there. He felt his body in the room but he was standing outside of it. It had occurred before and it was happening again.

Concentrate! he willed himself.

He heard his brother's words in his head. *"Do you want to go to prison?"*

Cutler closed his eyes tightly and opened them again. The woman was still there, the gun in front of her, waiting for his command. The tunnel vision had subsided. He had beaten the feelings once again.

"That's fine, Miss McCleary," he said in Dr. Cagle's voice. "You can put the gun down now."

But she didn't do it. Had she heard him?

"Miss McCleary? The exercise is over."

The gun blast was so loud that it made Hannah shriek and Cutler jump. He hadn't expected her to actually pull the trigger. The George Bush figure had a huge hole in the center of his chest. Cutler stood and went to the cut-out and looked behind it. Some of the books were obliterated. Thank goodness that the other side of the wall was another storage room for a different company. Chances were slim that someone might have been in there. He just hoped that the bullet hadn't gone through *two* walls.

"Oh my God," Hannah whispered as she lowered the gun. "I can't believe I did that."

"I thought you said it wasn't loaded," Cutler said, shaken.

"I lied."

Cutler smiled. "Well, I must say, it shows some progress in you taking a more, er, shall we say, *aggressive* approach to your life. How did it feel?"

"Wonderful." She almost laughed. "I've never fired a gun before. Ever!"

"Guns are dangerous, Hannah. I don't think it's a good idea for you to be carrying one."

"I'm sorry, Doctor Cagle. I think I ruined your president."

"That's all right. They had plenty more."

"I can't believe I actually hit the target!"

"You, uhm, did very well. Now why don't you put that thing away and sit down again."

He could see that she was very jazzed about what she had done. She no longer pulled on her fingers or fidgeted in her seat. Now she breathed steadily, her eyes fixed on the damaged cut-out.

"Now, when you feel this anxiety creep up on you again, or you feel that this man might be coming to get you, I want you to try and re-experience what you just did, *but without the gun.* Try to keep that feeling of empowerment and use your wits instead of a real weapon. The purpose of the exercise was for you to feel that self-confidence you gained with gun, but to try and recreate it without the gun."

She nodded slowly.

"Now what's happening with this boyfriend you mentioned last time?" he asked.

She shrugged. "I haven't seen him much. He's very busy. We went out to breakfast once but haven't seen each other since."

"Do you like him?"

"Yes. I wish he'd take the time to see me more, though. But it's typical. Most men realize very quickly that I'm a bore."

"Nonsense," Cutler said. "Be a little more aggressive with him. Use your sex. You'll be surprised at what it can do for you."

Hannah appeared shocked. "What?"

Cutler smiled. "It is my professional opinion that you, my dear lady, need some love and affection. You need intimacy. It will do wonders for you. All I'm saying is that women have the capacity to make a man interested. On the other hand, if he shows an interest in you, physically I mean, then by all means take him up on it!"

Hannah laughed. "You sound more like a matchmaker than a therapist!"

The doctor laughed, too. "In many ways I am. Now go take your pill. There's a water fountain in the hall. You're going to be fine, Hannah. I'll see you at our next scheduled appointment?"

"Yes." She stood and went over to the desk. She held out her hand. He carefully took it and let her shake it warmly.

"Thank you, Doctor Cagle," she said. "You've done a lot for me and I've only seen you twice."

"Well, that's my job," he said, quickly taking his hand away. He didn't want her to recognize the feel of Sean Flannery.

Then Hannah's brow creased. She looked at him oddly.

"What is it?" he asked.

"Nothing," she said. "You remind me of someone I know."

"Oh?"

"Yeah. Actually it's that policeman I told you about. You both are built the same way."

Uh oh, he thought. *Play it cool.* "That's a coincidence," he said. "As I keep saying, put your trust in him. As a figure of the law, I'm sure he won't steer you wrong."

"That's what I think too," she said. "Well, goodbye."

"See you next time."

Hannah went out and closed the door. Cutler breathed a sigh of relief and wiped his hands on his trousers. It would have ruined everything if she had recognized him as Sean Flannery but it would have been a disaster if she had remembered meeting Bill Cutler before the "dark time."

***

Hannah felt very strange in the elevator going down to the first floor. Something about the doctor had struck her, but she couldn't place her finger on it. He *did* remind her of Sean, but there were lots of men who were built similarly. There was something else… perhaps a smell? Was it cologne? Did they wear the same cologne? She wasn't sure, but she thought she was on the right track. His hand had been sweaty. Probably due to the shock of the gun going off in his office, she thought.

She exited the building and decided to visit her own apartment and pick up mail. She walked over to First Avenue and stood at the stop to wait for the Number One bus.

It would be nice breath of fresh air to see her own little home again.

Chapter 23

The truck driver had been a gentleman. He had talked very little on the short ride to Wauseon, mostly wanting to know things like where she was going and where she came from. He didn't mention the accident. He gave his name as "Rick" and told Sophia that he would be stuck in Toledo for a few days. It wasn't that far away, if she needed anything... But Sophia answered that she would be fine, thank you very much. He had dropped her at a Holiday Inn on the outskirts of the city and handed her a business card.

"My cell phone number is on there," he explained. He left after asking her name. Sophia had replied that it was "Hannah."

Sophia checked in, picked up a newspaper in the hotel lobby and went to her room, where she spent the first hour in the bathtub. She felt incredibly dirty after having spent the last twelve hours outdoors and sleeping in a pipe. She had bruises all over her body from the accident and the wound on her head, although apparently not serious, still hurt. She had covered it with a large band-aid and that seemed to do the trick.

Sophia decided that she had nothing to lose if she phoned the sheriff. She could claim that she had been disoriented and "not herself" after the accident and had wandered down the highway until she got a ride into town. It was the truth, mostly. She had to get hold of the suitcase that contained the money. Her own bag full of clothes and personal items had been in the trunk of the BMW as well. The only hitch would be the cocaine. If they'd found that, she could be in trouble. She supposed that she could gauge how they sounded over the phone and then make a decision as to what to do. Should she try to get some sleep first? That was probably best. She still felt a little hazy.

She reclined on the bed and began to look at the newspaper. She flipped through the pages until she found a photograph of John's BMW, upside-down, with several state troopers standing around it. A headline read: CHICAGO SUSPECT IN FATAL ACCIDENT.

"Oh my God," she muttered and then quickly scanned the article. It stated that John Cozzone had been sought for questioning in the murder of one George Williams in a Chicago hotel. Williams' body had been found in the garbage chute and that Cozzone's hotel room number had been written on a piece of paper found in the victim's pocket. Cozzone and an unidentified female companion had checked out of the hotel before the body was discovered. In what appeared to be a freak accident, Cozzone was killed when his BMW ran off the James W. Shocknessy Ohio Turnpike and overturned. Police were searching for the female companion who may or may not have been in the car with Cozzone and was described as an attractive model-type blonde in her twenties. The case had been turned over to the Fulton County Sheriff's Department. A toll-free number was listed for anyone who might have information.

"Shit," she said. Now what? How was she going to get her money? The police probably had it.

Then again, it didn't say that she was a suspect. They didn't know if she was in the car with him at the time. Sophia wondered if she might be able to concoct a story that the police would believe. She knew nothing about the killing in Chicago and had gone on to Ohio without John. She just wanted her luggage.

She opened her purse and removed the Colt. She immediately placed it in the hotel room safe and locked it away. The next thing she did was pull out the business card the truck driver had given her. She picked up the phone and made a call.

***

Hannah approached her building in a fairly good mood. The visit with Dr. Cagle had lifted her spirits tremendously and given her the most self-confidence that she had experienced in years. It was comforting to know that the handgun was in her purse if Timothy Lane decided to attack her again. She was still uncertain whether or not she'd be able to pull the trigger, but it seemed possible now. The man was a vile scum who preyed upon defenseless women and deserved to be blown away.

Hannah became concerned when she saw a police car parked in front of the building. She went ahead and entered, stopped at the mailbox, and found it empty. She then unlocked the inner door and went inside. The building was quiet, as it usually was at this time of day. The tenants were either at work or, in the case of some of the elderly ones, holed up in their rooms. She crept up the stairs; no matter how hard she tried, the old wooden steps invariably creaked. It was particularly bad when someone heavy, a man for instance, stomped up the stairway.

When she got to the second floor, she saw that Liz's apartment door was open and that two policemen were in the room. She wanted to ask what was going on, but she didn't have to. One of the officers saw her and said, "Excuse me."

"Yes?"

"Do you live in the building, ma'am?"

"Yes."

"Did you know the tenant who lived here?"

Lived? Did he say *lived*?

"Yes."

"How well did you know her?"

"What's this all about?" Hannah asked.

"Ma'am, we're investigating a homicide. Can we ask you some questions?"

"A homicide? What are you talking about?"

The two men looked at each other. The first man continued, "Ma'am, Miss Rosenthal was killed last night. Outside of the bar where she worked downtown."

"Oh my God," Hannah muttered. "Who did it?"

"That's what we're trying to find out. Come inside for a minute, would you?"

Hannah felt numb. She walked into her friend's apartment and saw that nothing was different. The policeman gestured to a chair, where she sat.

"How well did you know her?" he asked as he pulled out a notebook.

"Not really well. We were neighbors. I live upstairs on the next floor."

"May I have your name?"

"Hannah McCleary."

He wrote it down and asked, "Were you aware of anyone she may have been seeing, a boyfriend, perhaps?"

"No. She was gay."

The second policeman spoke to the first. "She worked at Alice's, Jimbo."

The first one, "Jimbo," smiled faintly. "Oh, yeah. My mistake."

Hannah didn't like the private joke that the two cops shared. It made her angry. "She wasn't seeing *anyone* that I know of," she said.

"Do you know if she has family in the area, or where her family might be?"

Hannah tried to remember what Liz had told her about relatives. "I know she has some, but I don't think she ever mentioned where they live."

"That's all right, we'll find them."

"Can you tell me what happened to her?" she asked.

"She was outside of the bar, apparently going to get some ice from the storeroom. Someone attacked her. Strangled her. Did some nasty things to her after she was dead."

"What do you mean?"

"We can't go into that, I'm sorry."

Hannah was horrified. Had another sex maniac such as Timothy Lane assaulted Liz? What if it had been Timothy Lane himself that had done it? After all, he was out on parole.

The officer asked her a few more questions and then told her that she could go. He gave her a card and said for her to call him if she should think of anything that might be of importance.

In a daze, Hannah left the apartment and walked upstairs to her own. Once she was inside, panic seized her. The earlier pleasant feelings completely dispersed. The terrible anxiety clutched and squeezed her heart, almost causing her to faint with fright. She wanted to scream but couldn't. Instead she gasped with a cat-like shrieking noise that emanated from the back of her throat, stumbled and fell onto the kitchen floor, and started to cry.

Poor Liz. She was a good soul. How could this have happened?

Hannah sat up on the floor and wiped her face. Why did she feel certain that it was Timothy Lane who had done this terrible thing? She had no proof and no rational reason to think that. Yet, from deep within her soul, something was telling her that what she suspected was the truth.

What should she do? Tell the police?

No, they were idiots. They snickered at Liz being a lesbian. She looked at the card and her hand and immediately tore it into pieces.

Sean. She should call Sean. He'd know what to do.

Hannah ran to her phone and dialed Sean's number.

"Flannery," he said, live and in person.

"Oh, Sean, thank God you're there."

"Hannah, what is it?"

"It's Liz. She's dead."

"Who?"

"Liz, my neighbor. I told you about her."

"Oh, right. What do you mean, she's dead?"

"I think Timothy Lane killed her. It happened last night, outside of the bar where she worked."

"Oh dear. I'm sorry, Hannah."

"It's terrible."

"How do you know Lane did it?"

"I don't know. It's just a feeling."

"Hannah, if a 'feeling' is all you've got to go on, then you're being a little too obsessive about this guy."

"I know, but I swear it just seems right, Sean."

"I'll, uhm, I'll make a couple of calls. That bar is not in my precinct, you know. But I'll see if I can find out anything."

"What are you doing now? Are you busy?"

"A little."

"I want to see you. Please, Sean. Can you come see me for just an hour or so?"

There was silence at the other end until he said, "I might be able to get away for a little while. Where, your apartment?"

"No, meet me at my cousin's townhouse."

"Give me an hour."

"Oh, thank you, Sean! I'll see you soon!"

"Bye."

"Bye."

Hannah hung up then took a look at her apartment. After staying in John's place for a week, she was certainly spoiled. Her apartment was so… *dreary*. She had forgotten exactly what she had come home for.

Hannah left the apartment, locked the door, and ran down the steps. Before going outside, though, she looked up and down the street. If Lane were out there, he would probably be watching the building. She scanned each parked car and determined that they were empty. Was it safe? Most likely. It was broad daylight.

Why would he kill Liz? Was Lane such a mad rapist that he would attack *any* woman? Did rapists really go after heavy women? Hannah had read that a rapist didn't discriminate. They went after old women, young girls, women of all races, pretty women, ugly women…

She stepped out of the building and began to walk quickly southward, toward Cozzone's residence. She was seething. She would teach Timothy Lane a lesson. The police were useless. They put him away but then let him out so that he could do more harm. There was no justice. They locked him away for a few years, just so he could think about and hone his craft. It did absolutely no good. Lane probably became more ruthless and vicious in prison. He most likely thought about her every day, plotting his revenge, working out how he was going to terrorize her and then kill her.

Hannah didn't stop anywhere on her way to the townhouse. She made it in eleven minutes, a record for her. She quickly let herself in, picked up Panther, who greeted her at the door, mewing and purring. Nothing appeared to be awry. Carrying the cat, she went up the stairs and into the office. The message indicator on the machine blinked "1." She pressed the "play" button and sat down with the cat in her lap.

The message was infinitely disturbing.

"Hello, this is Sergeant Thomas Ackerman of the Fulton County Sheriff's Department in Ohio. We're looking for any next-of-kin for a man named John Cozzone. We traced his driver's license to this address and phone number. If there are any next-of-kin at this address, we would appreciate a call back." The officer left a number.

What could this mean? Hannah feared the worst. The police wouldn't be calling about John unless...

She picked up the phone and dialed the number. A woman answered and Hannah asked to be connected to Sergeant Ackerman. When he came on the line she identified herself and then listened to what he had to say. As he spoke, Hannah thought she might be ill.

The sergeant told her that John had been killed in an automobile accident about five miles from Wauseon, Ohio. He said that he was "sorry for her loss" and relayed the necessary information for her to contact the coroner's office so that she could identify and claim the body, as well as pick up the deceased's belongings that were found in the car.

Hannah was stunned. She let Panther jump off her lap and then she put her head down on the desk. She hadn't been able to cry a lot for Liz earlier, but now she had enough tears for both Liz and John.

***

Dominic DeLauria stepped into Freddie Pontecorva's den and found his mentor and benefactor standing alone, looking out a bay window at his expansive backyard. Not much could be seen, as it was dark, but the moon was full and it illuminated the gazebo, the Roman statuary, and the surrounding maple trees.

"Come in, Dom," Pontecorva said without turning.

"Hello, Freddie."

DeLauria had been summoned that afternoon to dine with Pontecorva and "take a meeting." He had driven out to Glen Cove after leaving Favio to his own devices in front of the Cozzone residence. He had quickly become sick of the kid but needed him to take over when DeLauria wanted to sleep or do something else. Favio had phoned him to report that the McCleary woman had returned to the townhouse.

Tommy Salami brought the two men glasses, one filled with bourbon and the other with cranberry juice. Only then did Pontecorva turn from the window. He took the juice, raised it, and said, "*Salud.*"

After they both took sips, Salami left the room.

"You hungry, Dom?" Pontecorva asked.

DeLauria shrugged. "I guess so. What's on your mind, Freddie?"

Pontecorva waved his hand away, saying, "Ah, it's nothing. Just my gall bladder acting up again. I don't feel so good. Don't worry, I didn't call you out here for any particular reason other than I wanted someone to dine with besides my usual squad of ugly goons."

"Have you seen a doctor, Freddie?"

"Yeah, I'm probably gonna have to have surgery. What a pain in the ass. Anyway, let's talk. Have a seat."

The two men sat around the coffee table.

"Dom, I understand you've got this Hannah McCleary, the shooter, under surveillance?"

"Yeah," DeLauria answered. "She hasn't made a move. She knows I'm out there but she hasn't tried to run. I think she's waiting for Cozzone to get back, wherever he is."

Pontecorva nodded. "He isn't coming back. He's dead."

"Yeah?"

"We got the news this morning. Apparently he was in a car accident near Toledo, coming back from Chicago."

"Is that so? Was he alone?"

"It looks that way."

DeLauria rubbed his chin. "You know what I think? I think he probably sold the stuff in Chicago and was coming back with the dough."

"That's what I think, too."

"So where's his car? All his stuff?"

"In Wauseon, Ohio. Little whistle-stop of a town. Waiting to be picked up by next-of-kin."

"Who would that be?"

"We have no idea. But I want you to stay on top of this shooter-lady. She's gonna want that money, too."

"I should think so."

"So don't kill her yet. Follow her. Maybe she'll lead you to the money. Then, after you get hold of it, then do the deed."

DeLauria took another sip of bourbon. "Fine by me," he said.

Chapter 24

It was nearly 7:30 when Bill Cutler arrived at the townhouse. Hannah opened the door and fell into his arms, surprising him.

"Oh, Sean, I've been worried!" she said. "What took you so long?"

He stroked her silky hair and held her close. "I'm sorry, darling. This other case I'm on…"

"It's all right. You're here now. Come inside."

He removed his trenchcoat and tossed it over the stair railing. He noticed that her eyes were red. "You poor thing," he said. "Was Liz that good a friend?"

"Oh, it's not just her. I got some bad news from the police in Ohio. John was killed in a car accident."

"John, your cousin?"

"Yes. I have to see about stuff like identifying the body. I sure don't want to have to do that."

"Jesus, Hannah. Doesn't he have other family?"

"No. Just me." She embraced him again and said, "He was a nice guy. I'm gonna miss him."

Cutler held her tightly again. He knew enough about women to know that at times like this they were at their most vulnerable… and receptive.

He put his hand under her chin and lifted her head. Even without makeup she was terribly beautiful, he thought. There was an intangible innocence to her face that was so desirable.

Cutler leaned in to kiss her. She let him do it, but she didn't open her mouth. He moved his hand from her chin and placed it on the back of her head, holding her in position. He continued to kiss her and tried working her lips open so that he could slip his tongue inside. He sensed that she was resisting it at first, but then she succumbed and pressed into him. Her own tongue entered his mouth and he felt her passion rising.

He lost himself in her for a moment and then they parted. She continued to look into his eyes, studying them as if she were attempting to peer into his mind.

"What are you looking for?" he asked, smiling.

"I just want to remember your face," she said. "I, uhm, sometimes have trouble doing that. Remembering people's features."

He had to remind himself that Dr. Cagle knew this but Sean Flannery didn't. "Really?"

"Never mind that. Kiss me again."

He brought her head to him a second time and the kiss was even more intimate and lingering. When they separated, she sighed. Cutler felt a surge of excitement. He was getting to her. He was going to put another notch in the Quest List. And in this particular case, Hannah McCleary was a very special conquest.

"Let's not stand in the hallway," she said.

They went into the living room, where Panther was perched on the back of the couch. Cutler went to the cat and held out his hand.

"Hello, cat," he said.

Panther hissed at him, jumped off the couch, and ran under a chair.

"Gee, was it something I said?" he asked.

"Panther!" Hannah scolded. "That wasn't nice!" She addressed the man she thought was Sean Flannery. "He doesn't usually do that. He likes people. Most people, anyway."

"That's all right. Animals never take to me," he said.

"I don't see why not." They stood looking at each other until she broke the awkwardness with, "Can I get you anything? Something to drink? Have you eaten?"

"Uh, yeah, I've eaten. Something to drink, perhaps?"

She went into the kitchen. "There's quite a selection. I think I'll have a little Jack Daniel's."

"That sounds good."

She poured two small glasses, came out from behind the counter, and handed him his drink.

"Cheers," he said, clinking the glasses.

"Cheers," she repeated. They took sips and Hannah coughed once. "Excuse me… burns!"

"You all right?"

"Uh huh."

He put his free hand behind her head again and pulled her to him. They kissed a third time and it caused Cutler's heart to race. He made a concerted effort to study his feelings, for he didn't want to experience what used to occur in the past. Those days were gone, he told himself. He had to remember what his therapist had drilled into him, even though he hated the man and no longer went to see him.

Focus on what was right. Keep your mind on the path. Resist temptation.

Nevertheless, it started happening. He opened his eyes to that awkward close-up view of another person's face in the act of kissing. The tunnel was forming. Darkness appeared on the periphery of his eyesight. The dreaded pounding in his head began and his loins reacted to the stimuli.

No! Control yourself! he commanded silently.

But he couldn't help it. The woman represented not only his latest object of conquest but also something from his past with which he never felt closure.

Suddenly, Cutler pushed Hannah over the back of the couch. Their drinks spilled and Hannah dropped her glass.

"Sean!" she cried.

"Never mind, we'll clean it later," he whispered. He was breathing heavily, kissing her again and again. She fell into the couch and let him get on top of her. They embraced and he sensed that she was into it and that she was opening up to him.

"Sean…" she murmured.

She was calling his name in passion. Yes! Yes! He was going to make it!

"Sean, wait…!"

He felt her struggle beneath him and it was glorious. The pounding in his head encouraged him to keep going. He couldn't stop now – the old feelings had taken over once again. He had missed them so much!

"Sean, STOP!"

She pushed him with all her might and he rolled off the couch onto the floor. "What's wrong with you?" she asked. She appeared to be agitated, even a little frightened.

Cutler saw that her T-shirt was torn just below the right breast. Had he done that?

"Hannah, I – "

"You hurt me," she said.

"Hannah, I… I… want to make love to you. I can't stand it any longer. I've wanted it since we first met." He got up off the carpet and moved in to her once again. This time she pushed him away, reacting like an animal that had been cornered. She leaped over the back of the couch and moved away.

"Hannah!"

"Sean, what's come over you? I can't do that… not yet… I just…"

He could see that she was upset and confused. "Hannah, I'm sorry. I just… well, I like you. No, that's not true. I *love* you. There, I said it."

She looked at him incredulously. "You what?"

"You heard me."

"Sean, I… I… you have an odd way of showing… I mean…" She turned away. "This is happening too fast. I'm not ready for this. It's not –"

The symptoms of Cutler's tunnel vision increased dramatically. Now he felt the anger rising. He wanted to scream but he held himself in check. Instead he got off the couch and said, "Fine. If that's the way you want to play it, then we'll take our *fucking time*!" He walked toward the hallway and Hannah ran after him.

"Sean, wait! Don't go!"

"I'll see you later, when you're a bit more *ready*!"

He grabbed his trenchcoat, opened the front door, and left without another word.

"Sean!" she cried after him.

Cutler hoped that she wasn't following him. He didn't look back. He went straight to the Toyota, unlocked it, and got inside.

The anger was subsiding, but the old feelings remained. As he drove away, Cutler realized that he would never be rid of them.

He would never change.

***

Hannah stood in the entry hall and stared at the closed door.

What had just happened?

Everything seemed to be going so well when suddenly he was… different. She didn't understand. He had frightened her. He had moved too quickly. She had felt violated in a way that reminded her of…

Hannah turned and went back to the living room. She picked up the glasses and carried them to the kitchen. She wet a rag and returned to clean up the spilled whiskey. When she was done, she poured another glass and sipped it.

The kisses had been so nice. Sean had a distinctive taste to his mouth and his touch had been warm and knowing. The scent of his cologne still lingered in the air. Hannah instantly felt more alone than she had in a long time.

She now realized why she kept to herself and never dated. Her neurological disability notwithstanding, the stress of second-guessing a partner at the beginning of a relationship was enough to give her a thousand panic attacks.

Luckily, the whiskey helped.

***

Sophia bucked and writhed, screaming the truck driver's name over and over as he looked up at her, sweating and moaning. She didn't have to fake it for long, for the guy was decent in the sack and he filled her to the brim. She straddled his waist and moved appropriately until she genuinely satisfied herself, then allowed him to finish inside her. Spent, she slipped off and lay on her back beside him on the bed.

The young man named Rick sighed heavily and grabbed his pack of Marlboroughs from the bedside table. He offered one to Sophia, who took it and let him light if for her with a silver-plated lighter.

"Hannah, that was fantastic," he said. "I am *so* glad you decided to call."

"Me too, baby," Sophia said. "There's more where that came from."

"God, I hope so. I think I've died and gone to heaven." He turned to her and kissed her. He touched the bandage on her forehead and asked, "Still hurt?"

"Only when you *press* on it!"

"Sorry."

"It's all right."

"So what exactly happened to you, anyway? You never did tell me."

"When, the other night?"

"Yeah. When I was in the diner they were talking about you coming in a few hours before. I figured you was the same woman when I saw you in the morning."

"I was in a car accident. In fact, I need your help with something."

"Honey, if I can do it for you, I will."

Sophia sat up and crossed her legs beneath her. "I was hoping you'd say that, baby. Look, I need you to do a little acting. Have you ever done any acting?"

"Uh, no."

"Well, it'll be easy. You just need to pretend that you're my husband."

He grinned. "That won't be too hard."

"And that your name is Cozzone. What would you like your first name to be?"

"What?"

"You need to pretend that you're the brother of someone I know. Er, that I knew. We need to go claim his belongings and identify the body, but we have to pretend that we're next-of-kin. It can't be me, because they're looking for me, but if I come in as the deceased's brother's *wife*, there shouldn't be a problem. Got it?"

"Not really." Rick sat up and stubbed the butt into the ashtray. "Is this illegal?"

"No, of course not. It's just that I need a suitcase that the police have got. They'll gladly turn it over to next-of-kin, so we have to pretend we're next-of-kin. It's easy."

Rick eyed her suspiciously but then grinned. "And what do I get out of it?"

She put her arms around him and kissed him again. "Baby, you can have me every which way and then some. Until you're so sore that you'll need a crutch to take a piss."

"I like that kind of pain."

"Good. But first we need to get us some fake IDs. Got any ideas?"

***

The phone awoke her at 8:15 on Monday morning. Hannah rolled over, picked up the receiver, and answered it in a hoarse whisper.

"Hello?"

"Yes, is this the residence of John Cozzone?" It was a man's voice. Authoritative but friendly.

"Yes."

"I'm sorry, did I wake you?"

"Yes."

"I'm very sorry. Who am I speaking with?"

"Who is this?"

"This is Doctor Charles Webber at the Fulton County Health Center in Wauseon, Ohio. I'm the deputy coroner for the county. Is this Miss McCleary?"

Hannah remembered now. She had placed a call to Ohio before going to bed last night. She had left a message.

"Yes. That's me."

"Hello, you left a message last night regarding Mister Cozzone?"

"Yes. I talked to some sheriff yesterday. Ackerman, I think. I'm, uhm, I'm house sitting for my cousin. John."

"I see. Are you the next-of-kin?"

"I guess. I'm his cousin. But not by blood. I work for him."

"I see. I'm sorry for your loss. We have Mister Cozzone's body at the county morgue here. We need someone from the family to come and identify him and make funeral arrangements. He had some personal things in the car with him as well that we can turn over to you."

"What happened exactly?" she asked.

"The sheriff's department has ruled it an accident. It occurred on the Turnpike, not too far from our little town of Wauseon. It appears that Mister Cozzone's BMW went off the road, flipped over, and hit an embankment. We don't believe he suffered. The neck was broken, so death must have been instantaneous."

Hannah felt a sudden pang at this news. John was her only family and a man she looked up to and admired. She wondered if his drug use had anything to do with the accident.

"Just a minute, let me get a piece of paper and a pencil," she said, forcing herself out of bed. Panther thought it was breakfast time, so he jumped off the bed and went to the door, meowing.

Hannah found something to write with and picked up the phone again. "All right, you'd better give me all the information," she said.

***

Bill Cutler didn't show up for work on Monday. He called the office and Debbie answered the phone. He explained that he wasn't feeling well. Debbie said that she and Kathy could handle it, but that Patrick left word twice for Bill to call him. Cutler winced and hung up the phone.

The pounding hadn't stopped. He had had no sleep since leaving Hannah's house. He spent the night pacing his apartment and finally going outside and walking through the neighborhoods in the dark.

He couldn't shake the damned tunnel vision that was the red flag indicator of slipping off the wagon. As he walked by a city park in Queens he had come across some teenaged girls sitting in a car. Cutler smelled the marijuana and was tempted to show them his phony badge and tell them that they were under arrest. Then, he would bargain with them and perhaps get them to do something in exchange for their release.

Instead, he had resisted the demons in his head, turned around, and gone home. He knew that the next time he might not be so strong.

Cutler picked up the phone and called his brother.

"Patrick Cutler."

"It's me," Bill said.

"How come you're not at work?"

"I'm sick."

"Really?" Cutler hated the way his brother sounded so judgmental.

"Yes, really."

"Okay. Listen, I spoke to your probation officer."

"You what?"

"I talked to him. I told him you hadn't been seeing your therapist."

"You… what?!"

"Bill, I'm doing you a favor, damn it. You're my brother!"

"It's none of your business!"

"Hey! Are you out of your mind? Have you forgotten that if it hadn't been for my intervention, you might be in jail? It was *my* lawyer who got those charges dropped. You got off pretty goddamned lucky with probation."

"Patrick?"

"What?"

"Fuck you, Patrick. Fuck you very much." He said it calmly and then slammed the phone down.

You want to go to prison? The words hung in his head, first spoken by his brother, then by the therapist and probation officer.

Cutler put his hands over his ears in an attempt to shut out the voices, but it was no good.

The demons had returned.

***

After a full day of anxiety and worry, Hannah decided that she would go to Ohio the next morning. Best to get the task over with. She didn't want to go. She hated traveling, although she often fantasized about doing so. She remembered the New Mexico brochure that she had at her apartment and how much she would have liked to see Santa Fe. Unfortunately, the thought of being on a crowded train or airplane gave her palpitations.

She had spent most of the day in a nervous state. She had pulled out the Jack Daniel's and had downed two glasses after lunch in the hope that it would calm her down as it had in the past. Unfortunately, all it did was disorient her more. Hannah was still on the edge of panic and the anxiety was about to drive her mad. At one point she picked up Panther and stroked him mercilessly until the cat meowed and tried to bite her hand. He jumped from her arms and ran away to hide. He had never done that before, indicating to Hannah that even he could sense that she was falling to pieces.

By nightfall on Monday, she had summoned the resolve to make the trip, but she wanted to take a quick walk to her apartment, check her mailbox, and pick up a couple of things she might need.

She left the townhouse and began the walk north. Once again she carefully scanned the parked cars, but as it was now night it was difficult to see anything in them.

As she turned the corner onto Second Avenue, Hannah didn't notice the man emerge from the Malibu parked a few doors down from the townhouse. She concentrated solely on moving forward, much like she did that fateful night when Timothy Lane decided to stalk her. She walked quickly, almost like someone who was walking fast for exercise. The adrenaline that pumped through her body for the last few hours propelled her with the strength and stamina of a star athlete. Her nerves were screaming and her heart was pounding in her chest, but she realized that her fright somehow served to give her self-confidence. The gun in her handbag also provided her with a feeling of invincibility. She hoped that no one stepped out of the darkness to hassle her; otherwise she just might shoot him.

Hannah looked back just to make sure she was safe. There was the usual number of people on the avenue, as it wasn't late. It was difficult to tell if any one of them was out of the ordinary. However, there was one guy whose shape and stance seemed familiar. He was a little over a block behind her, but he was walking in her direction. Her immediate thought was that it was the same man who had been pretending to read the newspaper across from the diner when she and Sean had eaten breakfast. Was it he? If so, it was the man who assaulted her. She knew it. It was Timothy Lane.

Hannah continued to walk faster, turning east on 72nd because it was a wide street and more people populated it. Looking back, she saw that the man had also turned the corner and was continuing to follow her.

She started to run.

The street between Second and First Avenues was long and it took her nearly a minute to reach the corner. She stopped to catch her breath and looked back. He was still there, although he had not bothered to run. She had put considerable distance between them. Could she possibly lose him completely? It was worth a try.

Hannah jogged down First Avenue and reached Wong's Laundry. It usually stayed open until ten o'clock for people who wanted to operate the self-service machines. Two customers were inside, both of them young people who were probably students. She ducked into the building and saw Mister Wong in the back.

"Mister Wong?" she called quietly.

He looked up and came out from his workroom. "Hello, Miss McCreary! You pick up something?"

"No, no, I want to hide. Can I hide in your back room?"

Wong's brow wrinkled. "Hide?"

Hannah looked back at the street. "Please. Someone's following me. I'm frightened."

Wong could see that she was distraught. "Come," he said. He gestured for her to follow him. The two students watched them but then went back to their laundry. Hannah stepped into the back where dry cleaning machines, industrial laundry machines, and other equipment was kept. There were shelves covered with customers' laundry bags, waiting to be picked up. Hannah moved out of sight and stood against the wall. Wong gestured to a chair. "Sit," he said. She did and began her finger pulling routine.

She waited five minutes before moving. Finally she got up and looked out the front. The man was nowhere in sight.

"Did you see a man walk past?" she asked Wong. "About five feet, eleven inches tall?"

He shrugged. "Maybe. Lots men walk past. Busy street."

Was she safe to go on home? She decided to risk it.

"Thanks, Mister Wong. I'll see you later," she said as she scooted out the door. She continued the walk north until she got within a block of her building and then she saw him again. He was standing at the corner in front of her, but his back was to her. She recognized his stance and clothing. He appeared to be looking around – possibly for her.

She couldn't go home. He was in the way.

The Browning in her handbag beckoned to her. She could easily pull it out, walk up behind him, and pull the trigger. She would be free of Timothy Lane once and for all. Surely the police would see that it was self-defense. The man had been stalking her. He had left her threatening notes and messages. He had killed her neighbor. If that wasn't justification for shooting him, what was?

What was she thinking? She couldn't shoot him on the street. Not like that, not in the back. She would be arrested, tried for murder. Even though she had killed a killer, she would be punished.

She couldn't do it.

Hannah turned around and started to walk back to the townhouse. She stopped at a pay phone and dialed Flannery's number. She groaned to herself when she got the voice mail.

"Sean, it's Hannah. I can't get to my apartment. Timothy Lane is standing on the corner, watching for me. I know it's him, he followed me from John's place. I don't know what to do. I'm going to head back to John's and I'll call you again from there."

She hung up and started to cross First Avenue so that she could walk west. A rider-less taxicab appeared on the street, traveling in the same direction. This gave Hannah an idea, so she flagged the driver. The cab pulled up to the opposite corner and she ran to get inside.

After she shut the door she told the driver to take her to East 55th Street and Fifth. Traffic wasn't bad, so it was a quick ride down Second Avenue and then crosstown. She paid the fare and ran into the building where Dr. Cagle's office was located. He was usually there this time of night. He would know what she should do.

Under the scrutiny of the African-American night watchman, Hannah signed in to enter the building. The form required her to write what office number she was visiting but she didn't remember it.

"Excuse me," she said to the guard. "What's the number of Dr. Cagle's office?"

The guard looked confused. "Who?"

"Dr. Cagle. Tom Cagle. He's a therapist on the sixth floor."

The guard shook his head. "You must be mistaken, lady. There ain't no doctor on the sixth floor. Not that I know of, anyway."

"Well, he is there, I've been to see him before. Can I just go on up? I don't know the number."

The guard frowned, looked at the form, and then waved her on.

"Thank you," she said. She ran to the elevator, pushed the button, and waited a few seconds for it to arrive. It took her up to the sixth floor in no time.

Hannah was breathless as she ran down the deserted hallway to Dr. Cagle's office. She got to the end and stopped, totally bewildered. Did she miss it? She had looked at each door on her left, searching for the familiar sign with the doctor's name on it. She turned around and retraced her steps back to the elevator.

She must have got off on the wrong floor. That was it. She rang for the elevator again, stepped on, and saw that she was indeed on the correct floor. She held the doors open and got out once again. This time she walked slowly past every door until she found the one it *should* have been.

This was it. It had to be. What happened to his sign? Perhaps it had come off and he hadn't gotten around to putting it back on. Hannah tried the knob, but the door was locked. She knocked loudly, but nothing happened.

What was going on? What happened to her therapist? Was she going completely mad?

She heard a noise at the end of the hall and saw a janitor pushing a mop bucket.

"Excuse me," she called. The man looked up. "Do you know what happened to Dr. Cagle?"

"Ma'am?"

"Dr. Cagle. This is his office. But the sign is gone and no one's there."

The man shook his head. "I think you have the wrong place, ma'am. There is no Dr. Cagle here. That there is a storage room."

"A storage room? No it isn't, I was just here as a patient."

"No, ma'am. I'm sorry, but that's a storage room."

"Open it please."

"I can't do that, ma'am. The only people who have keys work for the company that rents the room."

"What company is that?"

"MedScript. They're on the floor below us. But I'm pretty sure they're closed. It's after hours." The man went back to mopping, signaling that he was through with the conversation.

Hannah's nightmare was becoming worse. She wanted to scream in frustration but instead turned around and ran for the elevator. She took it down one floor, got off, and looked for the MedScript office.

Sure enough, there it was. The lights were on, and she could see a man alone at a desk in an office in the back. She knocked on the door loudly.

The man looked up and seemed to be alarmed.

"Hello? Can you help me? I need to ask you something!" she called through the glass door.

The man stood and cautiously walked out of the office. He was some forty feet away and acted like he was afraid to approach her.

"Please? Mister? I need to ask you something?"

The man slowly walked forward until he was ten feet away.

"Can you tell me what happened to Dr. Cagle? The janitor on the floor above told me that his office is really your storage room. I don't understand. Where did he go?"

The man studied her for a moment, then walked to the door and unlocked it.

"May I help you ma'am?" he asked.

"I'm sorry to bother you, but I'm looking for my therapist. His name is Dr. Tom Cagle and his office is...was... on the floor above this one. But the janitor said that the room now belongs to you. It's your storage room, or something. Do you know what's going on?"

"I'm sorry, ma'am," the man said. "I'm afraid I don't know a Dr. Cagle. And that storage room has been ours as long as our office has been here. Are you sure you've got the right building?"

Hannah felt completely dejected. Had she walked into the wrong place? Was she going insane?

Finally she said, "Sorry to bother you," and walked away. Only then did something strike her as odd. The smell. The man's smell. It was familiar. His cologne, or something. Something was oddly familiar about that man. But that couldn't be. She had never met him before in her life.

She *was* going crazy.

***

Bill Cutler locked the door and breathed a sigh of relief. She hadn't recognized him. She hadn't been able to tell that he was Dr. Tom Cagle, or Sean Flannery for that matter.

Poor woman. He almost hated to do what he was planning, but there was no other way. His course was clear. Once he had determined that it was his only option, Cutler had gone into MedScript after hours to try and get his mind off the unpleasant, yet necessary, tasks that were his destiny to fulfill.

He went back to his desk to finish sorting his resumes and head shots. He had an important audition the next day.

Chapter 25

The taxi dropped Hannah off in front of the Cozzone townhouse just before ten o'clock. She paid the driver and quickly ran inside, slamming and locking the door behind her. Panther was immediately at her feet with a greeting but she stepped past him and went straight for the Jack Daniel's. She poured a tall glass that she could nurse over the next hour or two, turned out the downstairs lights, and went upstairs.

She was in a state of total confusion. She didn't understand what had happened to her therapist's office. She didn't know why Sean had acted so badly the night before. Her cousin was dead and she needed to face her fear of traveling to Ohio.

And then there was Timothy Lane. He was outside the townhouse, most likely. He was probably sitting in a car, watching the place, waiting for the perfect moment when he could attack her. He would stall the inevitable until he could surprise her and scare her half to death. Maybe he knew that she was armed now and could defend herself. He would want to find just the right time to pounce, when she least expected it and when she was vulnerable and helpless.

She sat at her desk in the office and pulled out the therapist's business card. She dialed the number and got the familiar voice message. Apparently he still had an office. Had she been so flustered by the events of the last few days that she had walked into the wrong building earlier that evening? She didn't think it was possible, but perhaps that was the only explanation.

When the beep sounded, she said, "Doctor Cagle, this is Hannah McCleary. I tried to come by your office tonight but for some reason it wasn't there. I mean, your office wasn't where it was before. Did you move? Please give me a call at your earliest convenience." She gave out the number again and hung up.

With a sigh, she leaned back in the chair and took a swig of whiskey.

It burned her throat going down, but it was a burn that she had learned to like.

She fingered Sean Flannery's card and debated whether or not to call him back. There was something incredibly fishy going on with him. Hannah had resisted her instincts in the matter up to now but after the events of last evening, she had begun to smell a rat. Perhaps he wasn't as sincere about her as she had originally thought. Perhaps her first reaction to him had been correct – that no man could ever have an interest in her. He had told her that he loved her, but it had rung false. She didn't believe it at all. It seemed to her that he just wanted to have sex with her. If she let him, he would probably never call again. Men rarely did the right thing and just admitted that they wanted out of a relationship. They always hemmed and hawed or simply didn't call anymore. Hannah could remember in the *old days,* before the face blindness, when she went on dates with men. They would seem interested for a while and then ultimately disappear without any explanation.

Panther mewed and jumped into her lap. She thought that he was probably hungry, but she didn't feel like standing and going downstairs. The Jack Daniel's was already doing its stuff.

"Go eat your dry food," she told the cat. "There's still some in the bowl downstairs."

Instead, the cat kneaded her stomach with his front paws the way he liked to do when he wanted affection. She stroked him and he settled there, purring loudly.

The sound of glass shattering downstairs startled her so badly that she screamed, causing the cat to jump off and run out of the room.

Hannah grabbed her purse, pulled out the Browning, checked to see if the safety was off, and stood. She listened for any sounds downstairs that might indicate the presence of an intruder, but there was nothing.

She moved to the door and for a moment had to reach out and hold on to the sill to steady herself. Her heart was beating furiously and the sensation was on the verge of being painful. She told herself to take a deep breath and be brave. She then proceeded to go downstairs, one step at a time.

Holding the gun in front of her, ready to squeeze the trigger, Hannah descended. She could see the entry hall. It was empty and the door was still shut and locked. A little further down the stairs she could see the hallway leading back into the living room and the small parlor off to the side of the door. It was there that she saw the broken glass. A stone lay on the carpet.

Hannah moved all the way to the bottom of the stairs and looked into the parlor. As she suspected, the front window was broken. She peered out but couldn't see anything unusual. Whoever had thrown the stone had disappeared. She went over to it and picked it up. A note attached to the stone read, "Pay us back, baby. You have twenty-four hours."

Hannah dropped the stone as if it were hot. What the hell did he mean? "Pay us back?" For what? For sending him to prison? Timothy Lane was insane. He wanted her to pay him back somehow. With what? Money? She had no money. What did he expect her to do?

Never mind that creep, she thought. The first thing she had to do was plug up the hole in the window. She would have to call a guy to come and fix it, but for now she just needed something to cover it. She got an idea and went back upstairs to the office, where she found the large cardboard display that advertised John's in-store appearance for *The Apples of the Cosmos*. The colors on it had long since faded, but the poster-board was thick enough to do the trick. She grabbed some masking tape as well and took it back down to the parlor. In five minutes, the hole was covered – not exactly aesthetically, but at this point she didn't care.

She went back upstairs, put the gun back in the purse, and sat at the desk. The glass of Jack Daniel's was only half finished. She picked it up and swallowed a long, fiery gulp that made her cough violently.

Then she started to cry.

***

Favio got back into the Malibu and looked at DeLauria. "Okay, that's done. I broke the window. Now what?" he asked.

"We wait."

"What for? Why don't we just go in there and make her tell us where the money is?"

"Because she hasn't got it."

"How do you know?"

"Because Cozzone died in Ohio. He had the money. She's gonna have to go get it. We wait until she leaves and then we follow her. As soon as she's got her hands on it, then we make our move."

Favio opened a can of beer. It had become warm sitting in the car and the brew spurted out over them both.

"Goddamn it!" DeLauria shouted. "You fuck!"

"Sorry, man," Favio said. "I guess it got shook up something."

DeLauria pulled out his Walther and shoved the barrel against Favio's temple.

"Hey!" Favio yelled. "Dominic, whoa, take it easy!"

"You little shit, I'm getting sick and tired of you. Get the fuck out of here."

"What?"

"Go on, get out of here before I blow your brains out the side of your head."

DeLauria didn't have to say it twice. Favio opened the car door, spilling the rest of the beer as he fell out onto the sidewalk. "What do I tell Jimmy?" he asked.

"I don't give a shit what you tell him. Tell him I didn't need you anymore. Go on, I'll take care of this myself." DeLauria holstered his gun and turned away. Favio, dejected, walked away, toward the Lexington Avenue subway stop.

DeLauria fumed. He should never have taken on the kid. He preferred to work alone. As he watched Favio disappear at the end of the block, DeLauria noticed the Toyota Corolla he had seen before pull up in front of the townhouse. The same cop with the trenchcoat got out and went to the door.

Who *was* he? Was the cop McCleary's boyfriend? What about Cozzone? Wasn't he the boyfriend? Maybe not. Maybe they were just business partners and this cop was the boyfriend. DeLauria really didn't give a fuck who the bitch slept with since she was going to be dead soon. The cop worried him, though. It wasn't cool to have the law so close to a job. How much did the guy know? Had she confessed everything to him? What if she had managed to twist the facts and make it sound like she wasn't responsible for the Patrone killings and wasn't in on the cocaine deal? What if she blamed everything on the mysterious stalker who'd been harassing her?

DeLauria decided to wait and see. He was a patient man.

***

Hannah dialed Sean's number and waited for the expected voice mail message. Sure enough, he didn't pick up.

"Sean, it's Hannah." She cleared her throat and tried not to slur her words. She was very drunk.

"Timothy Lane was here tonight. He threw a rock through the front window." She coughed twice and continued. "I, uhm, I don't know what happened last night, but I miss you and wish you were here. I… feel funny about… about us. I don't know what's going on, but I think I'm going crazy."

She knew she was rambling but she let the recording go on.

"Do you really love me? You said you did, but you know something, Sean? I don't believe you. I think you just want… well, I don't know… don't listen to me, I'm not making any sense."

She coughed again. Tears came to her eyes.

"I gotta go to Ohio tomorrow. I have to identify John's body and pick up his things. Arrange for him to be buried, or something. I'll probably just have him cremated. That'll be easier." She paused for a few seconds because she could barely keep her head up. "I don't want to go. I'm scared. I'm scared that Timothy Lane will follow me and try to kill me in Ohio." She coughed again. "Maybe that would be best, huh, Sean? Maybe I should just let Timothy Lane kill me."

She took the empty glass of whiskey and considered pouring some more, but the bottle was downstairs.

"I've always *wanted* to travel," she said, continuing to ramble. "In fact, I'd like to leave New York for good. I just don't have the guts. I'd like to go to… I don't know, New Mexico, maybe. I think it would suit me. I'd go somewhere where there weren't a lot of people to deal with. Somewhere where I could live alone and just… exist… without too much worry."

A thought came to her head. She snorted and started to laugh. "Maybe I could go to Hollywood and be a casting director. That would definitely be up my alley!" She snorted again. "Never mind, you wouldn't understand."

She was silent for a few seconds.

"Well, anyway. I guess I'll let you go. Even if you aren't even there. Maybe I'll call you from Ohio when I'm not so drunk."

She started to hang up when she thought of one more thing to say. "Sean, if you do love me, don't… well, I just… don't… " She couldn't finish. She didn't know what she wanted to say, so she just hung up.

Hannah supported herself against the desk and stood. She slowly left the office and went upstairs to the master bedroom. She removed her shoes, jeans, and T-shirt, and fell into bed.

She sank into the mattress as if it were quicksand.

Chapter 26

It took Rick a half-day to obtain phony ID's for them both. He knew a guy in Toledo who made a living creating false identifications. Rick wasn't much of a criminal-type, but he knew plenty of people who were. It came with the truck driving territory. He told Sophia that he ran into all kinds of human beings in his job, and more often than not they had connections to most anything one might want.

Sophia examined her new Ohio driver's license, which displayed her photo and her name as "Hannah Cozzone." Rick's new license bore the name "Frank Cozzone." Their address was listed at an apartment in Cleveland. The building actually existed, but in reality it was in the process of being built. Apartments had already been rented to prospective tenants, which made the licenses valid at least for a few days.

The Fulton County Health Center was located in the rural town of Wauseon, not far from the turnpike. The community of approximately 42,000 people was made up of primarily farmers. The sheriff's department was a low-key, laid-back outfit that never had to deal with anything too serious. Sophia figured that it wouldn't be very difficult to procure what they needed.

It was late afternoon by the time Rick parked his pickup truck in front of the health center. He had left his rig at his employers' place and driven his own vehicle to fetch Sophia at the hotel.

"You better park a block away," she told him. "We don't want them checking your plates."

Rick swallowed and nodded. Sophia could see that he was nervous. His hands shook a little and he had that wide-eyed, deer-in-the-headlights look about him. Would he blow the whole thing? Sophia creased her brow and wondered if she might have made a mistake bringing him in.

"You better take it easy," she said. "I can tell you're scared."

"It's that obvious?" he asked.

"Uh huh. Listen, I'll do most of the talking. You just say 'yes' and 'no' when you have to. If they ask you anything direct about John, just make it up. You remember what we talked about this morning?"

"Yeah."

"What were the names of his books?"

"*The Apples of the Cosmos* and *The Loose Lips of Lucinda Leone.*"

"*Lucretia.* Not Lucinda. But pretty good. I keep forgetting that lady's name myself. I can't imagine these local yokels knowing that stuff. Come on."

She got out of the truck and he followed her. They walked the block to the front of the building and went inside. A woman behind a glass partition looked up and smiled.

"We're here to see the coroner's deputy." She consulted a slip of paper. "A Mr. Webber."

"And you are...?"

"Mr. and Mrs. Frank Cozzone. He's expecting us."

"Certainly." The woman made a call, said a few words, and hung up. "Have a seat over there. He'll be right out."

"Thanks."

They sat in a waiting area. The table in front of them contained the usual assortment of subscription magazines. Sophia picked up a *People* and started to turn the pages when a man came through a door marked "Employees Only." He looked to be in his late thirties, was bald, and had glasses.

"Mr. and Mrs. Cozzone?"

"Yes?" Sophia said.

"Hello, I'm Doctor Webber." They stood and he shook hands with both of them. "I'm terribly sorry for your loss," he said.

"Thank you," Sophia said. Rick was silent, so she looked at him.

"Oh, thank you," he muttered.

"I'm afraid my husband's had a pretty big shock," she explained. "Forgive him if he doesn't say much."

"That's quite all right," Webber said. "I understand. Why don't you both come this way?"

He led them through the door, down a cold and antiseptic hallway, and into a small office.

"Have a seat," Webber said as he moved around a desk and sat down. He gestured at two black chairs that faced him. Sophia and Rich sat and looked at him expectantly.

Webber opened a file and studied at it. "Someone from the sheriff's office wants to speak with you, but before that happens I – "

"The sheriff's office?" Sophia interrupted. "What for?"

"It appears that the autopsy revealed a few things about your... about your brother-in-law, ma'am." He didn't acknowledge Rick. "The toxicology report gave us some concern and the sheriff's office got involved."

"Why, what's wrong?"

"I'll let them explain that, ma'am. In the meantime, I need to see some identification. There's some paperwork I need you to fill out here, and then we'll go in and take a look. Have either of you ever identified a body before?"

"No," she answered. She looked at Rick.

"No," he echoed.

"Well, keep in mind that we haven't done anything yet to preserve the body or clean it up so that he's presentable for a funeral. The funeral home will do that. He hasn't been embalmed. The injuries Mister Cozzone sustained are still quite evident. I'm sorry, but you'll have to look at him this way before we can release the body to the funeral home of your choice. Let's see, you're from Cleveland, right?"

"Yes." Sophia took control as Rick looked at the floor, giving a decent performance of a bereaved brother.

"Have you selected a funeral home?"

"No. We would just as soon have him cremated here."

The coroner's deputy raised his eyebrows. "Here?"

"That's right. We really can't afford... I mean, you know how it is. To tell you the truth, Frank and John weren't very close, you see. They were only children and their parents are dead. There's no one else. They tended to fight a lot. John didn't even come to our wedding. I met him only once before."

"I see. So you're saying that you want a funeral home in Wauseon to take care of the arrangements?"

"I guess so. Is that going to cost money?"

"There will be some expenses, yes," Webber explained. "If you want the body cremated without embalming, I suppose that can be done. I'll send you over to the Morris Funeral Home after we're done. That's nearby and we use them a lot. You can discuss all that with Mister Morris there."

"Okay. Did John have stuff in the car with him?" After she asked the question, she realized that it might have popped out too soon and too eagerly.

"You mean personal effects?"

"Yes."

"Yes, he did. Three pieces of luggage were in the trunk of the car. I'm afraid the car is totaled. It was towed from the site and went straight to the impounding yard. You'll have to contact Mister Cozzone's insurance company with regard to the car."

Rick spoke up for the first time. "It wasn't our car." Webber looked at him. Rick shrugged. "So what's the use?"

"As a living relative, you may be entitled to some money," Webber said.

"Did you determine how the accident happened?"

"The sheriff's deputy will go over that with you. I can tell you that Mister Cozzone died as a result of injuries sustained from the accident. I could go into specific detail about the injuries if you want me to."

"No thanks," Sophia said. She looked at Rick and asked, "Unless you want to know, baby?"

Rick shook his head.

"Fine. I'll let you go over the paperwork for a few minutes, and then we'll go inside."

Sophia handed him the two driver's licenses and then she and Rick filled out the forms together, whispering quietly to each other as to what the answers should be. Webber examined the licenses and scribbled something onto a sheet of paper he had in front of him.

"Mister Cozzone, how long have you lived in Cleveland?" Webber asked.

Rick looked up and answered, "Seven years."

"And where were you before that?"

"New York. My brother and I are from New York. He still lives – er, he lived there alone."

"And there are no other relatives?"

"Our parents are dead. There's no one else."

"What about…" Webber turned over the paper and read the name, "Hannah McCleary? A cousin?"

Shit, Sophia thought.

Rick looked at Sophia. She answered for him. "Oh, her. She's Frank and John's cousin, yeah. She doesn't have much to do with the family."

"I spoke to her yesterday. She said that she worked for your brother?"

Sophia shook her head. "That's not really true. She did some secretarial work for him, but that's it. Nothing on the books, if you know what I mean."

"She has the same name as you. Hannah."

Sophia rolled her eyes as if she had heard it a million times before. "Yeah. That's a total coincidence." *Shit, shit, shit!* she thought. How could she have been so dumb as to use that name again?

"Miss McCleary indicated that she would probably be coming to identify the body as well. Did you know about this?"

"No." Sophia looked at Rick. "Did you, honey?"

"Nope. I don't talk to her."

Sophia nodded. He was catching on.

Webber sighed. "Well, since you're Mister Cozzone's brother, you have preferential weight in this matter. Why don't we go ahead and look at the body and then we'll take it from there."

The three of them got up and went out of the office. Webber led them down the hall to the mortuary. The cooler temperature of the room was like a slap in the face to Sophia. An involuntary shiver ran down her back. Rick instinctively put his arm around her.

Webber opened one of the refrigerator doors and slid out a tray. A sheet covered the body.

"Why don't you move up here closer?" he suggested. Both Rick and Sophia crowded in behind him. Webber lifted the sheet off the corpse's head to give them a view.

Sophia gasped. John Cozzone was definitely dead. His skin was sickly pale and there were two prominent bruises on his face.

"Oh, God," Rick said. He turned away and put his face in his hands. Sophia was impressed with his act.

Webber looked at her for a verdict. She nodded and said, "Yeah, that's John." Webber nodded and replaced the sheet over the head. He slid the tray back into the cubicle and shut the door.

"Once again, I'm sorry for your loss," he said. "Now if you'll come this way, Sergeant Ackerman wants to talk to you."

"Who?" Sophia asked.

"From the county sheriff's office."

"Oh, right."

He led them out of the cold room and back down the hall. They went into a small conference room where a grey-haired man sat at a table. He stood when they entered. He was wearing a uniform that consisted of black pants and a grey shirt.

"Good afternoon," he said, extending his hand. "I'm Sergeant Ackerman of the Fulton County Sheriff's Department."

"Frank Cozzone," Rick said, shaking his head. "My wife Hannah." Ackerman shook her hand as well.

"Have a seat," the sergeant said and then addressed the coroner's deputy. "Thanks, Chuck. I'll give you a holler when I'm done." Webber nodded and left the room, shutting the door behind him.

"Very sorry for your loss," the sergeant began.

"Thanks," Sophia said. "What's this about?"

"Well, there are a couple of things I need to bring up about Mister Cozzone. Now I understand you didn't have much contact with your brother?" This last he addressed to Rick.

"That's right. We haven't spoken in years."

"I see. The Ohio State Highway Patrol turned over this case to us. I have to inform you that we believe that the accident was caused while your brother was under the influence of narcotics."

Rick did the surprise routine quite well. "Really?"

The sergeant nodded. "Cocaine was found in his blood. A lot of it. Not only that, we found traces of cocaine all over the front seat of the car."

Rick shook his head, looked at Sophia, and said, "Tsk, tsk, tsk. That sounds like John, doesn't it, honey?"

"I'm not surprised," she said.

"Were you aware that your brother was using cocaine?" the sergeant asked.

"No. But I figure he was the type to do that. He was, you know, an *artist*." Rick said it as if the word itself was some kind of disease. "Like I said, we didn't have much to do with each other."

The sergeant studied them both for a moment and then said, "There's something else. Your brother was a suspect in a murder case in Chicago."

"What?" Rick exclaimed.

"What do you mean?" Sophia asked.

"He was apparently driving back to New York from Chicago. A man was found shot to death in the hotel where your brother was staying. The victim had a piece of paper in his pocket with your brother's room number written on it."

There was silence in the room. Finally, Rick said, "I, uhm, I don't know what to say about that."

The sergeant nodded. "Unfortunately, we couldn't find any other evidence linking him to the crime. There was no weapon in the car. The victim was a known cocaine dealer in Chicago, though. So there's that."

"So what does this mean for us?" Sophia asked. She was becoming impatient. She wanted that suitcase. Then a horrific thought struck her. "Did you open his luggage?" she asked.

The sergeant nodded. "Yeah, we had to. In view of the circumstances, you understand. With the cocaine on the seat and in his blood, and the incident in Chicago."

Sophia thought her stomach was going to shoot up into her throat. "And?" she asked, hesitantly.

Ackerman shook his head. "We didn't find anything of interest. I suppose we can sign everything over to you. It's a closed case."

Sophia didn't know what to think. They didn't find the money? They opened the suitcases and didn't find a million dollars? And what about the cocaine that they never sold in Chicago? Where the hell was that?

Rick and the sergeant stood. Ackerman said, "Oh, there's one other thing."

"What's that?" Rick asked.

"Your brother was with a woman in Chicago. Witnesses there reported seeing him with an attractive blonde woman. Do you know who that might be?"

Rick and Sophia looked at each other. "No," they said in unison. They turned back to Ackerman, who was studying Sophia carefully. She could see that the sergeant thought *she* was an attractive blonde woman.

Was the game over? she wondered. Had they been found out? Had she walked right into a spider's web?

After a long and torturous silence, Ackerman finally said, "Well. I guess there's nothing to be done now. Both the suspect and the victim are dead. I guess it's Chicago's responsibility to find the mystery woman. Apparently she didn't leave Chicago with your brother. If she did, then he dropped her off somewhere before the accident. As no one else was hurt in the mishap, it's a closed case."

Rick said, "Okay, thanks." Sophia stood and the sergeant opened the door. He called for Webber and said, "Chuck, you can release the personal effects to these people now."

"Okay, Tommy," Webber said. "This way, folks."

Ackerman said, "I'm sorry again for your loss."

"Thank you," Rick said.

Webber led them back down the hall to another room. Three suitcases, including the one containing nearly a million dollars, were on a table.

"This is everything that was in the trunk of the car," Webber said. "If you'll just sign here, you can take it." He handed them a clipboard with a form on it. Rick signed it. Webber gave them back the driver's licenses.

"Here you go. And here's the name and number at the funeral home. I've already told Mister Morris that you'll be right over."

"Thanks," Rick replied.

"And once again, we're very sorry for your loss."

Rick and Sophia nodded.

***

When they got to the pickup truck, Sophia threw the big suitcase down in the back and examined the locks. Cozzone had originally locked the thing, but the officers had obviously broken the latches.

She took a deep breath and opened it.

The suitcase was full of clothing and newspapers. There was no sign of any money.

"Well I'll be fucked," she said to herself.

"What is it?" Rick asked.

"It's gone."

"What do you mean?"

"It's *gone,* you idiot!" she said. "The money's gone! It's not here! John must have hidden it. He did something with it. That *bastard!* That no-good, fucking, shit-eating, yellow-bellied, piece-of-crap *bastard*!"

Rick let her stew for a bit and then asked, "So what do we do now?"

"I don't fucking know," she said. "Let's go back to the hotel."

They drove in silence back to the Holiday Inn, grabbed the suitcases, and went to her room. Once again, she looked through the suitcase and searched the other two as well. Although they had been moved around when her bag was searched, all of her belongings were intact as she had packed them.

"Well, that was fun," Rick said. "You never said 'thank you.'"

"What?"

"You never said 'thank you' for helping you. I thought I did a pretty good job pretending."

"You asshole, we didn't get the money," she said. "The plan didn't work."

"The plan worked, it's just that there wasn't any money."

"Shut the fuck up. I'm thinking."

"So were you that blonde in Chicago he was talking about?" Rick asked.

"I said shut up!"

Rick stood there for a moment and then said, "I'm going to take a shower." He started to take off his clothes as he walked toward the bathroom.

Sophia thought about the new situation. What could John have possibly done with the money? He must have gone out of the Chicago hotel room when she was passed out, drunk. That was it. He had gone out and done something with the cash. Hidden it somewhere. But where? And why? Didn't he trust her? That prick. She should have known that he wasn't reliable when he balked at her using her gun.

So if the money was hidden in Chicago, that meant that John would have had to go back there to get it. Wouldn't that have been a pain in the ass? Didn't make sense.

He must have sent the cash back to New York somehow. It was going to be delivered to his home. That had to be it. He had packed it up and shipped it while she slept off all the booze she had consumed. But where in New York?

And it came to her. Obviously, John had sent the money to his cousin.

Sophia first heard the shower start and then Rick singing to himself. What was she going to do with *him* now? He was no use to her anymore. She had to get rid of him. The problem was that he knew too much. If there had been some money, she could have bought his silence, paid him off with some of it, and could still retire rich. Unfortunately Rick was now a liability.

Sophia squatted by the safe and opened it. She removed the Colt, checked to see if it was loaded, then walked to the bathroom. As she opened the door, the sound of the water hitting the shower stall tiles and Rick's singing grew louder. Sophia stepped inside and shut the door.

She opened the shower and asked, "Can I join you, baby?"

"Sure!" Rick said with a smile.

His expression changed when he saw the gun pointed at him.

Chapter 27

The footsteps grew louder behind her as she hurried toward her apartment. She knew that he was following her and that he would attack as soon as she entered the building.

"Hey, baby, where ya goin'?"

The voice sent chills down her spine as she struggled to move one foot in front of the other. Once again, she found it difficult to move. The dream world always had its own rules and Hannah could never change them. She wanted to scream but the sound that came out of her voice was a mere whisper, a squeak of helplessness.

Then she remembered something – she had a gun in her handbag. How could she have forgotten?

Hannah reached into the purse that hung around her neck. The gun was there, waiting to be released from its hideaway. She grasped the butt and felt the solid comfort that it always gave her when she held it. Hannah drew it out of the handbag, turned around, and pointed it at the assailant, the man she knew as Timothy Edward Lane.

He was there, just a few feet away. The figure was bathed in shadow, as the light on First Avenue was uncharacteristically non-existent.

"Whatcha got, baby? A toy?"

She pointed it at the man, but he kept coming. He was almost upon her.

Hannah squeezed the trigger and nothing happened. The shadowy figure grew larger, increasing its mass and body shape like a genie.

She pulled the trigger again. And again. And again… but it was fruitless. Finally, all she could do was scream as the horrible mass of evil enveloped her.

***

"Ma'am? Ma'am?"

The hand on her shoulder shook her a little more.

"Next stop is Bryan. Ma'am?"

Hannah opened her eyes and jerked awake. It took a few seconds for her to realize that she was still on the train. The conductor was standing in the aisle beside her, his hand on her arm.

"I'm sorry to disturb you, ma'am. You asked to be woken when we got to Bryan," he said.

"Yes, thank you," she said. The man walked away and left her, shaken and disoriented. The dream had been especially disturbing.

The coach was dark and the rest of the passengers were asleep. Hannah understood now that it had taken the conductor a few tries to wake her. He had been trying to keep his voice down so as not to disturb the others. She looked at her watch and saw that it was 3:55 in the morning. Outside, the flat landscape of Ohio shot past her at a brisk speed, but as it was very dark and nothing could be seen but a blurry motion of blackness.

Hannah stretched and pulled her one bag down from the ledge above her seat. The number 49 Amtrak train from New York's Penn Station to Chicago had been her only option to reach Wauseon at a rate she could afford. Actually, the train shot past Wauseon without stopping. The nearest station to Wauseon was about twenty miles further west, in Bryan. She would have to take a taxi back to Wauseon. At this time of the morning, she wondered how difficult it would be to obtain one.

It had been a long journey. She couldn't imagine traveling all the way to Chicago in a coach seat. If she could have afforded it, she would have splurged for a sleeper compartment. Hell, if she could have afforded it, she would have *flown*. As it was, going to identify John's body and collect his things was costing her more than she wanted to spend. She was terribly sorry about her cousin and she would miss him. Hannah just didn't want the responsibility of taking care of his arrangements. She had enough to worry about right now.

The train slowed to a stop in what appeared to be the middle of nowhere. The sky was littered with stars and Hannah could see that the land was flat and featureless as she stepped off onto the platform. The Bryan station was a small, wooden structure that seemed deserted. Considering the time, Hannah wasn't surprised. She was the only one who got off the train.

She went inside the little station and saw a pay phone on the wall. A quick call to directory assistance put her in contact with a taxi service. The dispatcher sounded as if she had been woken abruptly as well. Hannah was promised that a taxi would be there in fifteen minutes to pick her up. She asked the dispatcher if there were any inexpensive hotels in Wauseon where she might stay. The Holiday Inn was recommended.

***

The cab let her out in front of the hotel. There appeared to be some activity going on, as there were three police vehicles and an ambulance parked in front with the emergency lights flashing. She took her bag and purse and went inside. A sleepy-eyed man with a worried look on his face was behind the reception desk with a large cup of coffee. Hannah was able to read the emotion on his face but wouldn't have been able to pick him out of a lineup an hour later.

"Yes, ma'am?" he asked.

"I hope you have a room? I need to check in," she said.

"Yes, we do. How many nights?"

"I'm not sure. Tonight for sure, what's left of it, anyway. Probably tomorrow night. Hopefully that will be all."

He took her credit card and she filled out the registration form. "What's going on?" she asked.

"Oh, we had, uhm, we had some trouble. Nothing to worry about."

"I hope not."

He gave her a key and told her how to get to the room. He didn't offer to help with the one bag.

When she got to the room, she spent a couple of minutes in the bathroom, removed her shoes, and then crawled into bed with her clothes on.

***

Hannah slept until 10:30 and was woken by the alarm she had set. She figured that there was no rush to get to the Fulton County Health Center. John's body was certainly not going anywhere. She showered and got dressed, then made a phone call to the coroner's deputy who had first contacted her. He sounded distracted when he finally answered.

"Mister Webber? It's Hannah McCleary from New York."

"It's Doctor Webber. Can I help you?" he asked.

"You called me the other day regarding my cousin, John Cozzone."

"John – You're… wait, tell me again who you are?"

"Hannah McCleary."

"Miss McCleary! I've tried to phone you again. The police – I mean, we need to speak with you. Are you still planning to come to Wauseon?"

"I'm here. I got in early this morning."

"You're in Wauseon?"

"Yes. I thought – "

"When can you come in? The sheriff would like to speak to you."

"The sheriff? What for?"

"We'll explain when you get here. Where are you staying? We can send a patrol car over to pick you up."

She made arrangements to come in within the hour and then hung up the phone. She was bewildered. Why did she have to talk to the police? Had John gotten himself into some kind of trouble before the accident? What was going on?

Sergeant Ackerman arrived in a black Crown Vic on time and met her in the hotel lobby. He introduced himself and led her to the car.

"What's going on?" she asked as she got in.

"The sheriff would like to speak to you, ma'am," he answered. "We're a bit confused on a few matters."

"So am I."

They drove in silence through the rural town until they reached the small health facility. Two other patrol cars were parked in front and Ackerman pulled in beside them. They got out of the car and went inside. Ackerman was able to bypass the reception barrier and go right through to the back. He led Hannah down the hall and into the conference room, where a middle-aged man with grey hair and a mustache sat with Dr. Webber.

Ackerman made the introductions. "Gentlemen, this is Hannah McCleary. Hannah, this is Sheriff Rumley and Doctor Webber. I believe you've spoken to Doctor Webber."

They shook hands and sat down.

"What's all this about?" she asked.

"Miss McCleary," the sheriff began. "I understand that you're John Cozzone's cousin?"

"That's right."

He frowned and continued. "Yesterday a man and woman came in to the health center to identify your cousin's body and claim his belongings. The man identified himself as Frank Cozzone, the deceased's brother. With him was his wife, Hannah Cozzone."

Hannah didn't understand. "But John didn't have a brother. I'm not sure I follow you..."

The sheriff and Webber gave each other a look. "That's what we were afraid of," the sheriff said. "Do you know this man?" He handed her a driver's license. She examined it. The holder's name was indeed Frank Cozzone and the home address was somewhere in Cleveland. She couldn't decipher the face, of course. It meant nothing to her and it wouldn't have even if she knew the person.

"I've never seen him before," she said. She had no idea if that was the truth.

She gave it back to the sheriff, who drummed the tabletop with his fingers.

"We have a problem," he said. "I suppose you can prove that you're the deceased's cousin?"

Hannah thought about it. Could she?

"I'm not sure. I mean, I have my ID with me, but that doesn't say he's my cousin. What kind of proof would you need?"

"Some kind of family record? Something that indicates that you're related?"

Hannah shook her head. "It's complicated. He's a distant cousin. He's my mother's sister's first husband's son from a previous marriage. So we're not really related by blood. And all those people are dead."

"I see. Is it true that you were employed by Mister Cozzone?"

"That's right. I'm – I was his personal assistant. I typed things for him, that kind of stuff."

"And you live in New York as well?"

"Yes."

Webber leaned over to Sheriff Rumley and murmured into his ear. The sheriff nodded and turned back to her. "Miss McCleary, your cousin was a suspect in a murder in Chicago a few days ago. The police there were searching for him when he had the unfortunate accident outside our little town. According to Chicago, there was a woman with him. Would you happen to know anything about that?"

"Yes. Her name was Sophia. I don't know her last name. She was his girlfriend."

"How well do you know her?"

"Not well at all. I've met her once, er, twice, and very briefly."

"Would you recognize her if you saw her again?"

Hannah hesitated. She wouldn't recognize her out of context under any circumstances. "I don't think so. To tell you the truth, John had a lot of girlfriends and they all looked alike. Model types."

"Okay, here's the thing," the sheriff said. He tapped Frank Cozzone's driver's license, which still lay on the table. "This man and a woman, a pretty blonde 'model type,' as you say, came in here yesterday and claimed to be Mister Cozzone's kin. They filled out the proper forms, looked at the body and identified him, and then took away all of the personal effects that had been in the car. Last night, this man was found murdered in a hotel room. The same hotel where you're staying, the Holiday Inn. Not only that, but there's a match with the ballistics in the Chicago killing."

Hannah didn't know what to think. It was all very confusing and bizarre.

"I saw the police cars in front of the hotel when I arrived last night – er, this morning. It was between 4:30 and 5:00," she said.

"The woman is missing. All of the luggage and belongings were still in the hotel room except for one piece that appeared to belong to a woman. It was filled with women's clothing and toiletries. We believe that the woman who claimed to be Mister Cozzone's sister-in-law killed this man, took that one bag, and fled."

It was all a bit overwhelming for Hannah. "Whew. So what am I supposed to do? I mean, what is it you want *me* to do?"

"We're not sure," the sheriff said. "Your cousin had cocaine in his blood and there were traces of the drug on the front seat of the car. Were you aware that he was a drug user?"

"Yes," she said truthfully. "I didn't approve. But he's always been into that, I suppose. You know, he's a celebrity. Or was. He was more famous about twenty years ago."

"Do you know what he was in Chicago for?"

"Not really. He and Sophia went for a few days. I figured it was some kind of romantic getaway."

"Do you know why Sophia would use the name 'Hannah'?"

"She did?" Hannah was appalled. "Not at all. That's just weird. And creepy," she answered. "Who was killed in Chicago?"

"A drug dealer. He had your cousin's hotel room number written on a slip of paper that he had in his pocket. Does the name George Williams mean anything to you?"

"No."

As the conversation went on, Hannah realized that it was really an interrogation. The police were dealing with a couple of murder cases and they believed that she was some kind of link. The sheriff continued to ask her questions about her job for Cozzone, where he lived, what he did for money, and then began to probe into her own personal business. He wanted to know her whereabouts over the past few days and if she could account for the answers.

"Listen, I have nothing to do with any of this," she said, finally. "I came all the way from New York to identify my cousin and collect his stuff. Frankly, I really didn't want to do it. I loved my cousin; he was the only family I had left. But I'm just not up for… any of this. How come you let those two people in yesterday to identify the body?"

Webber answered that one. "At the time we thought their identifications were reliable. There was no reason to suspect otherwise. We're very sorry."

"So now what, I just go back to New York?" she asked.

"If that's what you want," the sheriff said. "However, we might need to get in touch with you again. No telling what might turn up. We'd like to solve this murder and we'd especially like to find this Sophia. Do you think she'll contact you?"

"I don't see why she would. Why would she go to the trouble of hiding her identify and coming in here to identify John's body? What's in it for her?" Hannah asked.

The sheriff answered, "Good question. We're wondering the same thing. If indeed this 'Mrs. Cozzone' is the same person as your Sophia. She took the woman's suitcase with her and if what you say is true, then it probably belonged to Sophia. Maybe she thought there was something hidden in the luggage. After all, these are drug dealers. Who knows?"

Hannah sat back, frustrated and angry. "Great. Here I am in the middle of nowhere and I have to go all the way back to New York. Do you know how long of a train ride that is?"

"We're sorry, ma'am," Ackerman said.

"There is still the matter of what to do with your cousin," Webber said.

"What do you mean?"

"He needs to go to a funeral home. And be buried. The couple who was here yesterday were supposed to have gone to a local funeral home to make arrangements, but they never did."

"Look, I don't care," Hannah said. "I don't have money. Just cremate him or something. Can you do that?"

"That's what the couple yesterday wanted us to do."

"Well, I'm the real next-of-kin, and that's what I'm telling you to do."

Webber asked, "If your cousin was famous, wouldn't he have money? As his only relative, I imagine you would have access to his estate."

Hannah was beginning to understand the full extent of her responsibilities with regard to Cozzone. It was all very frightening.

"I don't know. Do I need to talk to a lawyer?"

"That probably wouldn't be a bad idea," Ackerman said.

The sheriff spoke up and addressed Webber. "I'll speak to Morris at the funeral home and see if we can treat this like a John Doe case. That way Miss McCleary won't be troubled any more. If it's a cremation she wants then I'm sure the county can cover that expense." He looked at her. "Is that all right?"

"Yes, thank you."

"You'll still need to do something about his estate, especially if there is no one else to do so," the sheriff said.

She nodded. "Yeah."

Webber said, "Oh, and we'd like you to identify your cousin before you leave, since you're the real next of kin."

Hannah sighed and said, "All right. But afterwards I'll just go back to the hotel. The train back to New York stops here and leaves around midnight tonight. I think I'll try to get some sleep this afternoon and go home tonight."

"Fine," the sheriff said. "Sergeant Ackerman will drive you back to the Holiday Inn."

Viewing the body wasn't as bad as Hannah had feared. She truthfully didn't recognize the man on the table as John without his familiar smell, height, and friendly voice. But Hannah stated that it was he and then walked out of the room. Goodbyes were said and hands were shaken. Ackerman led Hannah out of the building and into the car.

They didn't notice the man inside the Chevy Malibu that was parked across the street.

Chapter 28

Sophia removed her black wig and sunglasses and looked at herself in the mirror. The bruises had faded somewhat but the gash on her forehead was still ugly. In fact, it appeared to be infected. She opened the mirror, revealing her pathetic medicine cabinet, and found a used tube of Neosporin anti-bacterial ointment. The expiration date had come and gone six months ago, but she figured it still had some strength. She dabbed some over the cut and put a fresh band-aid over it.

Damn, she thought. Probably should have had those stitches after all.

Her Greenwich Village apartment was a mess. When she had walked in that morning, fresh from the Greyhound bus ride from Ohio, she realized that she hadn't been there since she and John Cozzone had left for Chicago over a week ago. She had left in a rush without arranging for her mail to be stopped or telling anyone she knew that she'd be away. Her answering machine was full, mostly from her friends, wondering where the hell she was.

It was the one message from her uncle that got her attention.

"Sophia? We need to talk. Please call me as soon as you get this."

That was all he needed to say. The command, plus the tone of voice that indicated displeasure, was enough to plunge an ice pick of terror into her heart.

What did he know? Surely he wouldn't connect the shooting of Charlie Patrone to her? There was no way that he could. She had set it up so that the Pontecorvas would think someone in their own organization had done it.

She reached for the phone but hesitated. This was going to be difficult. She took a deep breath, picked up the receiver, and dialed.

Benny, her uncle's right-hand man, answered.

"Yeah?"

"Benny, it's Sophia."

"Sophia! Where the hell you been? Your uncle's going crazy."

"I've been away. Jeez, Benny, I don't tell my uncle every place I go. He knows that. What's the problem?"

"Just a minute, he'll want to talk to you." There was silence for a few seconds and then she heard the raspy voice of her uncle, Carlo Castellano.

"Sophia?"

"Hi Uncle Carlo. How are you?" She attempted to sound pleasant and cheerful.

"Never mind that. Where the hell you been?" he snapped.

"What do you mean? I was away for a week. I went to Chicago to see a friend. What's the big deal?"

"When did you leave?"

"Last Friday. Why?"

"We've got a problem. Have you been doing something you shouldn't be doing?"

"What are you talking about, Uncle Carlo?" She tried to infuse her speech with the innocent manner of a teenager. She knew that her uncle tended to go easy on her when he pictured her as his "little girl."

"Don't give me that bullshit, Sophia. A couple of Pontecorva's men were shot and killed a week ago Thursday by a woman who claimed that Marco had sent her. The Pontecorvas think they know who she is, but the description of the shooter that *we* got sounded an awful lot like you."

"Oh, Uncle Carlo, don't tell me you believe something like that?"

"Sophia, we've been through this before. If it hadn't been for my friends in the justice system, you'd be behind bars. Everyone knows it was you who whacked Billy Sorvino two years ago. Even the Pontecorvas know that. I'm surprised Freddie hasn't come over here and demanded to see you. The hit on their men is very similar to what you pulled on Sorvino."

"Oh, come on, I had nothing to do with it."

"Sophia? Listen to me."

"What."

"The Pontecorvas hit Marco. They thought he was in on it. He's dead."

"Oh my God!" She winced. Marco was a cousin, the man who was in charge of the drug distribution on the East Coast. She never thought that he would take any heat from what she had done. "When did that happen?"

"Three days ago. Some goons picked him up outside of his office, took him somewhere, and apparently worked him over pretty good trying to get information out of him. They dumped his body near one of our fruit stands in the Bronx."

"That's terrible!"

"Yeah. Well, I just want you to know that we've got a little war going now, and unless the shooter's head is brought to the Pontecorvas real soon, it's gonna get ugly. I've spoken to Freddie, trying to reason with him. He admitted that he has a guy working on the case and thinks he's found her. I was relieved to hear that, but when I heard what this woman looked like – "

"Uncle Carlo, it wasn't me. You can forget about that."

"Are you doing drugs again, Sophia?"

"Of course not!"

He was silent. She could imagine his face as he thought about the situation. He would rub his double chin and his mouth would become an upside-down "U." The fact that he was actually considering what she told him indicated that she might be off the hook.

Finally he said, "Sophia, you had better be telling the truth. If you did this, and Freddie and his boys find out, I'm not sure I'll be able to protect you."

"Don't worry, I haven't done anything. How's Aunt Anna?"

"She's fine. When you gonna come over and see her?"

"How about tonight? I just got in and I have a few things to do."

"All right. We'll expect you for dinner. And it might be a good idea to come stay with us until this thing blows over. I don't like the idea of my niece out and about while there's a war on."

He hung up. Sophia closed her eyes and exhaled. It wasn't as bad as she thought it might be. She hung up the phone and sat on the couch that was situated in front of the big screen television. Her luxurious two-bedroom apartment had plenty of space – quite fitting for the niece of a mafia kingpin – but somehow it just wasn't enough. She always wanted more. More money, more possessions, and more excitement.

Sophia's feelings of entitlement originated from the resentment she felt toward her uncle. He was actually more like a father. He and Aunt Anna had raised her because her own parents had perished in some kind of accident. Uncle Carlo had kept an iron hand on her as she was growing up. He was abusive, demanding, cruel, and manipulative. He had claimed to love her, but he had a funny way of showing it. The man was a monster. He treated her aunt like a slave and his own sons and daughter like laboratory mice – to play with, experiment with, or torture as he saw fit. This had contributed to her juvenile delinquency and her eventual troubles with the law. The first time she had "acted out" was in second grade, when she had kicked a classmate in the testicles so hard that he had to go to the hospital. Sophia had felt the boy had deserved it because he had called her a "hyena." She had committed her first murder at the age of fourteen, but no one knew about that. She had been in and out of drug rehab five times during her high school years and had the pleasure of one extended stay that had interrupted her attendance at college. She had never gone back to school after that and her uncle had been "disappointed", as he liked to say. He cut off her allowance and threw her to the dogs. That was when she decided to take matters into her own hands and use the skills she had learned growing up in a mafia family.

She looked at her watch. It was time to find Hannah McCleary and see what she knew about the money and cocaine that John had seen fit to keep out of Sophia's hands.

If John had told anyone what he had done with it, it would be her.

***

Hannah slept for three hours in the hotel room and then showered, got dressed, and packed her overnight bag for the trip back to New York. The hotel manager had been very kind in allowing her to stay past the noon checkout time until that evening without charging her for an extra night's stay. She had promised to be out before six o'clock, however, and her train wasn't until 12:16 that night. What was she going to do in Wauseon, Ohio, before taking a taxi to Bryan? She hated going to movies because she couldn't follow the plots. If a character showed up in a different costume she always had trouble recognizing him. She supposed that she would just have to sit in the hotel lobby with a couple of magazines and wait it out.

She decided to call Sean. She bought a pre-paid phone card at the front desk and used it to dial him on the pay phone, expecting to get the voice mail. Surprisingly, he answered.

"Sean Flannery," he said.

"Hi Sean, it's Hannah!"

"Hannah, where are you?"

"I'm still in Ohio. My train leaves around midnight and I'll be home tomorrow afternoon. Will I see you?"

There was an uncomfortable pause and then he said, "I'll come over tomorrow evening if you're not too tired."

"I'm exhausted already but I don't think I'll be too tired to see you. Hey and Sean, I think I might have left you a pretty strange message the other night. I was pretty drunk."

"Don't worry about it."

She thought he sounded odd. Emotionless. It wasn't like him. "Well, I'll see you tomorrow then?"

"Yeah," he said. "I just might have a big surprise for you."

The way he said it made it sound as if it wasn't a pleasant surprise.

"What do you mean? What is it?"

"Uh uh. It's a surprise. Just get back here in one piece."

"You've got me curious now."

"I gotta run. See you soon, baby." He hung up without waiting for her to answer.

A wave of anxiety shot through her chest. There was something about the way he had said the word "baby" that set off all kinds of alarms.

She hung up the phone and stood there for a moment. Her imagination was playing tricks on her again. She was ultra-sensitive about that word. That was it. Being referred to as "baby" by any man brought back the ugly memories of that night and she just didn't like it.

Hannah walked back to the middle of the small lobby and sat down, ready to plunge into the latest *People* magazine. She looked at the cover and realized that she didn't care what Harrison Ford was doing now. She knew that he was a big star and was rich and famous, but that meant nothing to her. His face on the magazine certainly was a blank slate. How could she possibly care about celebrities when she couldn't recognize them?

She decided to go for a walk. The summer air was pleasant and it wasn't dark yet. She asked the teenaged male clerk behind the desk if she could leave her bag there while she took a stroll. She went outside, walked past the hotel's garbage dumpster, up the driveway and onto a wide thoroughfare. This intersected with a rural two-lane road that led out of town toward the Interstate. She figured that she would walk a mile or two and then turn around and head back.

As she strolled along, she thought about Sean and how unusual it was that he had come into her life. He had appeared from out of the blue, already interested in and attracted to her. Nothing like that had ever happened before in her life. Perhaps when she got back to the city she would let him sleep with her. She had been resisting it but now the time was right. They had known each other for over a week. She was afraid that if she didn't do something like that then he would lose interest and move on.

"Hey, baby."

Hannah froze in her tracks. The voice came from behind her.

My God! Was he there? Was he behind her? Had Timothy Lane followed her to Ohio?

She slowly turned around and saw him. He was standing twenty feet away and was wearing blue jeans and a black shirt. She didn't recognize him, of course, but she was quite familiar with the menace that he exuded. It was like an aura, something that only she could see. It telegraphed that this was a dangerous man. A stalker of women. A rapist.

"What are you doing way out here in the middle of nowhere, baby?" he asked.

"What do you want?" she whispered. She clutched her purse and held it in front of her. Could she get the handgun out before he made his move?

She looked around and saw that there was no one else in sight. Although the landscape was flat and one could see for miles, Timothy Lane could pounce on her right here on the road, kill her, and leave her for dead – and there would be no witnesses.

"You know what I want, *baby*," the man said. "You took something that isn't yours. The owner wants it back."

He wasn't making any sense again. Hanna's mind computed his words and attempted to understand the meaning behind them. Was he talking about his time in prison? She had taken away his *time*?

"Look, I'm sorry you were in prison," she said. "Please. Leave me alone."

The man began to walk forward. "This is your last chance, baby," he said. "Give it back now. You came all the way to Ohio to get it, now turn it over. Where is it, at the hotel? In your luggage?"

"What are you talking about?" she asked.

The man shook his head and laughed. "You're good, baby, I gotta tell you that. If I didn't know better, I'd say it's an Oscar-worthy performance. Now, my patience is at an end. I've been watching you long enough. This is the moment that it all comes down to. Surely you must know what the penalty is for what you did. I can ease that for you, baby, make it a bit more... *pleasant*... if you tell me what I want to know. Otherwise..." He shrugged as if it were out of his hands.

"You're crazy," she said. "Go away. I'll scream."

"Scream away. Who's gonna hear you?"

He was right but she did it anyway. She started screaming at the top of her lungs. When he realized that she was much louder than he wanted her to be, he rushed toward her. Simultaneously, she pulled the Browning out of the handbag, pointed it at the charging man, closed her eyes, and squeezed the trigger. The gun recoiled in her hand and the noise startled her so badly that she jumped, cried out in surprise, and dropped the weapon.

Hannah opened her eyes and saw that the man she knew as Timothy Lane had stopped approaching. One of his hands held his stomach as blood seeped through his shirt. The other hand waved erratically in front of him, as if he were blindly searching for a railing to hold on to.

She had hit him in the stomach. Hannah put her hand to her mouth as she watched in horror.

The man plummeted to his knees and remained there, clutching his abdomen and staring at her. His free hand then swung around to his back and struggled with something there. His upper body began to sway and he coughed twice.

He brought a handgun out from behind his back. She gasped as he pointed it at her.

She immediately began to run past him, back toward town. A shot rang out behind her but the pain she expected never came. She ran for at least a minute before she dared to look behind her. When she did she saw that the man was lying on the road, face up.

Had she killed Timothy Lane? Was it over? Was the nightmare finished?

Hannah continued to run. What was she going to do now? Should she call the sheriff or Sergeant Ackerman? Or by doing that would she land herself in more trouble? The police in New York were inept and only cared about the bottom line. Here in the boondocks of America, they were probably much worse. She had visions of rotting away in a cold, smelly cell in a forgotten town in a lonely state.

Forget the police, she thought.

She reached the Holiday Inn, burst into the lobby, and breathlessly addressed the clerk behind the counter.

"Can I get that taxi now?"

The boy stared at her. He wasn't used to customers in a panic. Wauseon was a laid-back, slow motion town.

"Did you hear me?" she asked, a little louder. "I want my taxi to Bryan now. Can you call them?"

"Yes, ma'am." The kid picked up the phone and began to dial. She reached behind the partition, picked up her bag, and then went to the window. It was dusk now, and the sunset cast broad strokes of orange and red across the sky. The angle was bad but she could just glimpse the beginning of the road she had been on. There was no sign of Timothy Lane. Had she killed him? Had she got him out of her life, once and for all?

She had to sit. Her heart was pounding the inside of her chest cavity and it felt as if it would puncture a hole there. Dizzy, she fell into a chair as an intense surge of panic and anxiety attacked her nervous system. She suddenly felt nauseated and knew that she would vomit at any moment. She looked up and saw the Men and Women washroom doors at the other side of the lobby. Summoning every ounce of strength that she had left, Hannah pulled herself up and struggled toward the bathroom. She pushed open the door and went straight to a stall, bent over, and threw up.

Ten minutes later, she emerged from the bathroom after having washed her face. She wished that she had some of her beloved Jack Daniel's, but that would probably just make her sick again. She thought that perhaps she was going through withdrawal from it. She hadn't had any in two days.

The clerk stared at her. "Are you all right, ma'am?" he asked.

"Yes," she whispered as she sat down.

"Your taxi will be here any minute."

"Thank you."

Then she remembered the gun. It was still in her handbag. Should she carry it back to New York? What if the police stopped her? It was evidence, wasn't it? Perhaps it was best to get rid of it. After all, John didn't need it any more. And Timothy Lane was finally dead. She had no reason to keep it. She didn't *want* to keep it.

She took her purse and a section of the newspaper that was on one of the lobby seats and then went back into the washroom. When she was alone, she removed the gun from her purse, wiped it clean with wet paper towels, and wrapped it in several sheets of newspaper. She kept wrapping it until she had formed a football-sized bundle. She went back to the lobby and, without looking at the clerk, went outside to the side of the hotel. Hannah carefully looked around to make sure that no one was watching, then she dropped the bundle into the garbage dumpster.

The taxicab pulled up in front of the hotel just as she came back to retrieve her bag.

"I think that's your taxi, ma'am," the clerk said.

"Thank you." Hannah went outside to begin her long journey back home, away from the horror and unpleasantness of Wauseon, Ohio.

Chapter 29

Hannah was exhausted. She had planned to take the subway from Penn Station but in the end opted for a taxicab. She knew that Panther would have a fit as soon as she walked into John's townhouse. He was probably starving. Hannah had put plenty of dry food in his bowl, but the cat wasn't used to being left alone overnight, much less two.

The train had been delayed for a while in Pennsylvania and got in to New York three hours late, so by the time she arrived at the house it was nearly seven o'clock.

She paid the driver, took her bag, and went to the front door. Nothing seemed out of the ordinary. After all, Timothy Lane was dead. She had nothing to fear now. The only thing that she didn't look forward to was dealing with John's estate. Did she know any lawyers? Not really. Only the one who had prosecuted the case against Lane, and she doubted that estate resolution was his forte. Perhaps he could refer her to someone.

As she unlocked the door, she suddenly realized that the townhouse could be hers. Since she was John's only living relative, might it become her property? She wasn't sure how these things worked. On the other hand, it might have to be sold. She had no idea. Still, wouldn't it be nice…?

Panther meowed loudly as soon as she walked inside. The cat slinked around her legs and let his annoyance be known in no uncertain terms.

"Hello, Panther," she said. "I'm so sorry, did you miss me? I'm home now. Let me put down these things and I'll give you a good meal of canned tuna. How would you like that?"

The cat raised up on its hind legs and propped his front paws on her thigh. This was a sign that he wanted to be picked up. Hannah dropped the bag, lifted the fifteen- pound cat, and held him to her chest.

"You're getting heavy, Panther. No one would ever know that you were starving for two days!"

The meowing was replaced by purring as he closed his eyes and allowed her to stroke him. Hannah walked with him into the living room and saw that the open bottle of Jack Daniel's was on the counter. Next to it sat a dirty plate and utensils.

What was that?

Hannah let Panther leap out of her hands as she approached the counter to get a closer look. This wasn't hers. She was sure that she had left the kitchen clean. She had put away the Jack Daniel's and clearly remembered loading the dishwasher with dirty dishes before leaving the townhouse two days ago.

Was someone in the house?

"Hello?" she called.

There was a noise upstairs, the sound of something being dropped.

Suddenly Hannah wished that she still had that gun. She walked slowly to the foot of the stairs. The front door behind her was still open. Should she make a run for it?

"Who's there?" she called again. "I'm calling the police!"

A woman appeared on the first floor landing.

"There you are," she said. "I was wondering when you'd come home."

Hannah didn't know who she was. She was young, a model-type… one of John's girlfriends? And then she knew.

"Sophia?"

"Sorry to frighten you," the woman said as she descended the stairs. "John had given me a key to the house. I, uhm, came back without him."

Hannah didn't know what to think. She backed up a little, allowing some space between them when Sophia got to the ground floor. If the police in Wauseon had been correct, Sophia was involved with that murder in Chicago, and possibly with the one in Wauseon. Even if she was innocent, Hannah knew that the woman was no good.

"You do know what happened to John, don't you?" Sophia asked.

"Yes. I just got back from Ohio."

"Yeah?" She walked past Hannah and into the living room. "You didn't bring back any more of his stuff, did you?"

"What do you mean?"

"Anything he might have left in the car. I don't know."

"Was it you who claimed to be his sister-in-law?"

Sophia stopped. She turned around and smiled. "Why, what are you talking about, Hannah?"

Hannah felt herself becoming anxious but this time it was fueled by anger. This woman was up to something and Hannah didn't like it.

"You know what I'm talking about," Hannah said. "You and some guy pretended to be John's relatives and went in to claim his stuff. You got it all. There was nothing else. All I came home with is the responsibility of settling his estate. Now I think you had better turn over what you have of his. I don't normally like the police, but I'll be happy to call them. I bet they're looking for you."

"My, my, don't we talk tough?" Sophia said. She moved to the couch and sat down. There was a glass on the coffee table, half-full of what appeared to be Hannah's Jack Daniel's. Sophia took it and had a sip, then replaced it on the table. "I tell you what, Hannah. I left all of John's stuff in Ohio. I brought back my own bag. If you want John's stuff you'll have to go back to Ohio to get it."

Hannah recalled that the sheriff had said that bags had been left in the Holiday Inn room where the man had been shot.

"Did you kill that guy in the hotel?" Hannah asked.

"What guy?"

"John's stuff was in the same room as a dead guy. He had been shot."

"I wouldn't know about that," Sophia said as she took another drink.

"I don't believe you."

"Well, that's your problem, honey. Now I have a question for you."

"What."

"Did John send you anything? Any messages?"

"No, I only heard from him once. When he was in Chicago. Weren't you with him there?"

"Yeah, I was with him. But he left without me," Sophia said. "We had a fight."

"I'm sorry," Hannah said, but she couldn't avoid sounding sarcastic.

"Look, Hannah, I'm going to ask one more time," Sophia said as a gun materialized in her hand. Hannah blinked. Where did it come from? Had it been in her waist this entire time?

"John had something that belonged to me. Actually it belonged to both of us, but I want my half. Do you know anything about it?" Sophia casually pointed the gun at Hannah.

"No, I don't. Put that away. You're scaring me."

"That's the idea, honey. Listen, why don't I believe you about this? I think I got to know John pretty good. He did something with my property – hid it, shipped it somewhere, I don't know. But he *did* do *something* with it. And the only person I can think of that he might let in on it is you. Now you had better tell me everything he said to you. Maybe he gave you a message but you didn't realize he was doing so."

"I don't think so," Hannah replied. "We just had a normal conversation. 'How are you doing?', 'Are you having fun?', that kind of thing."

The gun went off, scaring Hannah out of her wits. The outstanding acoustics of John's living room intensified the sound of the shot. Panther leaped from a perch on the counter, ran across the room, and hid under a chair.

Sophia had shot the counter just below where Panther had been sitting.

"The next one will put a hole through him," Sophia said. "By the way, his litter box really needs to be changed. It stinks upstairs something awful."

"You... you tried to shoot my cat!" Hannah cried.

She started to walk across the room to retrieve him, but Sophia waved the gun at her. "Uh uh uh! Stay right there. I need to find out if you're telling the truth or not."

Sophia stood and stepped around the coffee table. Hannah was incredibly frightened now. The pounding of her heart and the anxiety sickness made her weak in the knees, threatening to cause her to collapse. The nausea she had experienced in Ohio returned with a vengeance.

"I... I..." she struggled to say.

"What?" Sophia asked. "You have something to say? Spit it out, girl."

"I don't know what you're talking about! Honest!"

"Why do I not believe you?"

"You killed that man in Ohio, didn't you? And someone in Chicago! I'll bet you killed John, too." Hannah was breathing heavily, barely able to spit out the words.

"John was a wimp," Sophia said. "He wanted to play with the big boys but couldn't catch the ball. Good looking guy, though, I'll give him that. Pretty good in bed, too."

Hannah's face flushed and she looked down.

"Whoa, looks to me like you had the hots for your cousin," Sophia said. "Don't tell me that you slept with him?"

Sophia's words reverberated in Hannah's ears, increasing the amount of anger that was bubbling inside of her. The ferocity she felt overcame the nausea and anxiety and suddenly became empowered. Hannah looked at the woman with hate in her eyes and snarled, "No, I didn't!"

Then she lunged at Sophia with all her might, knocking her back against the coffee table. This caused Sophia to trip backwards. The Colt fired into the ceiling but Sophia held on to it. Hannah grabbed Sophia's right arm with both hands and attempted to loosen the woman's grip on the gun.

"Get off of me, you crazy bitch!" Sophia spat.

Hannah leaned in and clamped her teeth down on Sophia's forearm. Sophia screamed bloody murder and reflexively brought her knee up into Hannah's stomach, knocking the breath out of her attacker. Hannah gasped and struggled for air, releasing Sophia momentarily. Sophia rolled out from under her and got to her feet. She held her arm where Hannah had broken the skin.

"You shit," Sophia said, pointing the Colt at Hannah, who was crawling on the floor, face down, trying to regain her breath. "You better not have any diseases." With that, Sophia kicked Hannah hard in the side, knocking her flat and exacerbating her struggle for oxygen.

"I oughta shoot you right now," Sophia said, her finger on the trigger.

Hannah shut her eyes, realizing that the inevitable was seconds away. Then she heard not one but two gunshots. She knew she was dead but oddly there was no pain and no immediate curtain of blackness. She was still conscious and the shock of the gunfire had forced air into her lungs. She rolled onto her back as she gulped oxygen and coughed, and then she saw that Sophia was staring off toward the front of the house. Although Hannah couldn't put the features of faces together, she could read emotion and there was a bewildered, disbelieving expression on Sophia's face. A bloody patch spread across the right side of her chest.

Someone had shot her.

Hannah turned her head and saw a man leaning in the archway between the living room and the front entry hall. He, too, was wounded, blood spurting out of his stomach. No, it was coming out of his chest. The stomach wound looked… older. His pants were soiled with dried blood. The pallor of his face was like death. He looked like he had died yesterday and had come back from the grave.

Of course, Hannah didn't recognize him, but there was something about him that was familiar.

It was Timothy Lane.

Hannah scrambled back along the carpet in a reverse spider position. She wanted to scream but couldn't find the right brain-to-voice command. Nothing worked but her flight response.

"The door was open," the man said hoarsely, addressing them both. He coughed once and said, "You can't imagine what it's like to drive all the way from Ohio to New York with a bullet in your gut." He looked at his chest and saw the new blood, then spoke to Sophia. "Damn, you're a better shot… than *she* is!"

"Who… the fuck… are you?" Sophia managed to say. She wobbled on her feet, still pointing the gun at the man but she was having trouble holding it steady.

"It's Timothy Lane!" Hannah cried. She had backed herself to the couch but was still in a sitting position.

"Who?" Sophia asked.

It took a few seconds for Hannah's answer to register with the man. Then he looked at her and echoed Sophia. "*Who?*"

"Shoot him again!" Hannah cried to Sophia. "He's a rapist and a killer!"

Dominic DeLauria raised his Walther again and pointed it at Sophia. Sophia, in pain and confusion, squeezed the trigger. Despite her bad aim, the slug hit DeLauria in the abdomen, knocking him back. His gun recoiled again, blasting a hole in the wall behind Sophia. DeLauria's body made a splattering sound as he hit the carpet. The blood gushed out of him.

"Is he dead?" Hannah jumped to her feet but was afraid to run over to him. The man certainly appeared to be dead. He wasn't moving and there was more blood around him than she'd ever seen in her life.

Hannah turned and looked at the other woman. Now it was Sophia's turn to look like death. All the color had drained from her face as she clutched the red wound on her breast. She dropped the Colt and careened sideways into the china cabinet. The glass door shattered as Sophia fell into it. She tried to steady herself against the piece of furniture but she was only able to delay her inescapable crash to the floor.

The room was quiet. The only sounds Hannah was aware of were her own rapid breathing and the pounding of her heart.

"Sophia?" she whispered. She moved forward and stood over the woman. Sophia's eyes were still open but they stared blankly at the ceiling. Her tongue jutted out of her mouth grotesquely and a thin stream of blood trickled down her chin to the carpet.

Hannah felt as if a sledgehammer had hit her. What was she supposed to do now? She had to get away. She had to leave the townhouse and never return. She wanted to crawl under a rock and hide. She felt like crying and screaming but couldn't find the strength.

"Hannah?"

She was so out of it that she imagined someone was calling her.

"Hannah?"

It was louder this time. The voice belonged to someone she knew.

She saw movement out the corner of her eye. A man had come in the open front door and walked into the house.

"My God, Hannah! Who is… Hannah!"

Hannah looked up and saw him. She couldn't help herself.

"Sean!"

She ran to him and flung her arms around the one man who might be able to take her away from all this. The dam finally burst and the tears poured out. She sobbed loudly against his chest, releasing the demons that had been torturing her for the last hour.

Chapter 30

"My God, Hannah, what happened here? Who are these people? Are they dead?" Cutler held her close, taking in the sight of the living room. The bloody bodies were so incongruous, as if they existed in a nightmare and would go away if he woke up.

"Oh, Sean," Hannah sobbed. She pointed at DeLauria. "That's Timothy Lane! Don't you recognize him?"

Cutler turned his head to look again and said, "Oh, yes, I see. It *is* him, isn't it."

What the hell? he thought. Did this guy really exist? Had she been telling the truth all this time? He had thought that Hannah was completely nuts, was imagining things, was ultra-paranoid…

"And who's that girl?" he asked, gesturing to Sophia.

"That was John's girlfriend. Her name is Sophia. I don't know her last name."

"What's she got to do with all this?"

"I don't know. She and John were up to no good. Selling drugs or something. I think she killed John and may have killed some other people in Chicago and in Ohio. She tried to kill me."

"Whatever for?"

"She thought I knew something. Something about John. I really don't know! It's all so upsetting."

"Come on, let's sit down somewhere."

"What should we do, Sean? Are you going to call more police to come?" she asked.

Can't do that! he thought. No, he had to keep the police away.

"I can handle this," he answered. "I'll call them in a minute. I want to make sure you're not going to fall apart first."

He released her and she backed up to the kitchen counter. She saw the bottle of Jack Daniel's and said, "I need a drink."

"Pour me one, too," Cutler said.

She took two glasses from the pantry and poured what was left of the whiskey into them. As she did so, Panther jumped onto the counter.

"Oh, hello, Panther," she said. She grabbed the cat and hugged him close. "You poor thing. You're probably scared to death. Look, Sean, he's shedding like crazy."

"I can imagine." He took the glass and had a large swallow. With one arm holding the cat, Hannah used her free hand to take a long drink as well. She coughed twice.

"Sean, I just don't understand any of this." She sat on one of the barstools by the kitchen counter. She released the cat and it lay beside the empty whiskey bottle. Cutler watched her as she withdrew into herself, much like she had the first time she had visited "Dr. Cagle."

Cutler walked back to the open front door, shut and locked it. It was amazing that no one on the street had heard the gunshots, but then again, this was New York. The townhouse was situated atop several stone steps and one couldn't see inside the door easily from the sidewalk.

He came back to the kitchen. Hannah was still motionless, save for her tic of pulling on her fingers.

She looked so defenseless sitting there. Like a waif, an orphan from the Charles Dickens stories he used to read as a child. She was disheveled, of course, and there was a bruise or something on her face. Part of her shirt was torn, exposing a bit of her pale shoulder. Cutler found the image incredibly exciting. It was erotic.

The pounding in his head was relentless and the tunnel vision was sharper than ever.

Hannah was indeed a beautiful woman and what made her particularly attractive was the vulnerability that he had exploited over the past two weeks. Cutler knew that she was the perfect victim, the ideal conquest, and the ultimate notch on his Quest List.

He narrowed his gaze on her, drawing his eyes up and down from her feet to the top of her head. He imagined her sprawled out beneath him. He could hear her protesting as she tried to fight him, but she was also screaming with pleasure as he forced her to do what he wanted. He knew that was what she really hoped for. She was in love with him. She desired him. All women craved to be taken by force and made to do the bidding of their masters.

It was happening. Cutler felt his surroundings fade away and the only thing that mattered was to fulfill the quest. She was sitting there, ready for him. All he could see was Hannah and she was begging him to take her. He could hear the woman's words in his head as she implored him to ravage her.

Cutler surrendered to the ritual. It was a ceremony that he had to perform or he would go mad. Perhaps he was already mad. They had told him that he was. Patrick had frequently accused him of being insane. The shrink at Bellevue and his therapist warned him not to stop taking his medications. He might "act out" again. He might commit a crime again. Like he had before. He could hear his therapist warning him, *"Do you want to go to prison? Do you want to spend the rest of your life there?"*

They didn't know anything, Cutler told himself. He was in control. He knew exactly what he was doing. The Quest List was everything – it was his Ten Commandments, his Constitution, and his Magna Carta. Hannah McCleary's name was on the list and he had to mark it off. It was time to do so. He could postpone it no longer. He could see that she was ready to be sacrificed.

Cutler involuntarily moved into the kitchen and stood behind the barstool. He put his hands on Hannah's forearms and leaned in to smell her hair and nuzzle her ear.

Yes, finally, it was time.

***

Hannah was completely unaware that Sean had moved behind her. She had entered that never-never land that she sometimes went to when things got to be too much for her. She could see what was in front of her and she was acutely aware of Panther lying on the counter beside her, but she felt as if her mind was not inside her body. She wondered if it was one of those "out of body experiences" that she had heard about. Probably not, because those were attributed to people who were dying. Then again, there were the psychics and Shirley MacLaines of this world who claimed to be able to do it. In a way, Hannah had two different views of herself at that moment. One was inside her head, looking out through her own eyes, seeing what she would normally be seeing. The other camera angle was suspended above, from the ceiling, looking down onto the kitchen with omniscient knowledge. By switching to that view, Hannah could see that Sean was directly behind her.

Then something about this image disturbed her. The comfort she normally felt with Sean was no longer present. Hannah felt the dreaded anxiety rush up inside her chest cavity and then her heartbeat increased dramatically. Adrenaline pumped into her veins, sending a wake-up call to her shell-shocked brain. Something was terribly wrong. There was danger very near. Alarms sounded, red flags were thrown, and warnings flashed on the intangible monitor in her mind.

Then there was the smell. That sweet cologne that Hannah knew she was familiar with but couldn't quite place. It was all around her. It was strong, almost like the musty scent of sweat in a locker room except that it was not unpleasant. Where had she smelled it before? Was it Sean's cologne or after-shave? It seemed that she was reminded of the scent when she was around him. Yes, that was it. She had smelled it the first time she met Sean, that time on the street in front of her building. And she remembered the scent from when they had been nearly intimate, the night she rejected him.

But there was something else.

Hannah knew that smell from another place and a different time. It activated an unpleasant memory hidden in the dark recesses of her consciousness. She had smelled that cologne before and it was long before she had met Sean.

Hands caressed her shoulders. Sean was touching her.

"It's time, baby," he said.

What?

His voice was different. He didn't sound like Sean.

"You need to work on coming out of your shell, Hannah," he said. This time the accent was decidedly different. It had more of a New England lilt. It was... Bostonian.

What?

"You need to submit to your desires, Hannah. Give yourself to him."

The voice was Dr. Cagle's! Was her therapist in the room?

She slowly turned her head. Hannah wanted to see who was behind her. Even if the face was a blank to her, she must be able to discern who he really was. There had to be something that would give her a clue.

"What is it, Hannah?" Sean asked. It was his voice, that non-descript Virginia accent.

"You sounded different."

"Did I? I'm afraid you've had such a terrible shock this evening," he said. "Poor girl. Your mind is playing tricks on you."

"Sean, what's that cologne you're wearing?"

"Cologne? I don't wear cologne."

"Yes, you do. I smell it. I've smelled it before, too."

"Have you?

"Yes."

The voice changed again. "Where? In the therapist's office?" It was the Bostonian accent again.

Oh my God! My sweet Lord in Heaven!

Sean was Dr. Cagle!

"Sean…?"

"Yes, Hannah?" Back to the voice she knew as Sean. His hands continued to massage her shoulders and arms. She had turned completely around to face him now and his hands moved around to the back of her neck.

"Who are you?"

"Who do you think I am?" The voice changed again. It was neither Sean's nor Dr. Cagle's. Something different altogether.

"I… I… don't know."

"You're stuttering, Hannah," he said in Dr. Cagle's voice.

"D…Dr. Cagle?"

"Maybe." The hands closed around her neck, still rubbing gently.

"Sean, what are you doing?"

The completely strange voice spoke. "Who do you think I am, Hannah?" This time the voice was familiar. Where had she heard it?

"I'm a great actor, Hannah," he said. "The best in the city. One day I'll be on Broadway, or I'll be in the movies. I'll win an Oscar someday. You'll see. Oh, I almost forgot. I promised you a surprise." He kept one hand on her neck, continuing to rub, while the other hand reached into his trenchcoat pocket and pulled out a small white jewelry gift box. He handed it to her. "I thought you'd like to have this. As a keepsake."

Hannah took the box with trembling hands. She didn't want to open it but she knew that she must. She was afraid of what he might do if she refused.

She carefully lifted the lid, revealing a pad of cotton. She gingerly lifted the cotton and saw the item inside.

It was a gold *chai* on a chain. Liz's necklace.

The hands began to tighten around her neck. Hannah jerked back, dropped the box, and struggled against him. Cutler held on to her throat and squeezed.

She slipped off the barstool, tipping it over, and was now bent back over the counter.

"I couldn't let her live, Hannah," he said. "She was going to warn you about me. It would have spoiled my quest."

She tried to scream, speak his name and plead with him. She hit him on the shoulders but he was too strong.

"Still don't know who I am?" he asked. "Maybe this will help. *Hey, baby, where ya goin'?"*

The words drifted into Hannah's ears and floated through the sensory passages to her brain. Once the words registered, a tremendous blanket of terror enveloped her heart.

He was Timothy Lane! He was her rapist!

The hands tightened around her neck. She was truly choking now, struggling for air.

"It's time to finish what I tried to do five years ago," he said. "Oh, and by the way… that poor schmuck who went to prison… what was his name? Lane? He didn't know you from Eve. He was the wrong guy, Miss McCleary. The police were wrong. They never caught the man who followed you home that night. He got away, went about his own life, and lived to follow other women home."

This wasn't happening! Hannah struggled against him, desperately trying to breathe.

He continued to speak as he squeezed. "One of those women got away from him, as you did, and threatened to press charges. She dropped them, though, as long as he made an effort to combat the demons. That was the 'dark time' – two years of probation and therapy. The funny thing about it, though – it didn't work too well."

Hannah stared into the eyes of the man who hovered over her. She could see the face now. It all came together. The eyes, the nose, the mouth, the cheekbones, the dark hair… it was him. The man who had followed her home five years ago and tried to rape and kill her in the entry space of the building.

God help me… God help me…

She heard the meow of a cat nearby. What was it? Was it really a cat? Yes, it was Panther! The cat was still on the counter, watching the horrible scene, frightened but incensed that something bad was happening to his human master. The cat wasn't a dog, which might have immediately tried to defend a master who was in trouble. But the cat knew instinctively that something was wrong and he was issuing a protest.

Hannah reached behind her with one hand, groping for the furry animal as the vice-like grip around her neck grew ever tighter. She heard the meow again and she strained to touch him.

Don't move away, Panther! she willed. *Where are you? Come to me!*

Another meow. Blackness was falling around Hannah's vision. It was going to be over very quickly. She felt like succumbing, releasing herself into the void so that the pain and suffering would go away.

Her fingers felt fur. She bent them quickly, over and over, in a tickling motion that she knew Panther liked. He moved a little closer until she was able to grasp his underbelly and pull him toward her.

She flung the cat at her assailant's face. Panther screeched and dug his claws into Cutler's head. He yelled, let go of Hannah's neck, and knocked the cat away. It ran across the room and hid under a chair. Hannah fell to the floor, gasping for air and struggling to get to her feet at the same time. It was different from the earlier sensation, when Sophia had knocked the breath out of her. This was all in the throat, a feeling that her windpipe had been crushed.

Bill Cutler had a hand over one eye. The cat had scratched him hard and he couldn't see. With his other eye he attempted to focus on his prey, who was now crawling backwards across the kitchen floor. He lunged forward to catch her, but he tripped over the barstool, which was lying in front of him.

This gave Hannah the seconds she needed to stand and run.

"Come back here!" Cutler yelled.

Hannah made it to the stairs and went up, two steps at a time. He was right behind her, though. She got to the first landing and went into the office. Hannah heard him reach the top of the stairs just as she slammed the door and locked it.

Cutler beat on the door. "Open up, *baby*. Come on, we gotta finish something!" he yelled.

"I'm calling the police!" Hannah cried.

"Go ahead, baby. You do that!" he said with satisfaction in his voice.

What did he mean?

Hannah went to the phone and picked up the receiver. It was then that she noticed the message light blinking. She had not checked the messages since she returned from Ohio. No time for that now, though. She put the receiver to her head and heard no dial tone. She jabbed the receiver button several times, trying to connect to an outside line, but the thing was dead.

"What's the matter, baby? Does the phone not work?" Cutler asked through the door.

What had he done? Had he cut the line before coming into the house?

"Go away!" she cried.

"Nuh uh," he said. "We got unfinished business, baby. You and me."

Hannah backed away from the door and looked around the office for a weapon – anything that she could use to defend herself. Unfortunately, all she saw were manuscripts, desk supplies, and other useless items.

Cutler battered the door hard, causing it to splinter a bit at the hinges. Hannah thought that he must be using some kind of ram. It wouldn't be long before he was inside the room. She was helpless.

"I'm gonna count to three, baby," he said with glee. "Open up or I'm comin' in after ya!"

Then she remembered something. Hannah ran around to John's desk and opened the top drawer. She rummaged through it, looking for the one item that might be the thing to save her life. The drawer was full of junk – pieces of paper with notes scribbled on them, dozens of loose paper clips, pens, pencils, a ruler, a Scotch tape dispenser… Hannah slammed the drawer shut and opened the next one, a side drawer normally used for filing. John had thrown all kinds of office tools inside of it – a hole punch, a bottle of rubber cement, a stapler, boxes of staples, White-Out, a pair of scissors…

A pair of scissors. Could she use them?

Hannah grabbed them and then saw what she had been looking for in the first place – John's silver letter opener from the Book of the Month Club. She picked it up and held it in her hand. It was nearly eight inches long and was very sharp.

Cutler's battering ram collided with the door again. And again. The top hinge shattered as the wood splintered. Hannah screamed.

"Olly olly in-free!" Cutler called.

Hannah desperately tried to find other items that might help. She opted to push her desk away from the wall and shove it against the door. It was tremendously heavy, but the adrenaline pumping through her body gave her the strength she needed to get the job done. Cutler must have realized that she had placed a blockade behind the door, for he screeched in frustration.

"Goddamn it, Hannah, open up this door!"

The middle hinge snapped and now the only thing holding up the door was the bottom hinge and the desk in front of it. Cutler shoved and pushed, but the door wouldn't budge any further.

Then it became quiet. He had moved away from the door. But where to?

Hannah was aware that her breathing was rapid and shallow and she could hear her awful heartbeat in her ears. If she didn't calm down soon, she was afraid she might have a heart attack. But what could she do? There was no escape from the room. There was no window or ventilation passage that she could crawl into. The phone didn't work and all she had to protect herself was a letter opener. Was this the end? Had it all come down to this?

Oddly, she suddenly thought of Timothy Lane. The man had been wrongly convicted. She had pointed to him in the courtroom and told the jury that he was the one who had tried to rape her. He had gone to prison for five years. Was he still there? Was he dead or alive? Given the fact that Sean Flannery was an imposter and a psychopath, she had no way of knowing. How could she have been so gullible? Was she as blind as that? Had her neurological condition completely taken over her mental capacities?

She would have to deal with the guilt over Timothy Lane another time.

The sound of gunshots startled her back to the here and now. Bullet holes appeared in the door and she felt the rounds zipping past her head. She dived for the floor as the ammunition covered the wall behind her.

"How do you like that, Hannah?" he called. "Did you feel that? Are you hit?"

She hugged the floor and tried to steady her breathing.

"What's the matter? Are you dead? Did I get you? Don't die yet, baby, we still have some work to do!"

The door gave a little as he rammed it. The desk scooted an inch. He did it again, and again. There was nothing she could do now. He was going to make it inside the room.

Carefully and silently, Hannah got off the floor and climbed on top of the desk behind the door. She held the letter opener with both hands, pointed down, ready to stab the first body part that broke the barrier between her safety and the hallway outside. The door buckled again… and again. Each time the desk moved a little further. Finally, there was a foot of space through which her assailant could look.

Bill Cutler's face squeezed through the opening and looked inside. His eyes darted around the room and then finally noticed her on top of the desk behind the door.

He smiled. "Hey, baby!"

The letter opener jabbed into the man's face, creating a geyser of blood.

The man screamed and disappeared from the opening. Hannah felt her heart beating so hard that it made her dizzy. She listened as Cutler cried like a wounded animal, falling into the opposite wall in the hallway and thrashing around like a fish out of water.

Hannah considered her options. She could wait until he regained some composure. He would then find a new way to attack, storm the room, and overcome her. He would shoot her with the gun. He would disarm her of the letter opener and ultimately be the victor.

Or she could go out there and attack *him* while he was down. What was it that "Dr. Cagle" had taught her? Face her fear! Visualize the enemy in her mind and focus her anger on him!

Of course that was the only thing she could do. The man in the hallway was the monster who had ruined her life. He had tried to kill her, attempted to rape her, and he had caused the debilitating condition that kept Hannah McCleary from leading a normal, social life. She was well aware that she was mentally ill. She had come to understand that she had serious psychological problems – and they were all because of the *creep* outside the door.

Hannah slipped off the desk, pulled it out of the way, and opened the door.

Bill Cutler was on the floor, holding his face and moaning pathetically. He hadn't noticed that she had come out of the office. A hat rack from the downstairs entry hall was on the carpet beside him – the battering ram he had been using.

Hannah held the letter opener with both hands and stood above him. She raised the weapon high and then brought it down between the man's shoulder blades.

Cutler made a sharp grunting cry, jerked, and froze in that position. Hannah backed away in horror, unable to look at what she had done. She turned and waited for a sign – anything at all – that she had succeeded.

There was a groan and a sigh, and then the sound of a body hitting the carpet with a *tha-rump!*

She slowly turned toward the sound and saw that her assailant was lying face down, unmoving, in a pool of blood. The letter opener protruded from his back like a flagpole.

Hannah slumped against the wall, curled into a fetal position, and started crying.

Chapter 31

She didn't know how much time had passed.

When Hannah raised her head, the house was very quiet. She could faintly hear the sounds of the city streets outside and the ticking of a clock somewhere in the townhouse. She could also still feel and hear her heartbeat in her ears, although it had slowed to a normal rate. Nevertheless her head was pounding in pain. Sophia had hurt her, certainly, but Hannah always got headaches when she was under stress.

What to do now?

She couldn't stay in the townhouse. What was the point? John was dead. He wasn't coming back to give her the wages she was owed. The manuscripts would never be published.

She had to leave.

Hannah turned her head and looked at the body in the hallway. She had an impulsive desire to search his pockets for a wallet. Perhaps there was some kind of identification that would tell her who he really was. But did it matter? Probably not. She knew that he wasn't Timothy Lane. Timothy Lane had been innocent of the crime committed against her and now he was lying dead downstairs. The poor man. She didn't blame him for coming after her the way he did. Prison had made him more evil than when he went in. He probably wanted revenge against her so badly that he was unable to use common sense. It was all her fault. She had identified him in court and she had been wrong.

"Can you forgive me?" she asked no one.

And what should she do with the three bodies in the house? What *could* she to do? Call the police? They would take her "downtown" and put her in an interrogation room. They would shine a bright light on her for hours and make her tell her story over and over until they were satisfied.

She hadn't done anything wrong, had she? She had defended herself against a man who had tried to rape and kill her. He had also murdered her friend Liz. Sophia and Timothy Lane had shot each other – she had nothing to do with them. Still, the letter opener in the back of the assailant had her fingerprints on it. She was loath to touch it and pull it out.

She stood and walked slowly down the hallway to the bathroom. She took a towel, went back into the hall, knelt by the body, and wiped the letter opener clean. Surely there would be no fingerprints now.

Was he really a policeman? Probably not. He had pretended to be one, and he had masqueraded as her therapist as well.

He must have known about her face blindness. But how?

Hannah turned away and went into the office. She would never know the answers. It would always be a mystery – everything that had happened in the last week. John and Sophia – what had they been up to? What had really happened to her cousin? What did Sophia think was in the house that belonged to John? And her assailant – why had he gone to so much trouble over the past few days to gain her confidence? Did he just want to sleep with her without raping her? It was sick. The man was deranged. He deserved to be dead.

Hannah sat in the chair that used to be in front of her desk.

There was nothing in New York for her now. She had no job, no friends, and no family. Her apartment was the size of a jail cell. Her condition prevented her from going out and socializing in public. The city was one big intimidation, something she would never get used to again. Once upon a time, before the assault, she had enjoyed being in New York. Now it was the root cause of her problems.

So leave! What was to stop her? What if she just disappeared? She could do it. No one would miss her. The landlord of her apartment might report her missing, but after a month he would simply throw out her stuff and rent the room to someone else. The New York police didn't know that she worked for John. The Ohio police were dense – they wouldn't come looking for her. Any loose ends regarding the murders there and in Chicago would most likely end with the discovery of Sophia's body.

A blinking light on John's desk attracted her attention. Hannah turned to look and remembered that there was a message for John on the answering machine. She stood, pressed the button, and listened.

It was a Hispanic voice, the young man she knew as Manuel. "Hello, this is Boxes and Copies. There is a package here for Hannah McCleary. It was sent from Indiana. Please come by the shop at your convenience to pick it up. We are open twenty-four hours a day."

Hannah played the message twice and then erased it. What could it be? John must have sent it. Who else would send her something from Indiana? Was it the thing that Sophia was talking about?

Hannah looked around the office and took what trinkets that belonged to her. She wondered where her purse was and then remembered that it was downstairs in the kitchen. She had left it there when she had first walked into the townhouse with her bags.

She left the office, stepped over the dead body, and went down the stairs. The other two corpses were still lying where they had fallen. Hannah didn't spend time looking at them. She picked up her purse, put the office trinkets inside, and scanned the room for Panther.

"Panther? Kitty-kitty?"

She heard a sound and a soft meow. He was under a chair.

"Oh, there you are, poor guy." She went to him and picked him up. He immediately began to purr. "You were probably scared to death, weren't you? I'm sorry I threw you at that man, but you saved my life, did you know that? You *saved my life*! You're my hero!"

She opened the storage closet in the entry hall and removed the cat's travel case. She put him inside and then gathered his food and bowl from the kitchen. She opened her suitcase and put them inside. Hannah stepped into the middle of the living room and carefully scanned the area for any more of her belongings. Satisfied, she picked up her bags and the cat's travel case and went to the front door.

It wasn't quite ten o'clock. The city was still awake, there were people on the streets, and traffic was still flowing steadily.

Hannah closed the front door behind her, locked it, and then dropped the key into the drain that lay adjacent to the curb and the street. She walked to Second Avenue, turned the corner, and headed north. She stopped at the Boxes and Copies and found Manuel sitting alone, reading a comic book.

"Hello, Manuel," she said. "You left a message for me?"

"Yes, Miss McCleary!" he said. He smiled broadly when he saw her, the way he always did. Hannah could see the smile. It was warm and friendly. Too bad she couldn't put it into context with the rest of his face.

He went into the back and returned promptly with a box the size of a microwave oven.

"It's a little heavy," he said. "You have something to carry it with?"

Hannah looked at her suitcase, which was a pull-type on rollers. "Will it fit on here? You have something to tie it on with?"

"Sure, we can do that," Manuel said. He grabbed some twine and bound the box on top of the suitcase so that she could pull both objects with one hand. Her other hand was free to carry Panther's case. Manuel had her sign for the package and then she was on her way.

It took her fifteen minutes to walk to her building. When she entered the entry hall, Hannah checked her mailbox, which was empty, and then used her key to go inside. She carried Panther up the stairs first, unlocked her apartment, and put him inside. She then went back downstairs, grabbed the suitcase and box, and returned to her apartment.

Once she had shut the door and was alone, Hannah set the box in the middle of the kitchen. She took a knife and sliced the packing tape. She opened it to find newspaper wrapped around something. She tore the paper way and gasped.

The box was packed with stacks and stacks of money. All one hundred dollar bills. A note sat on the top –

"Dear Hannah – Please keep this safe until I return. If I don't come back, it's all yours. Be careful with it."

Much love,
John

Hannah, her eyes wide and her mouth open, picked up one stack and counted the bills. There were fifty. Five thousand dollars. The next thing she did was to count the stacks. There were so many of them! They had been packed in the box tightly and she was surprised at how little space one stack of fifty one hundred dollar bills actually took up. It took her twenty minutes, but she ended up with one hundred and ninety-eight stacks. Hannah stood and scribbled the figures on a scratch pad that she kept by the phone. Five thousand times one hundred and ninety-eight equaled…nine hundred and ninety thousand!

Almost a million dollars.

She wondered if there had originally been an even million. John had probably taken five stacks out. Who knew… who cared?

There was something else in the box – several neatly wrapped plastic baggies filled with white powder. She instinctively knew what it was and she didn't want it. Without hesitation, she took each plastic baggie and dumped the contents into the toilet in her bathroom. She had to flush the commode three times to get rid of it all.

Hannah opened her single, tiny closet and pulled out a larger suitcase. She emptied the small suitcase into the bigger one, opened her dresser drawers, and filled the big suitcase with what she thought she could use. She went around the apartment and picked up things that she felt she couldn't do without and put them in the suitcase as well. She transferred her toiletries into the bag and closed it up.

She spent the next half-hour carefully loading the smaller suitcase with the money. It barely fit, but only after she took twenty stacks out and put some in the big suitcase and the rest in her purse.

Hannah made one more round through the apartment to make sure that she had everything she wanted. She scribbled a note to the building's super, telling him that she has moved out. Anything left in the apartment he was free to sell or get rid of. The landlord could keep her deposit.

She didn't leave a forwarding address.

It took two trips to get everything down the stairs. She put the note in the super's mailbox, then made sure that her two suitcases were tied together securely. She was just able to roll both of them with the one hand, and carry Panther's case in the other. It would work.

Hannah went outside and hailed a taxicab. She ordered the driver to take her to Penn Station, where she paid him with a hundred-dollar bill.

"I can't make change for this!" he complained.

"Then keep the change," she said, smiling sweetly. She left the driver in a state of shock and pulled her stuff onto the pavement.

She made her way to the Amtrak ticket windows and bought a one-way to Santa Fe, New Mexico. It was a complicated route. She would have to take one train to Chicago, switch and travel into the western states, and then change services. It was do-able, but it would take several days. Hannah shrugged and paid the fare in cash. She was told that she would have to wait a few hours but that she could board a sleeper train just after one o'clock in the morning.

Hannah went to the waiting room and sat on one of the benches. She took a deep breath and felt very pleased with herself. Here she was, leaving the city that she thought she'd never abandon. A new life awaited her on the other side of the country. Best to turn her back on the world she had inhabited for the last thirty years of her life and start anew.

The waiting room was relatively empty. A few late travelers were passing the time by reading newspapers or books. Most of the homeless people who had used the station as a refuge had been swept out years ago during a big city clean-up – but there were a couple who managed to loiter there.

Hannah paid no attention to the people. They were strangers. Even if she had known them, they would still be strangers. Their faces meant nothing to her. Her face most likely meant nothing to them as well. She liked it that way. Hannah realized that anonymity was something to be embraced, something valued.

For the first time in her life, Hannah looked forward to living in a nameless place and losing herself in a sea of blank, featureless faces – where she could be one, too.

ABOUT THE AUTHOR

Raymond Benson is the author of the James Bond novels *The Man With the Red Tattoo, Never Dream of Dying, DoubleShot, High Time to Kill, The Facts of Death,* and *Zero Minus Ten,* as well as the novelizations of the films *Die Another Day, The World is Not Enough,* and *Tomorrow Never Dies.* His Bond short stories have been published in *Playboy* and *TV Guide* magazines. He is also the author of the suspense novel, *Evil Hours*, and the non-fiction books *The Pocket Essentials Guide to Jethro Tull* and *The James Bond Bedside Companion* (the latter was nominated for an Edgar Allan Poe Award for Best Biographical/Critical Work in 1984). Raymond also has extensive experience directing stage plays, composing music, and designing and writing adventure computer games. He is married, has one son, and is based in the Chicago area.

OTHER BOOKS AVAILABLE FROM TWENTY FIRST CENTURY PUBLISHERS LIMITED

RAMONA

How did a little girl come to be abandoned in the orange scented square of the Andalusian City of Seville? Find out, when the course of her life is resumed at age seventeen.

Ramona catches the mood of Europe in transition, as Ramona, brought up in a quiet village in southern Spain, moves into the cosmopolitan world. Her strange background holds a mystery, revealed as the novel develops, but then events take on a different hue as a new perspective emerges. But that is not all, and reality seems to bend further, but does it?

From a novel within a novel, we move on to ... well, let's not say. Read it, and the author challenges you to predict each step of the unfolding plot, and just when it defies belief, read on – you will believe.

Ramona by Johnny John Heinz
ISBN: 1-904433-01-4

MEANS TO AN END

Enter the world of money laundering, financial manipulation and greed, where a shadowy Middle Eastern organisation takes on a major corporation in the US. As the action shifts through exotic locations, who wins out in the end? Certainly, the author's first hand experience of international finance lends a chilling credibility to the plot.

As well as being a compelling work of fiction this book offers, in a style accessible to the layman, a financial insider's insight into the financial and moral crisis, which broke in the early millennium, in the top echelons of corporate America.

Means to an End by Johnny John Heinz
ISBN: 1-84375-008-2

THE SIGNATURE OF A VOICE

The Signature of a Voice is a cat-and-mouse-game between a violent trio, led by a psychopathic killer, and a police officer on suspension. Move and countermove in this chess game is planned and enacted. The reader, in the position of god, knows who is guilty and who plans what, but just as in chess, the opponents' plans thwart one another. The outcomes twist and turn to the final curtain fall.

There is a sense of suspense but also anger as the system seems to be working against those who are fighting on the side of right, while the perpetrators of vicious crimes seem able to operate freely and choose to do what they wish. They choose the route of ultra-violence to stay ahead of the law in an otherwise tranquil community: they plan and execute, in all senses of the word. Is it possible to triumph over this ruthlessness?

The Signature of a Voice by Johnny John Heinz
ISBN: 1-904433-00-6

TARNISHED COPPER

Tarnished Copper is a story of greed, deception and corruption in one of the most volatile of financial markets. The author, Geoffrey Sambrook, has been a metal trader for 20 years, seeing the collapse of the International Tin Council, the Sumitomo Affair and numerous other market shenanigans, and brings an insider's unique insight into the way markets can be manipulated for profit. The fictional characters of Tarnished Copper seem horrifyingly real as they follow their dance of deception, culminating in untold riches for some, and death for another. A new, cerebral voice in financial fiction.

Tarnished Copper by Geoffrey Sambrook
ISBN 1-904433-02-2

OVER A BARREL

From the moment you land at Heathrow on page one the plot grips you. Ed Burke, an American oil tycoon, jets through the world's financial centres and the Middle East to set up deals, but where does this lead him? Are his premonitions on the safety of his daughter Louise in Saudi Arabia well founded? Who are his hidden opponents? Is his corporate lawyer Nicole with him or against him?

As the plot unfolds his company is put into play in the tangle of events surrounding the 1990 invasion of Kuwait. Even his private life is drawn into the morass.

In this novel Peter depicts the grim machinations of political and commercial life, but the human spirit shines through. This is a thriller that will hold you to the last page.

Over a Barrel by Peter Driver
ISBN 1-904433-03-0

THE BLOWS OF FATE

It is a crisp clear day in Sofia and three young friends are starting out in life, buoyant with their hopes, aspirations, loves. But this is not to be, as post war Eastern Europe comes under the grip of its brutal communist regime. Driven from their homes and deprived of their basic rights, the three friends determine to escape ... but one of them cannot seize that moment. It may seem that life cannot become worse for the families who are ostracised and trapped in their own country, but the path of hopelessness descends to the concentration camps and unimaginable brutality.

For those who escape there is the struggle to survive, tempered by the kindness they encounter along their way. We see how talent and determination can win through. Yet, though they may have escaped those terrible years in Bulgaria, they can never escape their personal loss of family, homeland, friends and love that may have been.

While life is very difficult for the three friends, they do not forget each other. After forty years of separation, they meet. For each one fate has prepared a surprise....

Can beauty, art and love eclipse the manmade horrors of this world? You will think they can, as Antoinette Clair brings out the beautiful things in life, so that the poignancy of her novel reaches into the toughest of us, and moves to tears.

This is a tale of beauty, music and a grand love, but it is also expressive of the sad recurring tale of Europe's recent history.

The Blows of Fate by Antoinette Clair
ISBN 1-904433-04-9

THE GORE EXPERIMENT

William Gore is not a mad scientist: he is a dedicated medical researcher working on G.L.X.-14, an AIDS serum. He is on the brink of a major breakthrough and seeks to force the pace, spurred on by his knowledge of the suffering to be spared, if he is right, and the millions of lives of AIDS victims to be saved. But as things begin to go askew, how far dare he go? What level of risk is warranted? What, and who, is he prepared to sacrifice? The answers become worse than you can imagine as William Gore treads a path to horror.

The Gore Experiment may be fiction, but it addresses real issues in the world of experimental vaccines, disease-busting drugs and genetic engineering. Is science unknowingly exposing us to risk through overconfidence in ever narrowing fields of expertise, ignorant of ramifications? Or is the red tape of bureaucracy signing the death warrants of the terminally sick? Well, William Gore at least is confident. He is convinced of what he must do. Should he do it?

This is not a book for the faint-hearted. H.Jay Scheuermann adds a new high-tech dimension to the traditions of vampires, Jekylls and Hydes as William Gore paves his own road to hell. But there is a twist....

CASEY'S REVENGE

Is this the best of all possible worlds? Well, almost, or so Casey Forbes thinks. She is a college professor with a successful career and good friends; boyfriend trouble in the past, perhaps, but who hasn't? And her prospects are excellent.

But no woman can expect to descend into the real life nightmare, that envelopes Casey ... out of nowhere.

Mary Charles's heroine is forced to confront the darkest side of human nature and the most bestial of acts committed by man. Yet it is the strength of will, the trauma inflicted on Casey's personality and the resourcefulness of the female psyche that Mary Charles explores in this novel. What does it take to survive overwhelming adversity and does Casey have it?

Many dream of revenge but wonder if they have within themselves the capacity to carry it out. Can Casey? And is the price going to be too high?

Read this thriller and one thing is certain: don't ever let this happen to you.

Casey's Revenge by Mary Charles

ISBN 1-90443-06-5

SABRA'S SOUL

From the heart of the California rock music scene comes this story of much more than just love and betrayal.

Does Sabra know who she is? She thinks she is a loving mother and a trusting wife, but her husband Logan, a powerful figure in rock music, seems consumed by commitments to his latest band, 23 Mystique. Sabra begins to feel that something is missing, to feel a yearning for something more. Is she too trusting and too slow to spot Logan's lapses in behaviour?

When Sabra meets the pop idol of her sub-teen daughters, things begin to change. She can't believe the attraction growing in her for this youthful figure, her junior by several years.

Lisa Reed paints a picture of virtue and vice in this tale of love, lust, betrayal and drug-induced psychosis, set amidst the glitter of the rock scene. It is not fate that leads these people on but their own actions. Can they help it and where does it lead?

Who better than Lisa Reed, with her access to the centre of rock, to weave this tense plot as it descends from the social whirl into the deadly serious. If you are a successful rock star, this is a book for you, and if not ... well, read on and dream.

Health warning: this book contains salacious sex scenes demanded by its setting.

Lisa Reed is by vocation a sensational writer, by profession a teacher of children with special educational needs and, through her marriage to Dizzy Reed of Guns n' Roses, she is right at the centre of Californian rock.

A true Californian, where she still resides, Lisa is the mother of two beautiful daughters.

Sabra's Soul by Lisa Reed
ISBN 1-904433-07-3

CUPID AND THE SILENT GODDESS

The painting *Allegory with Venus and Cupid* has long fascinated visitors to London's National Gallery, as well as the millions more who have seen it reproduced in books. It is one of the most beautiful paintings of the nude ever made.

In 1544, Duke Cosimo de' Medici of Florence commissioned the artist Bronzino to create the painting to be sent as a diplomatic gift to King François I of France.

As well as the academic mystery of what the strange figures in the painting represent, there is a human mystery as well: who were the models in the Florence of 1544 who posed for the gods and strange creatures?

Alan Fisk's *Cupid and the Silent Goddess* imagines how the creation of this painting might have touched the lives of everyone who was involved with it: Bronzino's apprentice Giuseppe, the mute and mysterious Angelina who is forced to model for Venus, the brutal sculptor Baccio Bandinelli and his son, and the good-hearted nun Sister Benedicta and her friend the old English priest Father Fleccia, both secret practitioners of alchemy.

As the painting takes shape, it causes episodes of fear and cruelty, but the ending lies perhaps in the gift of Venus.

Cupid and the Silent Goddess by Alan Fisk
ISBN:1-904433-08-1